I AM
STILL
ALIVE

I AM
STILL
ALIVE

KATE ALICE MARSHALL

VIKING

VIKING
An imprint of Penguin Random House LLC
375 Hudson Street
New York, New York 10014

First published in the United States of America by Viking,
an imprint of Penguin Random House LLC, 2018

LIBRARY OF CONGRESS CATALOGING-IN-PUBLICATION DATA IS AVAILABLE
ISBN 9780425290989

Printed in the USA
10   9   8   7   6   5   4   3   2   1

To the gang on the mountain.

I AM

STILL

ALIVE

I'M ALONE. I don't have much food. The temperature is dropping.

No one is coming for me.

It will be winter soon, and there are so many ways to die out here. If the cold doesn't get me, the hunger will. If the hunger doesn't get me, the cold will. Or some wild animal. Or those men will come back . . .

But I'm not dead yet, and someone should know. Someone should know what happened. So I'm writing it down, as best I can. In pieces, because that's the way it is in my head, all tangled up.

There are two beginnings to this story. One of them is on a tarmac in Alaska. The other's standing on a lakeshore with the rain falling on me like mist, the cabin's timbers smoldering, sullen and red. I'll tell you both stories, what happened before my father died and what happened after. And when I'm done or when I'm too weak to write anymore, I'll leave this notebook where the cabin was. If someone comes looking for us, for me, maybe they'll find it.

So if you're reading this, I'm probably dead. But for a while, I survived.

My name is Jess Cooper, and I am still alive.

SUMMER

Before

IT TOOK TWO flights to get up to the town where Dad lived in Alaska—where I thought he lived. I spent the second flight studying a picture of him. Mom had gotten rid of the photos of them together but held on to one of him alone, just for me, and I clutched it in my hand. I was worried I might not recognize him. Or he might not recognize me. We could walk right past each other and not know it.

In the photo, he stood in the woods in a blue rain shell. Mist hung in the air, his breath making a thicker cloud in front of his bristly lips. He had a beard that needed trimming and bright eyes, crinkled up at the edges like he'd laughed right before the picture was taken. By the time I stepped onto the tarmac and scanned the thin crowd of people waiting, I had memorized every detail of his face.

He wasn't there. I imagined adding gray to his beard, taking his beard away, making it longer. Scrubbing out the laugh lines and adding the sort of wrinkles you get from frowning, because I figured he couldn't be that happy if he'd left his wife and kid.

No matter what I did to the picture in my mind, it didn't match anyone there, and soon everyone waiting for the plane had been claimed by one of my fellow passengers.

The only person left was a huge man wearing a puffy yellow jacket who stared straight at me, squinting, but didn't move or wave or anything. His bushy red-brown hair poked out from under a baseball cap that might have once been yellow but had faded to gray brown everywhere except the brim.

I hitched my bag over my shoulder. Dad must have sent someone to pick me up, that was all. I walked over, my right foot dragging slightly. I still couldn't lift it properly, and the ball of my foot scraped along the ground. The man watched my slow progress without budging.

"Hi," I said when I got close. It sounded like a bird chirping, high-pitched and spastic. "I'm Jess. Did my dad send you?"

"Jess?" the guy said. He scratched his beard. "I'm supposed to be meeting Sequoia. Could be I'm in the wrong place, though." He looked behind me as if another girl could be lurking there.

"No, that's me," I said. "Jess is my middle name. I never go by Sequoia."

"Oh, great." He grinned. He looked a lot less intimidating when he smiled, but he still could've closed a hand around my entire head. "Carl's waiting."

He'd turned around and started walking before I really remembered that was my father's name. Carl Green. Not Cooper; Mom hadn't changed her name.

"So he sent you?" I asked the man's back as I struggled to keep up. I had to take three steps to one of his, and that meant instead of taking slow, careful steps with my bad foot, I had to fling myself forward in a lurching limp. Which I wasn't supposed to do. Will, my physical therapist, had been really clear about that. Slow and steady and I'd walk almost normally someday.

"Uh-huh," the man said. I was puffing by the time we reached the fence that divided the tiny tarmac from the parking lot, and he stopped. He looked around at me and blinked rapidly. "Sorry. I can take the bag, if you want."

I shook my head, slinging the duffel around to my front and folding my arms over it. "It's fine," I said, jaw set.

He rubbed the back of his neck with his palm. "Forgot you were handicapped. Is that the right word? Handicapped? Or is it something else? I think it's something else. I think handicapped is wrong. Sorry."

"It's fine," I said again. I didn't want to have this conversation. I was grateful when he nodded. But when he set off again he walked slowly, peeking at me out of the corner of his eye, and I could keep up pretty well. I focused on lifting my foot all the way off the ground. If I let it drag, I'd trip eventually, and a fall was the worst thing I could do to my healing muscles and tendons and bones.

I hadn't realized before the car crash how much a body could break, and I hadn't realized until the months afterward how imperfectly it got put back together. Parts of me would always be broken.

"I'm Griff," the man said abruptly as we walked, and all I could think to do was nod.

THIS IS WHAT you need to know about Griff:

He's probably the nicest guy I've ever met, even though he's a bit odd. He looks like a mountain man but claims it's camouflage: mountain men won't eat you if they think you're one of them, he says. He tells a lot of jokes like that, but he has a totally deadpan delivery, so you can never tell if it's a joke or one of the strange things he believes. If you laugh at the wrong thing, he'll give you this sad look. He loves the color yellow. Jesus is his personal savior. And if anyone's coming for me, it's him.

But if he is coming, it's not for months. And maybe not at all.

These days I think about him a lot. He's on a list that cycles through my mind all day. Mom, Scott, Will, Dad, Griff. Lily. Not George so much, because George is an asshole. Michelle, Ronnie, and then I'm out of people I really knew, and I start picturing faces from all over the place. The guy who served me ice cream the day before the accident. The woman at the gas station with three blond kids who stood at the nose of her minivan and put a hand to her forehead like she didn't know if she was going to get back in it. The pilot who'd flown the first leg up to Alaska, who'd known my mom, who'd invited me up into the cockpit but hadn't said anything, and I hadn't said anything, and we just sat there being quiet and sad until I had to go take my seat.

I thought it would be food that I fantasized about, but so far it's people.

BACK THEN I was more than a little scared of Griff. Which was only smart—strange guy telling me to get in his car? Yeah, that seems safe. Only I didn't see another option. I had a phone number for my dad, but I'd already tried it during my layover and gotten a recording telling me it was disconnected.

I probably should have gone back to Seattle then. Explained to the social worker that something was wrong, and I couldn't go live with my dad after all. And yet I didn't. I didn't turn back when the call didn't go through, and I didn't turn back when Griff was waiting for me.

Griff's car was an old station wagon, probably older than he was. The back of it was full of takeout bags and soda bottles, a sleeping bag, three banker's boxes, a full set of suitcases, and two pairs of shoes. The front seat was full of receipts, which Griff scraped off onto the floor when he got in. I wedged my bag between my feet, making the receipts rustle, and shut the door.

"You didn't bring much," Griff said.

"I don't need much," I said. The lawyer who'd taken care of selling the house and the furniture had rented a storage place for the rest, for whenever I wanted it. My memories would be tucked away safe, he'd said.

It felt like he was giving me permission not to remember. I didn't want to think about my life before, because I loved it too much. Loved Mom too much. I could lock everything up and forget about it until it all healed over, however long that took. As long as it would take to teach my body to walk properly again, I thought. When I could take a step without thinking about how to lift my foot, maybe I'd go back to Seattle and remember.

Griff didn't make much conversation after that. We drove a

long time in silence, until I realized we were heading the wrong way.

"I thought my dad lived in town," I said.

"Got a house in town," Griff said. "But he doesn't live there. You'll see."

"Shouldn't I know where I'm going?" I asked.

"Wouldn't mean anything to you," he said. "I'm taking you to your dad, and that's what counts."

"Right." I looked out the window. The town had petered out. Now there were a few gray-sided houses that looked embarrassed to be interrupting the wilderness. The road was pocked and cracked, and my hand drifted to my leg. The skin on my right leg looked just like that, with red swapped for gray.

It had taken them hours to pick all the glass out of my skin. I had more scars on my shoulder, and on my neck and face. The scars on my face were deep and red, like claw marks. They made people stare.

I liked them. People who stared at my face, I could stare back at. People who stared at my limp, I couldn't do anything about.

Eventually Griff started singing. He was so off-key and he mumbled so much that I couldn't tell what he was singing, but he bobbed his head and tapped the wheel in time to *something*. He jammed a button and the heater came on, rattling and coughing, and the wheels scraped and bumped on the uneven road and something clattered and bounced in the backseat. And then we came around a bend and there was a bear in the road.

Griff pumped the brakes casually, slowing up without stopping, and the bear took off for the woods. We just kept sliding along the road.

"Look at him skeeedaddle," Griff said, pulling out that syllable with a twangy accent, and I laughed. He gave me a grin and laughed with me, and then both of us were laughing with the gray-blue sky sliding over our heads and the forest growing thick and deep and wild around us. It was the first time I'd laughed since the accident, since Mom died, and it felt like coughing up burrs. It felt good, too, though I only realized that after.

"Skeeedaddle," he said again, and as we started on the next few hundred miles we were friends.

After

I CAN'T QUITE comprehend what happened here. I know it but don't feel it, feel it but don't understand what I feel. Maybe writing it down like this will help. It doesn't feel like a story, the same way that *before* does. It feels like it's still happening. That even now I'm waking on the shore, smoke and fog mingling together until I can't tell one from the other.

It's morning, though the sunlight is weak and thin through the thick gray mass of clouds, which hang so low they shroud the jagged tops of the trees. The forest has never looked so much like teeth. It's never seemed to stretch so far.

I've slept all night curled on the shore while the cabin burned. The fire is out, but the timbers still smolder, shedding smoke and steam. I sit up and hunch against the rain. It's getting harder, pelting against my shoulders and hissing on the lake behind me. The noise is like static, and it drowns out any other sound—a kind of crowded silence that leaves no room for thought. Every living thing with any sense is hunkered down, sheltered among the dark, endless trees. Waiting out the rain. Waiting out the cold. Still I can't move, can't think at all.

My mind refuses to retrace my footsteps, to go further into the past than the night, the fire. I know only that I am alone, that I am hungry, that my tongue is like sandpaper in my mouth.

I tip my face up, closing my eyes. The rain spatters my cheeks, my eyelids. *You're alive*, I tell myself. I won't, can't, think about what happened, but I know that being alive is a miracle in itself. *Stay that way.*

But how?

My thoughts move reluctantly. There are too many places they can't go, like pockets of burning embers too hot to approach. Thinking about Dad burns worse than all the rest, but I force myself to seize on to the thought of him, hold it in my mind until I feel as if my skin will blister and crack from the pain of it.

Dad would know what to do. Somewhere in my smoke-shrouded, too-painful memories, he must have showed me what to do.

He told me cold will kill you quickest—so build a shelter. Thirst will kill you in a day or two—find water. Hunger won't kill you for a long time, but it'll make you weak—so find food. Fire is supposed to be last. Fire is warmth and food and clean water, but it's hard and time-consuming, and people die because they spend all their time making the fire and no time finding water or building a shelter.

So shelter first. But the cabin's gone. Everything's gone. I have *nothing*, I—

No. Stop. I don't have *nothing*. I have the rain. The rain, which kept the fire from spreading to the trees, which I can gather and drink without boiling (no way to boil the lake water, not yet, not without fire).

I have what I'm wearing: good boots, warm clothes, a rain shell.

I have everything I grabbed from the cabin before the fire. Not much—my duffel and backpack, the hatchet, a can of peaches, a can of salmon.

I have the rifle and the bow with all its arrows, and a box of ammunition.

And I have Bo. He's down by the lake, pacing, sniffing. Looking up sometimes like he's waiting and watching. Waiting for Dad? I'm not sure. But I'm not alone, not completely. Bo is here.

No one is coming for me. For us. If I'm going to live, I have to move.

Easier said than done. My body is still a map of pain, from the soles of my feet to my pounding head. But better than sitting here with nothing but the flame-scorched past, waiting to die.

One thing at a time.

I grab for my duffel and rummage in it until I find what I'm looking for: a pill bottle. I rattle it. Five pills. Painkillers, the powerful kind, left over from my prescription. I haven't taken them in weeks, but I shake one out now and swallow it dry. Just one, even though I long for two, for the complete blanketing numbness that even when it doesn't muffle the pain makes me not *care* about the pain.

But there are only four left, and I have to stay sharp, so I cap the bottle and tuck it safely back in the bag.

One thing at a time, and the next thing is to feed myself. I twist the lid off the jar of salmon and pop a greasy piece in my mouth. Bo must smell it, because seconds later he comes loping up to me, his pink tongue hanging between his teeth and his breath fogging the air. He halts two feet away and licks his chops. Waiting for permission.

"Nuh-uh," I say. "I need this." The salmon and peaches won't last long. A few days if I stretch them. Less if I split them with a hundred-pound dog.

Bo whines and ducks his head. And then I remember the jerky treats. I grabbed them this morning when we were heading out, and they're still crammed in my pocket. I dig in my pocket, get a handful, and toss them to Bo. He snatches one out of the air, then snuffles around the ground collecting the rest.

I don't know what kind of dog Bo is. Neither does Dad. Neither *did* Dad. He's mostly black, flecked through with gray, lighter around his muzzle. He looks like he's got some husky in him, some malamute, and almost definitely some wolf. He's got that wildness to him. Dad said that you can't tame a wolf-dog, just make an ally of him. Bo's never been on a leash in his life.

I chew slowly. Even though I'm starving, I feel queasy, an odd churning in my stomach. It takes me a minute to recognize it. I had the same feeling after the accident, when they told me Mom was dead. For two, three days, things swung between horrible, clawing grief that hurt more than my injuries and a pinched numbness. That pinching was awful, but it meant I didn't think about Mom. Her death didn't feel real to me, not for a long time.

That's how I feel now. Numb. Numb is good. Numb means I

can think, can figure everything out, before the grief comes.

Shelter, I think, forcing down another bite of salmon.

The fifth or sixth night I spent here, my dad called me over to the fire. *If you ever get stuck away from the cabin at night, you're going to need to know a few things,* he said. That's when he told me about the cold, the water, the food, the fire. I was only half listening. I didn't think I'd need to know any of it. Didn't want to need to know any of it.

Did he teach me anything about building a shelter? I can't remember, or else it hurts too much to remember. I reach further back, find a safe memory, one that doesn't burn. A "field trip" in fourth grade. A field trip all the way out to the trees behind our school. "Wilderness day." They taught us to stay where you are if you get lost, use white clothes as a signal because they're easy to spot, things like that.

They taught us how to build shelters, which was the fun part. We made them with one big branch propped up against a log or a rock like a spine, then we laid smaller branches and evergreen boughs across like ribs. The branches and needles layered over each other to keep rain out, and then we filled the shelters with dead leaves and stuff from the forest floor, which they said would keep us warm.

I laugh, choking laughs halfway to sobbing. I've had weeks with my dad, the king of the wilderness, and I was so busy being angry that I didn't listen to a thing he said. Instead I'm remembering some stupid field day with a bunch of suburban kids who'd never spent a night out in the open in their lives.

The grief almost finds me, teeth and claws at my throat. I

make a strangled sound as I remember—the terror, the sound of it, the way that second stretched out and out and out and then snapped back into an instant that was too short, too fast to do anything about.

My dad is dead.

However much it burns, I can't escape that knowledge.

I didn't know him. I didn't like him. But he was my dad, and I loved him.

I don't know how to live without him. Literally. When Mom died it was like the grief squeezed everything out of me, breath and blood and feeling. I didn't know how I would live, then, but I knew that I would.

The grief is different now. Not as bad, maybe. But the living part is so much worse. I don't know how to survive out here. I don't know if I can.

"That's enough," I snap. "That's *enough*. We are not doing this again."

I spent two weeks refusing to do physical therapy after the accident. Refusing to talk to anyone. Refusing to move out of bed except to drag myself, crying and swearing, to the bathroom.

If I do that now, I'm going to die. I've lived too long where it's hard to die. I don't know how to be properly afraid yet. I don't know how to tell the difference between one kind of fear and the next. The fear that makes you fast. The fear that makes you wary, lets you hear a twig snapping like it's a gunshot. The fear that makes you freeze. The fear that paralyzes you, and the fear that keeps you alive.

I'm going to die, I force myself to think, and then I say it out loud, shout it, because I need to believe it down in my gut or I'm never going to be able to move.

"I AM GOING TO DIE," I scream across the lake. The words tear from me and leave my throat raw.

Bo barks, backing away from me, then spinning to face whatever threat I'm screaming at. My hands shake. I press my palms against my eyes, shivering.

Bo quiets down, creeps up toward me with his head low and his tail wagging tentatively. I grab him around the neck, pull him close. His fur is wet and the smell of him is strong and musky, but I don't care. I bury my face in his ruff. He huffs against my shoulder. The rain gets stronger, drumming against the hood of my rain shell until I want to tear it off and let myself get soaked just to get a little silence. I shut my eyes.

"I'm going to die," I whisper. "I'm going to die." I'm stuck on it. *Unless*, I force myself to add. There are a hundred, a thousand things that come after that word, but I focus on one.

"I'm going to die unless I find shelter," I tell Bo. "Shelter first." Something to keep the rain off me, to keep the cold out. Something that can fit me and Bo and even a fire, which means it has to be more impressive than the little hutches we made in school. I can make a lean-to, I think, if only I have something to lean it *against*.

I had weeks with my dad, walking out in the woods. It all blurs together now into brown and green; I couldn't even keep track of which way the lake was, once we were in the thick of the trees. But I remember a boulder. Dropped here by some long-gone glacier, it leaned a bit, like it was drunk. The ground under it had been dry. Safe from the rain.

If only I can remember where it *is*.

We were checking the traps my dad set nearby. He said it was a bad spot and picked them up to set somewhere else later. He looked up at me, grinned.

"You've got dirt on your cheek," he said. I went to wipe it clean. He shook his head. *"Makes you look like a proper wild girl."*

I rolled my eyes. *"It's going to take more than a little dirt."* I scrubbed at my cheek with my sleeve until the skin stung. He reached over, his hands all mucked up from working in the dirt, and tapped my nose.

"It's a start," he said. I grabbed my nose defensively. He just laughed, and I almost laughed, too. Almost. Managed to keep glaring, but only just. Had to stomp away to keep from looking like it'd been funny. That's when I saw the boulder, and the sun was low between the trees.

What direction? Where did we go from there?

I keep my eyes closed until I think I know, drawing a mental line from the lake to the rock.

The pill is kicking in, so I'll have to be careful. The pills make it so it doesn't hurt when it should, and that's when you injure yourself. I know my injuries are going to be my biggest problem. It would be hard enough for a whole, healthy person to survive. I'm hurt. I have to survive *and* let my body knit up.

Which means walking as little as possible today. Which

means that I have to get this right on the first try, or I'll add a bunch of wandering around I can't afford.

"I've got it," I tell Bo. I don't sound convincing. I let go of him slowly. He sits down, watching me. Waiting for instructions.

I look at what I have with me. Backpack, duffel bag, rifle, bow, hatchet, arrows.

I reach for the duffel, stop. I shouldn't carry everything at once, not as hurt as I am. I have to prioritize. I grab a handful of clothes from the duffel along with the bottle of pills and stuff them into the backpack. I grab the hatchet and the rifle, leave the bow and arrows in the duffel. It's not like there's anyone out here to take them.

I get to my feet, stop. My first task should be the simplest thing in the world. Walk to the rock. And if I was whole, if I was healthy, maybe it would be simple.

But I'm not. Haven't been for a long time. After the accident, I couldn't walk for weeks. And now—my foot drags. My leg seizes up. Now I'm not supposed to walk on uneven ground. I'm not supposed to run or strain myself.

I look around, as if a sidewalk will manifest itself in the wilderness. I snort. Will said it would take me another year at least before things start feeling normal, before I don't have to take every step carefully. I shouldn't have run yesterday, throwing myself carelessly through the trees, tripping on roots. I shouldn't be walking now. But I don't have a choice.

"Come on, Bo," I say. "Let's go."

Before

I FELL ASLEEP in the car, lulled by Griff's tuneless singing, and when I woke up he was shaking my shoulder.

"Passport," I realized he was saying.

"What?" I said.

"Your dad said you have a passport. You need to get it out," he said.

I sat up, rubbing at my eyes. My bad leg had stiffened up from sitting crammed in the car for so long. I kneaded it and peered around. We were behind a couple of other cars in some sort of line. A border checkpoint. "Where are we?" I asked.

"Heading into Canada," Griff said. "You need your passport."

Confused, I dug around in my bag until I found it. It was full of stamps. My mom used to take me all over the world. Paris and London and Bangkok and Hong Kong. We hardly ever got far from the airport, but I got little tastes of everywhere.

We got to the front of the line. Griff rolled down the window, and a man in a baseball cap and windbreaker leaned down to squint inside.

"Good afternoon," he said. "How are you two doing today?"

"Good," Griff said, more of a grunt than a word. I just gave him a crooked smile that could have meant anything. I knew it exaggerated the scars on my cheek. It tended to stop questions dead.

Griff handed over the passports. "Got one of those letters, too," he said. He reached across me and popped the glove box. It was stuffed with paper napkins and wet wipes, along with more receipts and a folded, crumpled paper, which he held out to the border agent. "About the kid."

He looked at our passports, then at the letter, frowning slightly. I couldn't tell if it was a something's-wrong frown or just a paying-attention frown. "What's your reason for visiting Canada today?" he asked.

"Just visiting," Griff said. "Friends, I mean. Visiting friends." I couldn't tell if he was nervous or if this was just more of his odd self. I did my best to look normal. I didn't know why we were heading into Canada, either, but I didn't want to get Griff in trouble.

"This letter says your father's given permission for you to travel with Mr. Dawson," the border agent said, looking me in the eye. "Is that the case?"

I blinked, then realized that Mr. Dawson must be Griff. "Yeah," I said. I didn't sound completely convinced. I mean, I hadn't read the letter, and I hadn't talked to my dad for more than two minutes on the phone in the last ten years. "Yeah, he did. We're visiting friends."

He looked at me for another long moment. It made me afraid,

even knowing he was probably just looking out for me. He was like the lawyer who handled my mom's will and the pilot who flew me up to Alaska. Men who saw my scars and wanted to step up and protect me, even if they couldn't figure out anything to protect me from.

"All right, then," he said. He handed our passports back to us after a little more examination, and we filtered our way through. In five minutes we were out the other side and in Canada. Griff relaxed, and I gave him a puzzled look.

"Why *are* we in Canada?" I asked.

"It's where your dad is," he answered. That was all the explanation I got for hours.

GRIFF DROVE TO another airfield. This one was even smaller than the last. It was private, tucked away next to a lake where Griff's bright yellow plane waited, its bulbous floats keeping it crouched on the water like a bug.

In a building—not quite a cabin—beside the tarmac, he served us a dinner of fat, sizzling sausages on buns with yellow mustard and no ketchup, which I thought might be more of his odd obsession with yellow but turned out to just be because he ran out.

"The legendary Sequoia Green," he said. I didn't correct him. "Your daddy's one of my best friends. He saved my life once. We were rafting, you see, and we hit a big rock. I fell in, and he fished me out. So he saved my life."

Griff didn't tell very good stories. The way my dad told the same story, Griff and I laughed so hard we had to hold our sides because our ribs hurt, and Griff snorted beer out his nose and into his beard and then we all laughed about that. Only now I can't remember how he told it, and even if I did and I wrote it down it wouldn't be as funny, because Dad's just like that. Dad makes people laugh. It's why Mom married him even though she shouldn't have, even though anyone could see that.

Dad *made* people laugh. Past tense. He died and I'm alone, and no one is coming for me. Pretending won't bring him back. But in that moment with Griff at the airfield, Dad was an entirely different kind of gone. He was hovering in the future, not lost in the past. Somehow it worked out to nearly the same thing.

But meanwhile, Griff and I were eating our sausages and he was telling terrible stories and saying weird things. Things like: "God loves everybody, and when you die he can finally tell you direct. That's why heaven's so nice."

And: "I don't think a person should get married until they've punched someone and been punched at least once."

And: "You ever see a moose run sideways?"

When Griff asked you questions, you didn't have to answer. He'd move on before you could even think it through. He did all the talking for the two of us, which suited me fine. I was still trying to figure out what I felt about all of this, and what I should do. Like, say, run for help. But once you get talking with Griff, the notion of him hurting you goes right out the window. And it wasn't like I had anywhere else to go.

"We'll leave in the morning," Griff told me, slurping down coffee. "Not enough light left today."

"Where are we going?" I asked.

"You're going home. I'm going to the middle of nowhere," Griff said. I laughed because I thought it was a joke, and he looked pleased, so I guess it was. But only in the sense that it was supposed to be funny, not that it wasn't true. We really were going to the middle of nowhere. And it was going to be home.

Griff slept on the floor in his little shack on the airfield, and I slept in his cot. It smelled like him, like sweat and that musky smell guys get. Not bad, just strong. There wasn't any heat, and even bundled up in blankets with two layers of socks on I didn't sleep most of the night.

In the morning Griff poured me coffee that tasted like he'd mistaken jet fuel for Folgers, and then we loaded into his plane. I'd stopped asking questions about where we were going. It was obvious I wasn't going to know until we got there.

"Your dad tells me your mom was a pilot," Griff said when we got settled. "And that you're a bit of a pilot yourself."

"My mom was teaching me. I was working on getting my license." I'd been looking forward to that more than getting a driver's license. It's not that exciting to drive when you can fly.

"Why don't you run through the checklist for me, then?" Griff said, and handed me a clipboard.

My mom told me that checklists are why her job was so safe. Pilots don't have to depend on memory, which will always fail sooner or later. The checklist is God. It works so well that surgeons are studying the way pilots use checklists, to eliminate mistakes when they're operating. You have to assume that you know nothing and that you've forgotten something, because the moment you assume you've got it and don't check, something will go wrong.

Mom was right—I should probably write one right now. Except it would fill this whole notebook. There's always so much to do.

We went through, checking everything over as the plane came bit by bit to life. Call and response, like a ritual. Safety gear—*aboard*. Temperatures and pressures—*in the green*.

My finger trailed down the checklist Griff handed me one item at a time, and I could almost imagine it was Mom's voice responding. That if I looked up, I'd see her as I had so many times before, mouth set in concentration, the faintest line between her eyes as she frowned her way through the safety checks. Mom flew big airliners, but she never, ever got tired of taking us up just the two of us, with nothing but a thin metal skin between us and the sky.

I used to be afraid that my mother would die in a plane crash, and I'd spend the rest of my life wondering if she had time to be afraid. If she could see the ground rushing up. If she was grabbing for an oxygen mask. If she tried to comfort the passengers or if she was only focused on the instruments, on wrenching the giant metal beast back into the sky where it had finally realized it didn't belong.

And then she died on the ground. She died in a car accident, and I was there. The other car came at us from the side, its headlights blotting out any sense of its size. She had time to say my name and fling her arm out across my body, as if that could keep me safe, and then the world ended. Only half of it came back. My half. It was full of wet cold rain and wet hot blood. Of sirens and screaming. But my mother was silent.

GRIFF AND I didn't talk much on the flight up. We had to yell, even over the headsets we wore, and I wasn't much of a conversationalist. We flew over empty land and mangy trees, and then over thicker and thicker forests, and more forests, and I wondered if we would fly forever like this, time suspended around us. Lakes winked at us between the trees, and I remembered a book I'd read that was just like this. A kid going to see his father, in a tiny plane with a pilot he didn't know. The pilot died, had a heart attack, and the kid had no choice but to crash into one of the lakes and live alone on the shore for two months before he got rescued.

That wouldn't happen to me. If Griff had a heart attack, I'd turn the plane around, or I'd land on one of the lakes and radio for help. I'd been paying attention to our heading, and we had plenty of fuel. Griff was flying back from our destination, after all; of course there was enough fuel to get back to that airfield.

I'd never landed a float plane on the water, but I thought I could figure it out. I ran through all of that in my head, and I think it actually turned into a kind of fantasy. Not that I wanted Griff to die, but I enjoyed playing it through. How I'd turn the plane around, how I'd take control. How I'd land and call for help calmly, and when it arrived they'd all be amazed.

Look at her, they'd say. *She flew the plane all by herself. And don't you know her mother just died?* And they wouldn't feel sorry for me at all, just impressed. Except I couldn't help picturing my mom in that crowd, too. Telling me she was proud, she knew I could do it.

Stupid.

Griff didn't have a heart attack. We flew and flew, and then suddenly he said, "Here we are, then," and we banked and descended. We aimed for a lake. On the north shore was a bald patch, not a clearing so much as the trees shrinking back from the water, and in the middle of that was a cabin. Despite the dread of realizing that *this* is what Griff meant when he said I was going home, I thought, *It's beautiful.*

A man in red came out of the cabin. A dog loped along beside him, huge even from this distance. The man raised a hand, and I realized it was my father.

My belly did an odd flop. My father. I hadn't seen him in person in years. He was around when I was born and a little while after, and for one visit when I was four. He was a stranger, and he was out here in the middle of nowhere and not where he was supposed to be.

"I can't stay here," I said, but the engine drowned it out. We touched down on the water, and for one horrible moment I thought we would just go straight down under it. I don't know why I thought that, but I was so sick afraid that the fear got into everything. The lake could swallow us up. Or the dog on the shore could snarl and leap the moment we touched solid ground. And he was a fierce-looking dog, gray black and huge. His tail didn't wag; he just watched us warily with shiny black eyes.

We climbed out of the plane and paddled to shore in a tiny little raft, and my dad and the dog walked over to us slowly. My fear became a lump in my throat like a peach pit. And

After

SORRY. I HEARD a growl outside, and it wasn't Bo because he's right here with me. He snarled and went stiff when we heard it, but he didn't leave, and after a while I heard something move off. So maybe it's safe now.

I— Where was I? Right. My dad and the shore. And Bo.

Before

THE DOG STOOD stiff and unmoving. He stared hard at me, and I was convinced he was going to attack, but Dad ignored him. My dad looked exactly like the picture, except for a little gray in his beard. He still had the same wrinkly laugh lines, and when he saw me he threw his arms out to the side.

"Baby bear!" he said. I stood and stared at him, my peach-pit fear still lodged in my throat. His grin faltered. "Sequoia," he tried instead.

"Jess," I corrected. I'd told him that on the phone, too, and he hadn't seemed to notice. I hated my first name. It was such a hippy name. It had no good nicknames and no good story behind it; it was just a tree and my dad liked trees, so here I was. I'd been Jess since I was four. "My name is Jess."

"Jess," he said, as if teaching it to himself. He dropped his arms. I hugged my duffel to my chest. "I'm glad you're here."

I looked behind him, up at the cabin. It didn't look much bigger on the ground than it did from the air. I couldn't see how we'd both live in it.

"I'm going to build an extension," he said, following my gaze, his hand rubbing the back of his neck.

"I thought you lived in Alaska," I said.

"I did. As far as the government's concerned, I still do," he said. Chuckled. "But out here, nobody bothers me. I don't bother anybody. Works out better for everyone that way." He smiled like it was a joke, but I kept on staring. Mom always said Dad liked the outdoors. Camping and hiking and hunting. But this . . .

"Does anyone know you live out here?" I asked.

"Griff does," he said. "Now you do, too. Couple other people." Something about the way he said that didn't sit right, and his eyes tracked away from me a moment before he spoke again. "But that's the way I like it. You'll like it, too. You'll see. You won't have to go to school and learn all those useless so-called facts." He paused and rubbed the back of his neck again, like he'd been gearing up for a lecture and thought better of it. "I know it doesn't look like much, Seq—Jess, but you'll love it. You're my daughter, after all."

I looked at him a good long while. I wondered if Griff would take me back, if I asked him. And then I thought about what would happen if I did go back. I'd have to explain. I'd go back into foster care. Maybe even back to the Wilkersons, the family I lived with before.

But I *couldn't* stay up here. There wasn't a *here* up here. I'd thought we were going to a little town with maybe one tiny store and a bunch of grizzled people who hardly ever saw each other—but there'd still be *people*. I'd seen that forest stretching to the horizon. There were no roads, no vehicles. When Griff left, I'd be stuck out here.

I had to go back.

"Dinner's about ready," Dad said. "You all should come in and eat." Griff made a triumphant whooping sound and the dog started barking, so hard his teeth flashed and his paws bounced on the gravel. I froze up. I never really liked dogs before the accident. After, they terrified me. They didn't have to be mean to knock me over or crush me to the ground, and here was this dog as heavy as I was, looking ready to charge. I couldn't keep to my feet if it did. Couldn't keep its teeth off me, and even if it didn't bite, I'd be hurt. Hurt again.

Dad laughed. "Bo won't bite," he said. "Not unless I tell him." He winked.

"If he jumps—" I started.

"Not afraid of a little roughhousing, are you?" He gave a bass rumble of a laugh, eyes twinkling. I gaped at him, forgetting about the dog for a moment. I spent every second calculating how to step, how to walk, how to stand to avoid the sharp, immediate pains of a twisted muscle or the later aches of strain and misuse.

I spent every day worried I was getting worse instead of better. That I'd have to go back to walking with a cane, or on crutches. That I'd get hurt badly enough again that I wouldn't be able to walk at all. And here was my dad, seeing me for the first time in years, grinning at the notion.

The dog kept barking. Dad's smile dropped, crumbling away over a few seconds, and he shot a scowl in the dog's direction. "Shuddup, Bo," he snapped. The dog went quiet immediately and went back to watching me. That's how Bo and I met. I was still pretty sure he wanted to kill me. Funny since he's the main reason I haven't died yet.

After

I AM FINALLY on the move.

I force myself to walk slowly. The rain is thinner among the trees, my jeans are already as wet as they're going to get, and it's hours to dark. I have time to do things right. Not to avoid hurting myself—too late for that, with my leg aching and the muscles of my back twisted into knots. But to avoid hurting myself more.

I picture myself the way I was right after the accident, dragging myself step by step with my hands gripped tight around parallel bars for support.

We don't want a setback, Will would say when I pushed too hard. A setback then meant months of frustration. A setback now will kill me.

Will is another safe memory, untouched by fire. I hold on to his voice, his grin, his terrible jokes as I walk.

The trip is painfully slow. Bo sticks by my side the whole time. When I stop, he stops, watching the woods. Sometimes he whimpers, anxious. I wonder how much he understands about what happened. Does he think Dad's coming back?

"It'll be okay," I say over and over. Bo doesn't understand the words. I don't believe them. I keep on saying it anyway.

It takes an hour to get to the rock. Or what feels like an hour. I don't have a watch. My phone ran out of battery long ago. I've already let go of the need to know precise time. *There's only the time it takes,* Dad would probably say, if he were here to say anything at all.

The side of the rock is even more canted than I remember, making a wedge of sheltered space more than big enough for one small girl and one big dog. I can huddle against it and be protected from the rain—but the rain's letting up now, and I'd rather stay warm by moving around. As soon as I rest, my muscles are going to stiffen up, and I won't be going anywhere or getting anything done for a good long while. So I look around.

We had a windstorm a couple of nights ago, and there are a lot of thin, downed trees scattered around the clearing. They'll make a good wall for my lean-to, if I prop them up against the rock, extending the space under it into an inverted *V.* Two solid walls and enough room to sit or lie down beneath them. Once I cover up the gaps between the logs, it'll keep the wind and the rain out. It might even hold the heat in a little.

Thinking in practicalities is the safest thing of all. No sorrow there, no fear, no rage. No stink of burning gasoline or too-red spatter of blood. Only necessity. I focus all my thoughts on the work of survival, and the heat of memory fades until it's bearable again.

I set the backpack under the ledge. I limp around the clearing. I can tell the pill is masking my injuries, so I move slowly, paying attention to how I lift my bad leg.

There: a big, thin birch tree. It's snapped off at the base, the stump jagged and dark with rain. The trunk is only as thick as my forearm, and it's twice as long as it needs to be. I can't hope to move the whole thing. I'm going to have to cut it in half.

I get the hatchet out and test its weight. I can't quite manage a full overhead swing, not with my back as messed up as it is, so I settle for shorter, thwacking strikes. It's slow going, and by the time I'm through, my arm and shoulder have the hot acid feeling of strained muscles. Then I have to go along the length of the trunk, chopping off the protruding branches. But I have the beginning of my shelter. All I have to do is get the two sections over to the rock.

I gauge the distance. Twenty feet, maybe. Not far, but I know I won't be able to lift either of the sections up, and I don't want to walk hunched over—harder to keep my balance that way, and I'll only wrench my back further. I need something to loop around the trunk so I can drag it while standing up.

My belt's not long enough, but the strap from the rifle is. With the belt closed in a loop around the trunk and the strap threaded through the belt, it's long enough that I can stand up straight, lift the trunk a couple of inches—the belt hooked against the nubs of two removed branches—and drag it to the shelter.

I go a couple of feet at a time, stopping to rest. *Slow*, I remind myself, *slow*. Like the first few physical therapy sessions after the accident, with Will promising I'd be running marathons some-day, but urging me to focus on just a few steps right now.

One foot, three feet, nine feet, twenty. I'm at the shelter. I grin triumphantly at Bo, who sits a few yards away, panting. Success.

And then I realize that I still have to lift the trunk up. And get the other one, and repeat the process. I can already feel the trembly ache that means tomorrow I'll be in worse pain than today.

I let out a soft, wounded sound. I want to collapse. Cry. Instead I lower myself to the ground and call for Bo. He trots over and lets me wrap my arms around him, my forehead against his ruff.

Smart, not strong.

It's my father's voice. I don't touch the rest of the memory, but I clutch at that. *If you can't be strong, you have to be smart. And smart is better than strong, out here.*

"We need to be smart about this," I tell Bo. His chest rises and falls with his heavy breath. "I'm going to be useless tomorrow. I'm going to have to rest the whole day, or I'll just make things worse. So I'd better get everything I need *today*, and I have to get it now before the pill wears off."

Dad insisted that fire came last. The least important thing out of what you need to survive. *Shelter*, he said. But I *have* shelter, don't I? I have the overhang. It's not much, but as long as I tuck myself against it the rain can't reach me. And I'm so tired, and the logs are so heavy, and I'm so wet. A fire will dry me out.

Besides, I have food. The salmon will last me a day, at least. I don't know how I'm going to get the peaches open—they're store-bought cans, so there isn't just a lid to unscrew—but I have them with me. And with the rain there's plenty of water. Dad even showed me how to squeeze it out of the moss that grows on the rocks.

I picture a fire, warm and crackling. Contained, kind, not like the hungry, tearing beast that destroyed the cabin. I imagine heating my hands by it, cooking food over it. I'll need fire to survive out here, so I'd better figure it out fast.

Or maybe my dad was right. Maybe I should focus on finishing the shelter.

No. Fire is the smart decision. I've got a partial shelter already, after all. Finishing it can wait.

But how can I make a fire? I don't have matches. Maybe I can rub sticks together. I laugh. It comes out more of a cough.

Maybe there's something else at the cabin or down on the beach I can use. Dad had all sorts of tools. Not all of them can have burned, right?

I don't want to get up. I want to lie down and sleep, and never mind the cold. But I grit my teeth. I stand. I whistle to Bo. I walk.

It's harder this time. My foot drags worse than before, and my arms are tired from all the chopping. I carry only the backpack, now empty, and the rifle. I don't really need it. The things that are likely to kill me out here, I can't stop with a bullet. But when I go to set it down, I can't. I keep seeing my father's face, the instant his eyes met mine. Fear kicks me in the gut, and I can't bring myself to let go.

Halfway back to the beach, I find a long, straight stick. It's just the right size for a walking stick. Not quite as good as the metal cane I used to have—the one George hid the day I left, that I searched for until I had to leave or miss the plane—but it still helps.

I make steady progress until I get close enough to smell it. The smoke is gone, but the stink of char still hangs heavy in the air. I can make out the blistered, charred remnants of the cabin between the trees. I halt, swallow. I should search the cabin. But I can't bear to think about digging through the rubble.

I know I should, but digging around feels too much like digging up a grave. Like digging up my father's grave, and I can't do that, I can't even think about it, or what happened.

So I'll just look. I'll walk around the edge, and see if anything survived.

I start forward. Every step, my chest gets tighter, until I can hardly breathe. Even with the rain, the air stinks of soot and smoke.

My father built the cabin himself. He came up one summer and selected each tree, straight and strong. He felled them and trimmed off the branches, stripped the bark, smoothed them down. He cut notches in them so that they would sit firm and even against each other, crossing at the corners of the house, and he sanded and smoothed them until they fit together so perfectly not the slimmest breeze could steal its way inside. He even cut a window, fit it with glass, hung curtains. Built himself a chimney and a table and a pair of stools.

All of that is gone now. The floor is charred black. The walls have collapsed. A few segments of log remain, blackened and crumbling. The woodpile, stacked along the side of the cabin, is burned up completely. You can just make out where the bed was, and the interior wall, but that's about it. The fire was thorough.

I walk along the edge. The wind stirs the damp ash; metal glints. The head of Dad's ax. The handle's been burned away, and the head is completely black except for one little strip at the edge—but whole.

I creep close enough to lean out and drag it to me. It's heavy, but I can carry it. I can manage it. And if the ax head has survived, other things might have. *I'll search*, I promise myself, already shrinking back, as if the heat still lingers, as if it can still burn me.

Later.

I fit the ax head into the outer pocket of the backpack and zip it up. My fingers are stained black. I rub them on my jeans unsuccessfully, only managing to spread the stain around. The shed's next. The day before it burned—yesterday, was it only yesterday?—Dad hung a deer carcass in there. Stretched out its hide on a rack.

All burned now. I can't even tell what might have been deer. There are bits of metal here and there, but nothing whole enough to be useful that I can spot.

Somehow, though, the fire missed one corner of the shed almost completely. A section of unburned logs reaches as high as my hip, and in the corner sits a small pyramid of glass jars for canning. I bend over and pick the top one up. They're coated in soot, but I rub at it with my sleeve to read the label.

MOOSE, it says. My heart leaps with excitement.

Then sinks. The jars are empty. No moose meat for me. But the jars themselves can still be useful.

I tuck five of them into the main compartment of the backpack, where they shift and clink against each other. I can't fit any more without worrying they'll break; I'll come back for them later. I straighten up. Nothing more to do here; the outhouse certainly isn't going to have anything helpful.

I limp down to the water. Every step hurts. I've stopped trying to lift my bad leg, just lean hard on my walking stick and drag it forward across the pebbles.

At the shore I bend slowly, agonizingly, and fill one jar. Two. Three. Now the bag is getting heavy, and I stop. I'll sip slowly. I'll leave the jars out to collect the rain. I'll be fine. I'll need to boil the lake water in any case, which means fire is even more of a priority, and I can't waste time.

I look along the shore. It's so empty. The trees stand mutely; no birds flit or call in the branches. *Silent as a grave*, I think, and a shudder goes through me. Where's Bo? Not here. Gone again, because it's what he does, he's half wild and he belongs to this place. Not like me, shivering and cold and half-starved before I've even gotten through a single day.

Two cans of food, that's it, and after that it'll be the long slouch to starvation or one quick, cold night or a foot in the wrong place that leaves me dying of thirst on the forest floor. I'm not a wild girl. I've never lived outside the city, never been on my own at all. I've never been so alone, and the silence stretches out forever, for miles, through endless woods and endless empty sky, and the panic grabs hold of me, grabs hard, a bruising fist around my ribs.

And then a splash. A fish leaping up, falling back into the water, and a second one, ripples sprinting over the surface of the water before it turns back to glass. I take a deep breath. Fish. There are fish in the lake, and that's food, right there, if I can just figure out how to catch it. And then I see something else: a familiar green bulk. The canoe. It's sitting there, upended to keep the rain and debris out.

I should leave it, but I don't know that yet. I shouldn't be here in the first place. I should be building the shelter, or at least letting myself rest. Instead I walk down to the shore (mistake). I flip it over (mistake), groaning with the effort, and an oar falls out. There's a seat that lifts up for storage. Inside is a little first aid kit, which I gleefully tuck into my bag. And rope. And a tackle box.

The rope is thinner than my finger, white and blue. I can't guess at how much is coiled up—fifty feet? One hundred? But I'm grinning as I pack it away. I pull the tackle box out last and close the seat, standing a minute to admire the canoe.

The canoe means I can travel all along the lake. I'll have to paddle even though my back is wrenched, sure, but it's not nearly as bad as my leg, so using my arms and letting my leg rest is a good thing.

The lake hooks at the southern end, sort of boot-shaped, so you can't see a big section of it from the north shore where I stand. Who knows what's down there? My dad said there was good fishing and trapping on the south side. I don't have poles, but I have the tackle box with its fishing lines and hooks and lures—and a knife. I can fish.

I grin at the lake. "I think it's going to be okay," I say. "I think we'll be okay."

I start to think that I'm not going to die, just as I've begun to believe I will. This is the biggest mistake of all.

Before

AFTER MOM DIED, after I got out of the hospital, I spent three months living with a foster family while my lawyer and the state tracked Dad down. I'd wanted to stay with my friend Ronnie. I usually stayed with her when my mother was out of town. But her parents had five kids of their own, and I needed constant trips to the hospital and physical therapy, and so it was decided—by Ronnie's parents, by the lawyer, by the court, I'm not sure—that I needed a "medically experienced foster family." Which is how I ended up with the Wilkersons, a couple with identical round faces and identical sour frowns. They trudged their way around the house like they were dragging all their life's disappointments with them, and never left any doubt that their foster kids—me, Lily, and George—were some of those disappointments.

The first morning there, I stared up at the slats of the bunk bed and listened to the rest of the house wake up. Mr. Wilkerson grumbled and yelled his way through the morning, and Mrs. Wilkerson started yelling back about five minutes after he got up. They weren't angry; they just didn't know how to talk to each other without *sounding* angry.

Lily managed to sleep through it, or pretended to. But you wanted to get up before George did. If you were still asleep when he got up, he'd torment you. For little Lily, he liked to grab her feet and yank her off the bed so she banged onto the floor. George was fifteen. I was older, but he was bigger, and he thought that he could bully me, too.

We got up earlier and earlier to try to beat him. When I'd been there a few weeks and George realized that he'd get in trouble for harassing me, because I was so delicate, Lily would crawl into my bed with me before the sun came up. I'd wrap myself around her like she was a doll, and she'd snuggle in against me.

Lily's father was in jail for beating up her mother, and her mother was a drug addict. Lily was six years old and had been in foster care three times already. Being around her was strange, because one minute I would think, *At least your mother is alive,* and then the next minute I would think, *At least I had a mother who took care of me.*

You don't really need to know any of that. You don't need to know Lily and George's names. The world's going to forget them a lot in their lives, so I doubt they'd even be offended if I did. But it's important for me to remember, like it's important to re-member that my mother's favorite color was blue and she liked starfish and when she laughed she hid her mouth with her hand because she had crooked front teeth.

Because when I lose the little pieces like that, I lose *before.* And without before, I only have the lake and the woods and the winter that I can taste in the air, and that's not enough reason to stay alive. I cried when I said good-bye to Lily, and said I wished I could bring her with me. Now that thought is like a nightmare. It's better that I'm alone, because then I don't have to try to take care of anyone—try and fail.

The day Griff and I flew to the lake, though, I was missing her and missing home, messed up as it was, and I figured I was about as miserable as I could get. Which goes to show how whiny I could be back then. I might still whine, but at least now I've got a better reason.

After Bo and I had our not-so-friendly introduction, Dad led us all back up to the cabin. The path up was smooth, and he'd filled it in with pebbles from the shore. Two big rocks, painted white with ram skulls tied to them with thick twine, marked the transition from the beach to the cabin. Their empty eye sockets stared at me, and I shivered.

The cabin was small: two rooms, with no door between them. Just a doorway with a curtain. He didn't even have a wood-burning stove, just a rough stone fireplace and a big black pot to boil water in.

Everything smelled of smoke and dog. Bo collapsed by the fire right away, but he didn't stop watching me. Dad served us dinner. Venison flavored with wintergreen that grew nearby, and some blackberry preserves and a loaf of hot, crumbly bread. Except for what Griff brought in, all of Dad's food was what he'd caught. Birds, rabbits, deer, fish, even squirrels when pickings were slim. Mostly fish, though. Lots and lots of fish.

I picked at the venison, trying to be polite by getting down a couple of bites at a time. I figured if I was polite it would soften the blow when I told Dad there was no way in hell I was staying here. When Griff left, I'd be leaving, too.

Dad watched me as closely as Bo did. When he finally glanced at Griff, I palmed a piece of meat and wiggled it where the dog could see it, figuring it would make it look like I actually ate something. I meant to toss it so he wouldn't come close to me, but he lunged up and over immediately, and he was so big and the cabin was so small that he'd reached my dangling hand before I could whip it out of the way. But he stood there, nose to my fingers, whistling wetly into my palm, and didn't take the meat.

"You have to say 'take it,'" Dad said. He was grinning again.

"Take it," I said, looking at Dad instead of the dog. Bo snatched the meat out of my fingers and retreated to the fire to eat it. Then he licked his chops and went back to watching me. Only this time he had that begging-dog look instead of a wary one. "I think he's warming to you," Dad said. "And you don't have to worry about eating, kiddo. I know your appetite's probably pretty screwy. Moira never could eat when she was nervous."

Moira. Mom. He said her name with such affection. "I'm tired," I said.

"You can have the bed until I build that extension," Dad said. "I'll be fine outside unless it rains, and then I can take the floor with Bo."

I looked over at Griff. He wouldn't be leaving in the dark, I thought, and he was a couple of beers in, which really meant he shouldn't be leaving. He'd wait until the morning, and then I'd go with him. I was safe to sleep for the night.

I nodded and rose. I thought about asking if I should help with the dishes, but then I realized that I had no idea how he'd do the dishes. Probably wash them down in the lake. And it was all too much—back then washing dishes in a lake seemed like hardship—so I just grabbed my duffel and headed into the back room, closing the curtain behind me.

I stayed in my jeans and long-sleeved tee rather than changing. Griff and Dad were talking and eating, but maybe they'd want to check on me and pop their head through the curtain. I never undressed in front of people anymore. At the Wilkersons I had to change in the bathroom with George hammering on the door.

At least there, all of us were some kind of broken. I was just the only one that came labeled. And that's what the scars were: a big label that told people everything they thought they needed to know about me.

I sat on the bed, heaping the blankets over my lap. I hauled my duffel up beside me and slowly unpacked my things. Last of all I took out a photograph. This was my nightly ritual, staring at the one reminder of Mom I let myself carry.

The photo showed Mom and me, standing with our arms around each other and the wind whipping our hair over our faces. We look alike, everyone says so. Pointed chins and dark eyes, dark hair that's in constant rebellion and never stays where it's told. Except she was prettier than me, and I don't look like that anymore. The scars pull at my face, make it uneven. The skin over my eyelid is burned, and my lid droops a little. It doesn't bother my vision. The weird thing is, it usually makes people think I'm brain damaged or something. If I wear sunglasses, they treat me just about normal. If I take them off, they start talking really slowly and sweetly, like I'm a little kid.

It was hard to look at the old photo, and I'd thought about keeping one with just Mom in it, but it wasn't just Mom I wanted. It was the two of us. It was her arm around me, and the wind that carried us both up, up, to where there was no one else. I looked at it every night. It was like if I didn't check it every night, it might disappear, and my memory of Mom with it.

I must have fallen asleep at some point, because the next thing I knew I was waking up to the sound of plane engines, and I swore. I grabbed my duffel. And then I realized that my things were still out, on top of the blankets. I stuffed them back into the duffel, then yanked my shoes on. The engines were getting louder. *He's going through the checklist,* I told myself. *You've got time, you've got time, just hurry.*

I left my shoes unlaced. I thump-stepped through the cabin and outside, where my dad stood with his hands on his hips, watching Griff's plane as it glided across the water and its nose pulled up and it lifted smoothly into the sky.

I stumbled my way forward. "Wait, don't leave," I said, but my voice was a whisper and it hardly got out of my mouth. "I can't stay here."

But Griff was gone. Dad turned to me with a big grin.

"Hey, sleepyhead," he said.

"He left," I said stupidly. The plane was already getting far away, turning the size of a yellow jacket. I walked forward, almost to the water. As if he'd see me and turn around if I just tried to follow. But the plane was nearly gone, and with it any fantasy of a quick return.

I was stuck here, with no company for hundreds of miles except a father I didn't know at all.

After

THE DAY AFTER the fire, the lake lies still, as if waiting for a plane I know isn't going to come. I stand too long by the canoe, watching the water and the sky. By the time I turn away, I'm already feeling the impact of my mistakes, a trembling weakness in my limbs I know will spread.

I start back for the trees with the duffel and tackle box. Bo comes trotting down from the tree line to join me, seemingly as eager as I am to get away from here. Little ripples of pain go down my back, but I grit my teeth against them. The backpack straps dig into my shoulders.

When I bend to pick up the duffel, a big rip of pain goes down my side and I have to brace myself against a tree trunk, panting. Between the tackle box and the ax, it's too much to carry.

"I can't carry this by myself," I say with a moan dangerously close to despair.

I want my dad with me. The whole time I was with him, I resented him, and I resent him now, I *hate* him because all of this is his fault; none of it would have happened if he hadn't dragged me out here and I wish I had never seen him again and I wish he was here now.

I wish he could tell me it would be all right.

I wish he could laugh at me and smudge dirt on my nose and call me stupid nicknames.

Tears fill my eyes. Bo whuffs against my leg as if to say, *You're not alone.* Or maybe I just want to believe that's what he's saying. Bo's the most loyal dog I've ever met. He's warm and he's fierce, but he's also strong. If only he could carry things for me.

Maybe he can.

I'd put my belt back on at the rock, but now I take it off. "Bo, sit," I say. He obeys warily. "Okay, now hold on. I don't know if you've ever worn a collar..."

I start to put the belt around Bo's neck. He jerks away and dances a few steps farther from me, eyeing the belt warily.

"It's okay, Bo," I say. "Come on, honey." I wiggle my fingers. Slowly he creeps forward. This time I hold the belt out for him to sniff. He gives it a cursory whiff and then looks at me like I'm a crazy person. I laugh.

The look is so incredulous, his eyebrows twitching up and everything. "It's not going to hurt you," I promise. I lift the belt slowly up to his neck, talking to him the whole time, letting him know who's a good boy. Gently, I slide the end through the buckle and cinch it to the last hole. "Okay, hold on," I say.

I let go. Bo gives a great shake, casting off droplets of water in every direction. I shriek and throw up my hands to stop the doggy-smelling water from splattering all over my face.

Bo freezes. He inches to the right. Inches to the left. Whirls around, trying to see his new decoration. He whines.

"It's okay," I assure him. "You look handsome."

He lifts his paw and ducks his head like he wants to scrape it off, but then he looks at me. I give him as stern a look as I can muster, and he lowers his paw.

"It's not for long," I promise him.

Then for the real test. I take the strap off the rifle again. I'd have to carry the rifle in my hand. I tie one end of the strap to the belt. It's long enough, but I can already see that dragging the duffel will be awkward, pulling Bo to one side.

I remember the rope. It's way too long, but I get out the ax head and prop it up between my knees. The soot rubs off on my jeans, but I'm already so filthy it hardly makes a difference. And who's around to see, anyway?

I run the rope over the ax to cut it until I have two good lengths. I take the strap off the belt. The two pieces of rope go in its place. I put one to either side of Bo, who still acts like I've gone completely crazy and he's just indulging me. I tie them off to the duffel straps.

Now the big test. I walk in front of Bo a few feet and call to him. "Here, boy!"

He hesitates a long moment before stepping forward. The ropes pull taut. He stops immediately and looks back with a faint growl.

"Come here, Bo," I say firmly, trying to sound like my dad.

He obeys slowly, each step exaggerated. The duffel drags along behind him. When he reaches me, I lavish him with praise, ruffling his ears. He pants, pleased and puzzled.

We do it again. Five feet, then ten, and then when I snap my fingers, he follows alongside me. It isn't a great system. The duffel keeps getting caught on things, and a stick rips a hole in the side and I have to turn the whole thing over so the contents don't spill out over the ground, but we make it to the rock and I don't have to carry nearly as much.

I'm still exhausted, though. My eyelids are drooping and my limbs have gone past that trembly feeling. Now they just feel numb and limp. I can barely drag myself to the overhang. I call Bo over and fumble with the belt, but my fingers are stiff and cold, and I can't get the buckle to release.

Finally I slide the whole thing over his head, flattening his ears briefly against his skull. He shakes again when it's off, then races around the clearing like a madman, tail between his legs and tongue hanging out. He makes three wild laps and then skids to a halt, at complete attention.

I laugh at him. He gives me an affronted look. I pull the duffel over and unzip it. The rest of my clothes are in there, and they're dry. Thank God. The tackle box I set aside; I'll inventory it in a moment. I set my can and jars in order.

Canned peaches, one partially empty jar of salmon, three jars of water, two empty jars. I set the empty jars outside the shelter, open, to collect the rain whenever it starts falling again.

I set my pain pills next to the full jars. I could take another, but there are only four left. I might need them later, and it's not like pain is a new experience for me.

I set the ax head on the far side of the overhang. I don't want to accidentally kick it and slice my foot open in the night.

I sort through the rest quickly: wallet, keys, shampoo, deodorant, hairbrush, phone (I stare at it for about three minutes, wondering why it seemed so very important just a few days ago), phone charger, and a thriller I picked up in the airport book store. In the backpack I have a notebook—this notebook—and a bunch of pens as well, which at the time I dismiss as useless and set aside with the phone and all the rest.

I tuck everything under the ledge and pull the tackle box over to me. It takes a moment to force the box open, since the latches are stiff and my fingers are shaking.

Inside is a bounty. A knife, a flint and steel kit, fishing line, hooks, lures. If only I had a rod, I could be a fishing queen. And then my heart sinks.

The flint and steel kit. Fire. I haven't gathered firewood. I haven't even gathered tinder. I have to get up. I have to gather wood.

I think about getting to my feet, and start crying. I'm too tired. I hurt too much. I can't do it. "I can't," I say. "I can't get up. I can't."

I know I'm feeling sorry for myself, but I'm also right. I took the extra walk down to the canoe, and I flipped it over, which was idiotic when I was already hurting so much. I won't be able to stand up and wander and bend over again and again to pick up fallen twigs and sticks and branches. I took that whole trip to find supplies to make a fire, and I can't do it.

I've nearly killed myself by forgetting how close I already am to death, but I'm lucky, because I've forgotten about my most valuable possession: Bo.

I curl up under the overhang, tears wetting my cheeks. Bo

crawls in beside me and lays down. He's warm, his steady breathing soothing.

"We'll be okay," I tell him. "We'll be okay until . . ."

Until. I say that word and it all comes crashing back. There is no until. No one's coming for me. Which means that it isn't enough to find food that my dad left behind; that will run out. I don't need food; I need ways to get food, to make food. It isn't just today, it isn't just tomorrow, it isn't just this week. It's months and months, and maybe someday someone will come, but I can't count on it. Can't count on them. Just myself, and I'm one girl, who's been in the woods for only a few weeks, who's never had to survive. Who's been hurt again and again. Funny how one word can change everything for you. Can save your life.

I'm not strong. But I'm smart. "We need a plan," I say, resting against Bo's side. "A really, really good plan."

Bo whines.

With pain pulsing through my body, I slowly drift to sleep, the sound of rain pattering against the ground all around me.

Before

I WATCHED GRIFF'S plane shrink and vanish. My dad put his hand on my shoulder and I jerked around, startled. He looked wounded. "He'll be back," he said. "He'll bring in more supplies. But we've got plenty to do in the meantime. Let me show you around."

"I've already seen the whole cabin," I snapped. I'd seen the outhouse, too. I'd almost cried. I'd had to hold my breath the whole time I peed, flies buzzing all around me and bouncing against the wooden walls. *Stuck here, stuck here*, I thought, over and over again. "What more is there to see?"

"There's a whole lot of things to see," he said. He scratched his chin like he wasn't quite sure what to say next. "And you'll have to get to know how things run around here. I can't take care of everything myself, not with both of us here."

"You want me to do chores? Fine. Just point the way."

"Chores? Some, I guess. But you're going to have to learn to feed yourself. To look after yourself. Sometimes I'll be gone two, three weeks hunting and that sort of thing. And you'll have to look after yourself while I'm out there."

I stared at him. "You'll leave me alone here?"

He laughed. "You'll do fine, baby bear."

He'd called me that twice, and I had absolutely no recollec-
tion of it as a nickname. But he kept saying it like he expected me
to remember.

"Fine," I said. Whatever. It wasn't like I was going to be here
long. "Show me around."

We started with the cabin. Not getting to know the rooms,
obviously, since (as my dad said) you could stand at the door and
spit on the back wall, but the things in it.

There were three hunting rifles and many boxes of ammunition. There was an ax and a smaller hatchet, an iron poker for the
fire, flint for striking sparks, blankets, food, pots, knives, wood-
working tools, plastic tarps, hammers, saws, fishing rods, fishing
lures, fishing hooks, fishing nets, dried herbs, spices, vitamins,
painkillers, antibiotics, jugs of water, jugs of cider, jugs of beer,
biscuits, condensed milk, candy, an old can of soda—

I could keep going. I could fill pages. There was so much of it,
and *I had no idea*. I barely even listened as my dad rattled everything off.

When every item was named and inventoried, we walked
along the rim of the lake. Near the water a green canoe lay belly-
up, speckled with sand. Dad and I carried it down and set it into
the water. Or Dad did, hefting it at the middle, and I reached a
hand toward the stern as if to help but barely scraped the wood
with my fingernails.

My step dragged, and pebbles were harder to navigate than

asphalt. I didn't trust myself with a bulky, unfamiliar weight on top of all of that. Or at least, that's what I said. I don't remember anymore if I said it because it was true or because I didn't want to help. Helping meant giving in to this, even if just a little bit.

If I was going to stay, I wasn't going to do it cheerfully.

Bo seemed to know where we were going and set off along the shore. There were fish in the lake, trout and perch, and even on this short run Dad dropped a line over the side with a minnow speared on the hook. The rod hooked into an open loop on the side of the canoe, so it wouldn't get pulled over the side. We were halfway across when the line jerked and danced.

"Reel it in," Dad said. I hesitated. He swapped himself around and squeezed in next to me, crouching in the bottom of the boat. He put my hands in the proper positions.

I started ploddingly reeling it in. His hand closed over mine. I flinched.

"You can't let it get too slack," he told me. "Or he has room to get free of the hook. Bring him in quick."

I cranked rapidly. The line stretched out into the water, taut and trembling, but I couldn't see anything underneath. I only knew there was a fish because of the twitching and jerking of the rod in my hands. I could feel every movement as the fish tried to get away. He strained, got tired, strained again, but even at his most frantic the reel gave me the leverage to haul him in bit by bit.

Then suddenly he was at the surface, a speckled, gleaming back appearing for a moment before diving below again. I could feel how tired he'd gotten. The jerks of the line that shot all the way through my arms were slower now, a few strong ones instead of constant fluttering panic.

I wished we could let him go, but my dad was hooting encouragement. I hauled back and whipped the lever around again, and then the fish was out of the water completely, hanging from the hook. He was the length of my forearm, and he arched back and forth in the air, his tail curling to the side with force that would have sent him shooting through the water. Useless in the air, though.

"Bring him over the canoe," Dad said. It was an awkward procedure with the rod still jerking this way and that as he tried to make his escape, but soon he was flopping madly in the bottom of the boat. Dad trapped the fish with a boot to its speckled side, and then he hit it three times sharply on the back of the head with a little weighted club.

I jumped at every blow. Blood oozed from the fish's gills. They flared once, twice, slowly as the fish gasped and died. My stomach churned. I'd never killed anything. Or seen anything killed.

"It was just a fish," I whispered.

"It was just a fish," Dad echoed. He twisted the hook free. "But a very good fish who will feed us well. Out here, you have to get your food honestly. It doesn't come in plastic wrap and Styrofoam. You can feel bad for the fish. Or the deer, or the rabbit, or whatever's on your plate. But I think you should feel thankful instead. Its meat keeps you strong. Keeps you alive."

"I think it would rather stay alive itself than keep me alive," I said.

"The fish doesn't get a vote," Dad said gravely, and I stuffed down a laugh before it could escape. He waggled his eyebrows at me. "Now why don't we go make ourselves a little fire, and I'll show you how to make this fellow into lunch?"

My stomach growled. We'd had some dry pancakes for breakfast. They made the inside of my mouth feel gummy, like they soaked up all my spit, and I had only managed to force down one before I pushed my plate away.

We came ashore, and Dad hauled the canoe up halfway out of the water. "Your mission, should you choose to accept it, is to gather kindling and wood for the fire," he said. "It's just for lunch, so we don't need much. Look for—"

"I've been camping," I said. "I can figure out how to pick up sticks." I stomped toward the tree line.

"Stay close," Dad called.

I plunged into the trees. I kept moving until I couldn't see him directly, though I kept glancing back to make sure I could at least see where the trees ended. I didn't want to get lost in the middle of nowhere, Canada, on my first day here.

As I kicked through the underbrush, stacking my arms with fallen branches, I pictured the heading we'd been on. I calculated speed and tried to remember exactly how long we'd flown. But I didn't really know where we'd started from, and to me Canada was a big endless stretch from North Dakota to the North Pole.

No wonder Dad liked it out here, if what he wanted was to get away from people. Even if I wanted to, I didn't think I could tell anyone how to find us.

A growl rumbled behind me as I reached for a fallen branch. I froze. Bear, I thought, or maybe a wolf—but when I peered behind me slowly, it was Bo, standing with his fur bristling on his shoulders and his teeth bared.

"H-hey," I said, holding out a placating hand. Then I realized he wasn't looking at me. A hissing, rattling sound came behind me and I jumped toward Bo, *Snake!* running through my mind, but instead of a snake a fat porcupine came waddle-bolting out of the bush I'd been rummaging in and made for the deeper woods.

As soon as it was gone Bo's growl vanished and he sat, licking his chops and thumping his tail on the ground.

"Good boy!" I declared. I wrapped one arm around my bundle of sticks so I could scrub his ears. "Just about got a face full of quills, didn't I?"

My heart was beating pretty fast, but now I felt foolish. Getting stuck with quills would have hurt like crazy, but it wasn't like a porcupine was going to eat me.

I whistled to Bo, and we headed back to the beach. The dog never left my side. Maybe he sensed that there was no way I'd make it on my own out here. Or maybe he was enjoying the novelty of getting affection.

Dad didn't talk to the dog except to give him orders. The most praise Bo got was a grunted "g'boy." But still Bo ran to Dad when we got back to the pebbled beach. I dumped my armload near the canoe and waited for judgment.

"Make three piles. Different sizes," Dad said. "That way it'll be easy to pick out the next one to toss on."

"Won't it be faster if you just do it?" I asked. My stomach was rumbling and my leg hurt. When it hurt like this, it felt like there was still glass in it, and sometimes I found myself touching my thigh and calf gingerly as if they would slice my fingers open.

Dad looked at me with squinted eyes, and I could tell he was making a decision about more than just lunch. He finally nodded. "All right. We'll hold off on the lessons for now. Just watch what I do, and try to pay attention."

I looked around and located a log to sit on. I dragged it closer by a broken branch that was sticking up, but three steps in, pain jerked up my leg and my knee and ankle just collapsed.

Sometimes the muscles and the tendons don't do what they're supposed to fast enough, so it's like trying to put weight on a hinge. Just *snap* and shut, and I'm on my face or my ass. Luckily this time I was leaning backward to drag the log and I just landed hard on my butt, jarring my tailbone and my spine, and making my teeth click together hard.

My eyes watered, but I bit down on the inside of my lip to keep from crying or making any noise. My leg throbbed and sparked with pain in turns, but I knew it would fade. I hadn't wrenched it or anything, it was just acting up, and the pain would be gone if I could just count to a hundred and not pay attention to it.

Dad laughed. "Watch yourself there, baby bear. You always were a bit clumsy."

I twisted around to glare at him. My vision was blurry with tears. "Last time you spent any time with me I was a baby. All babies are clumsy. I'm *hurt*. My leg doesn't *work* anymore, and you made me sit all scrunched up in a canoe and then go walk around in the woods and collect sticks, and I'm supposed to avoid uneven ground. I'm *supposed* to stick to sidewalks, and I'm not even supposed to go up and down stairs without a handrail. So maybe you can tell me where to find the sidewalks out here. And how about a physical therapist? Because the social worker said you'd have to keep sending me to one. My doctors said it'll take a year for me to get better all the way, and if I'm not careful, I might not ever be able to walk right, and if you'd bothered to pay attention, you'd know that."

Dad gave me a patient, pitying look. "Honey. You don't need a physical therapist. You'll get strong out here," he said. "Who do you think knows what you need better? Some overworked social worker who can't even remember your name, or your dad?"

"*You* didn't know my name," I said. "I haven't been Sequoia since I was a baby." That wasn't completely true, but it felt true and hot and right in my chest, like a burning coal, and I wanted it to burn him. "Christ, Dad!"

"Don't say that," he said.

"What? Christ? You don't want me to take the Lord's name in vain?" I rolled my eyes.

"There is no Lord," Dad said. "God's just a lie the powerful people tell the little people to keep them in line." He gave me an even squintier look. "You're not religious, are you? Moira was never religious."

"We went to church all the time," I said. It was a complete lie. When Mom was out of town and I stayed with my friend Michelle, we went to church on Sundays and youth group on Saturdays, but that wasn't very often, and she moved away a couple of years ago. Usually I stayed with my friend Ronnie and her family because she already had four brothers and her mother said having an extra set of ovaries around could only improve the situation. Ronnie's mother didn't go to church, even though she believed in God, because she said that if God was everywhere she could talk to Him anywhere she damn well pleased.

And then for a couple of years I'd just stayed with Scott when Mom was gone, and then Sundays were for waffles and whatever I wanted on them, even chocolate chips and whipped cream five inches deep. I had the vicious urge to say something about Scott now, about how great he'd been, but thinking about him dragged me up close to all those memories I'd locked away with our stuff, and instead I just glared damply at Dad and crossed my arms.

"Well, I don't hold with that," Dad said. "There will be no praying under my roof."

"What roof?" I asked, and flung my arms out. Bo took this as an invitation to sidle over and lick my fingers, and I snatched them back. He tilted his head to the side and sat down, licking his lips. "Why do you do that?" I asked him. "I'm not a snack."

"It's a signal of submission," Dad said. "He's saying you're the boss." He scowled at the dog. "Took me three damn years to get that dog to listen to what I say."

"Maybe you should have tried asking nicely," I said.

Dad grunted, and he shifted around to put his side to me. He started piling up little twigs and stuffing something white and papery from his pockets underneath them, making a sort of cone. Apparently we were done talking.

"No wonder Mom divorced you," I muttered. He jerked his head toward me but didn't quite look in my direction, and then he put his head down and kept working. I pushed myself around with my hands and my good leg until I was sitting on the log, and hunched to watch. I wanted to put my back to him and sulk, but I really did want to see how to start a fire. Ronnie's dad had always just brought a lighter and some of that quick chemical kindling that lights up fast and keeps burning forever. Dad didn't even seem to have matches.

"There are a lot of different ways to start a fire," Dad said. It sounded like he was talking to himself, even though I knew he wanted me to listen. "If you're lucky enough to have a flint and steel kit like mine, it's easy as striking a spark and being a bit of a windbag."

He was still angry, but the humor I'd heard in his voice when he talked to Griff crept back with that last sentence. He took out a piece of dark rock and a C-shaped piece of metal. Despite myself I leaned forward to watch as the steel rasped and scraped along the flint, throwing sparks into the papery substance. *Bark*, I realized—shredded birch bark.

It took a few tries before sparks struck true enough to take, making pinpoints of glow on the bark. Dad bent over, bracing himself on the shore with his palms, and blew. The pinpoints flared and raced along the bark, making ragged gaps edged with molten orange as smoke boiled between the tiny twigs. Then another rough breath out and the glows spat out thin fingers of flame that grabbed at the bottom of the twigs.

Dad kept blowing, but more gently now, and more and more fingers leapt up until they got a good grip on the twigs. Dad started adding larger sticks, balancing them so the little cone wouldn't collapse.

He narrated everything he was doing as he took the fish and slit it along its belly. He told nobody in particular how to scoop out the guts. He tossed some of them to Bo, who gobbled them up and then nosed over the pebbles looking for more, and then Dad put some of them in a little bag to use as bait later.

"Bo was a gift, you know," Dad said. He speared the fish on a metal rod from a box in the stern of the canoe and set it propped up over the fire. "Got him when he was just a fuzzy puffball."

"Oh," I said, not sure what else I was supposed to contribute. Dad kept the fish turning slowly.

"Man who gave him to me bred dogs to guard against bears," Dad went on. "Didn't think much about me going off on my own, and Bo was a little runty, so he put him in my arms. Said that and a rifle was all the protection I'd need."

I looked at Bo, big-boned and rangy and probably weighing almost as much as me. "Runty?" I repeated.

Dad laughed. "You should've seen his big brother. I think he might have actually been part bear himself."

We lapsed into silence again as Dad turned the fish. He seemed content to sit and turn and sit and turn, but now I was bored and my leg had finally stopped hurting.

I stood up, pushing off so I didn't put any weight on my leg until everything was lined up, hip and knee and ankle. When the joints were stacked like that they didn't collapse, and I could bend slowly to make sure that the muscles had remembered how to work.

I dragged myself off down the beach.

"Don't go far," Dad said to the fire.

Bo, who'd been sitting at Dad's side and staring at the fish with his tongue hanging out, lifted himself with a martyr's sigh and trotted after me. "Don't trust me not to get myself killed?" I asked him. He gave me an apologetic look, and we set off together.

It was hard to pay attention to my surroundings when I had to pay so much attention to my walking. Step, BIG STEP, step, BIG STEP, step, BIG STEP, then step, WRONG STEP, DRAG, LIMP, step.

Will, my physical therapist, had huge shoulders and swoopy hair, and he wore this big doofy grin all the time. His favorite thing to say was "You can do it! You just need the *Will*!" like it was the funniest, cleverest thing anyone had ever come up with.

The first time he said it I glared at him. The next three times I rolled my eyes, but by the time we got up to ten, twenty, thirty times I started giggling or groaning. He said that if I was annoyed at him, I didn't *think* about how much it hurt, and if I was laughing, I didn't *mind* how much it hurt.

I didn't know if that was exactly true, but it didn't take long for me to want to make Will proud of me. And so I pushed and pushed, even when I wanted to cry. And then he had to start telling me to take it easy, but by then he'd done the important thing. He'd convinced me I would get better. He even told me it was okay to get frustrated, and to cry, and to want to give up. He gave me a trigger for when I felt like that, so I could get out of it again.

I would let myself feel awful for a while, because feeling awful can feel really good. But I had to decide on an amount of time—ten minutes, five minutes—and at the end of it I had to snap my fingers and say, "That's enough of that, mopey-head!" in as chirpy and happy a voice as I could.

After that, I was allowed to go back to moping if I really wanted to, but somehow it worked. It wouldn't have worked for everyone, but whenever I had to declare *That's enough of that!* in Will's crazy upbeat tone, I couldn't take myself seriously anymore. Which meant I couldn't stay mopey.

My leg was getting sore, and I stopped. There was a bit of a hill between Dad and me, so I couldn't see him, but I could see the smoke rising up, and I could smell the fish cooking. I looked out over the lake. The wind dragged a ripple across the surface. Out toward the center a fish twice as big as the one I'd got flopped up out of the water and down again. A duck skidded down into the water not far away and paddled by, and insects skimmed over the surface.

I turned around. The trees were the lushest green I'd ever seen. Their branches were thick and tangled with one another, and they netted shadows beneath them until it looked like evening instead of noon. Birds flickered among the branches. There were at least half a dozen different calls echoing among the trees, and the flat, raspy croak of a crow.

It was beautiful. It was nothing like when I'd been camping and there were twenty camping sites laid out next to one another and some guy's RV running a generator and daytime TV in the distance. Here the sounds that wrapped around me were wild sounds and the smells were wild smells and there was no light to stain the sky except the sun.

"That's enough of that, mopey-head!" I declared, channeling my very best Will impression.

Bo looked at me like I'd gone crazy and maybe he should go get help. I grinned at him and scratched him between the ears.

"This totally sucks and my dad is bonkers," I told the dog. I wanted to be clear on that. I was done feeling sorry for myself, but I wasn't done being pissed and out of place. "Now let's go learn how to cook a fish."

After

MY FIRST MORNING under the overhang I wake up warm on one side and frozen on the other. Every muscle in my body aches. I press myself against Bo and whimper. He licks my cheek, then heaves to his feet. I protest—*come back*—but he's already gone, trotting off into the clearing.

I stay curled on my side, my mom's photo in my hand. My thumb covers the version of me in the photo, leaving just Mom, looking right at me. I lie there for a long time. I don't think I can do anything else. I try to sleep again, but it's too cold; the clouds are still thick over the sky and dew dampens everything. I should have changed my clothes before I fell asleep. If it wasn't for Bo, I might have frozen to death in my wet jeans.

At least I have other clothes. And food and water—two rain-filled jars, safe to drink without boiling, and the three from the lake whenever I can get a fire started.

But my food and my water and my clothes are down at my feet, and I can barely move.

I gather my strength for about thirty seconds, and then I roll onto my belly. I pull myself with my arms and push with my good leg, and get myself facing around the other way. The overhang is even better than I thought. Even with the rain that fell overnight it's dry and dusty; I'm the only wet thing under here.

I have to get into dry clothing. My rain shell's kept my torso dry and relatively warm, but my legs are freezing. First, though, I grab the jar of salmon. Propping myself up on one arm, I cram three fingers into the jar and pull out chunks of pink meat.

I have never tasted anything so good. It's oily and salty and it breaks easily over my tongue, and I have to stop myself from wolfing down the whole jar. Just a few bites.

I won't be moving much, so I won't be expending many calories. I can afford to eat slowly. I can't afford to run out of food.

Then I take one of the moose jars I'd filled with water and sip down about a quarter of it. I didn't have much to drink yesterday, so I have a real drink today. But I'm still going to have to ration, in case it doesn't rain, in case I can't get the fire going.

Then it's the hard part. I flip onto my back and undo the fly of my jeans. I'm going to get dirty; there's no way around that. My legs are wet and I don't have anything underneath me to keep the dirt off, but dirt won't kill me.

I work my jeans down my hips. I brace my good leg against the ground and lift my butt up enough to shove them down farther.

The wet fabric clings to my skin and my back twinges with the effort, but the jeans slide down to my thighs. I hesitate a moment before shoving my underwear down, too.

My face heats with embarrassment. "Don't be stupid," I hiss to myself. "There's no one here to see you."

Still blushing and hating myself for it, I manage to get my jeans bunched down to my ankles. Only then do I think about taking off my boots. I groan.

I'm going to have to sit up.

I squeeze my eyes shut and breathe raggedly. I already hurt so much. Tears well behind my lids at the thought of having to do more.

I reach for the pill bottle, pop the lid off with my thumb. Not many left. But saving them won't do me any good if I don't last long enough to use them. I swallow one with a mouthful of moose water and let myself lie still, loose clothes covering my bare legs to keep them warm.

When the aches start to fade a bit, I know it's time. I brace my hands under me and ease myself up.

It's like everything is tearing all over again. I cry out, but I keep pushing. I wonder if Will would be proud or horrified that I'm pushing myself so hard. I haul myself around so I can put my shoulders against the rock, even though that means my neck leans forward at an uncomfortable angle. My neck isn't what I'm worried about.

I fight with my bootlaces. They're swollen from the water and they've worked themselves into tight knots. I rip a fingernail before they finally ease up enough to get my boots off my feet. I strip my socks. Then the jeans and underwear, and now I'm naked from the waist down and still freaking cold.

Getting new clothes on isn't quite as bad as getting the old clothes off. I use an extra pair of underwear to dry my legs off first. I figure no one's going to complain if I have to wear the same pair two days in a row out here, and better to use wet underwear I don't need than a wet shirt I do.

I put it with the rest of the wet clothes and wriggle into my other pair of jeans. Only two pairs. I have to get the other pair dry somehow. I need fire. It keeps coming back to that.

I decide to wait. See how I'm feeling in a couple of hours. The pill should last four, and maybe my muscles will loosen up a bit. Maybe I can gather a little bit of wood.

In the meantime I sit with my back to the rock and try to come up with a plan.

IT'S GOING TO be much, much harder to survive because I'm injured, but sitting here with the drugs kicking through my system and my stomach cramping over my tiny breakfast, I realize that it's helped me, too. Because I was injured, I met Will. And because I met Will, I know Will's Important True Things, which was a silly name for what were really just ways of getting me to think right, so that I'd be able to get better.

One of Will's Important True Things is that you should always know the goal. I have two goals, always: to survive, and to get rescued.

Another of the Important True Things is that you should always have a plan, even if it is only one small thing that you will do first while you come *up* with a plan. You should always be doing something, even if it's thinking, even if it's relaxing (Will says knowing when to rest is as important as knowing when to work).

You have to learn to assume that you will fail and assume that you will succeed at the same time. This is the only way to stay smart and careful *and* stay moving and motivated. You cannot give up and you cannot let up.

I have a third goal, too, I realize. I tell myself I shouldn't. I try not to think about it, because thinking about it means thinking about that day. About what happened.

Nothing is ever going to put it right. That's what I tell myself. I need to stay alive. To survive. Anything else is a distraction. Anything else is impossible, and surviving probably is, too.

I rest the rifle over my lap. My fingertip traces the curve of the trigger. My dad told me when you fire a bullet from a rifle, it can go faster than the speed of sound. Aimed right, and you're dead before you hear it. You never know it's coming.

One single second, that's all it takes.

I try not to think about it.

I think about Will instead. What would Will tell me to do? He'd tell me to make a plan, step by step, moment by moment. Which isn't so different from what my dad told me, not so long ago. *If you want a thing, make it happen*, he said. Days ago, a lifetime ago.

I want to stay alive. And no one's going to make that happen but me.

So I plan.

Before

THE FISH WAS done cooking by the time I got back to my dad. I couldn't remember the last time I'd been so hungry. Which was good, because just plain fish without even salt to season it isn't the tastiest thing I've ever had. But it filled my belly, and by the time we were done eating, Dad and I weren't quite as prickly toward each other.

What he'd wanted to show me over here, it turned out, was a berry patch. There weren't any berries—they'd peaked early this season. But he said next year we could come down and pick pounds and pounds of it, and make jam and preserves to last us all winter.

"Of course, we have to make sure to get to them before Rolly does," he said.

"Who?"

"Rolly. She's a bear," he said cheerfully. "Just a little one, and as long as you don't bother her babies she won't bother you, but she'll eat your berries and your fish and your breakfast out of your hand if you let her, which is definitely not a habit you should encourage. What you really have to worry about is moose."

"Moose? Really?" I said, skeptical. "Aren't they vegetarians?"

"Huge, angry vegetarians. You hear a moose coming for you, get up a tree," Dad said, nodding. "Don't go for the water, 'cause Mr. Moose can swim a whole lot faster than you can. But he can't climb. And you sit up in that tree as long as you need to for him to leave, and then sit up there a little while longer."

"What about a porcupine?" I asked. "What do you do about a porcupine?"

He laughed. "Don't step on 'em," he said. "Porcupine's about the easiest meat you can get out here. They're slow and dumb. You can pin 'em with a stick and hit 'em with a rock, and then you flip 'em over to get at that soft belly and finish them off. Of course, we've got no need, but if you're starving and you can find one . . ."

I must have been making a face at him, because he trailed off. I didn't want to hit anything with a rock. Okay, I thought I could manage catching and gutting fish. But a porcupine? I didn't want to try getting the guts out of that. And what if I stuck myself with the quills? I'd been a vegetarian before Mom died. I gave it up at the Wilkersons because otherwise I'd have gone hungry, but I didn't want to kill an animal myself.

Dad showed me a little stream next, which he said I shouldn't drink, but that would do for rinsing off our hands. He said there was good sweet water down by the south of the lake, a little waterfall, and that he usually went fishing and trapping down that way because for whatever reason, the fish and the "varmints" liked it better on the south side. Which was maybe why when he checked the traps he'd set around here, all of them were empty. He cussed a bit and re-baited them.

"I'll show you how to set these another time," he said, but that sounded even worse to me than killing a porcupine. An animal might be alive and suffering for hours and hours before you ever came to check on it.

We paddled back across the water, leaving Bo to run the lakeshore again. On our way up to the cabin we fetched water from the lake. I didn't carry much, just one half-gallon jug while Dad loaded up with five gallons in each hand. You had to do a lot of hauling to get much water, but Dad said it was sweeter than anything out of a tap.

"Winter's easier in a way, because you can just melt snow," he said, and I pictured myself wading through snow with my bad leg. I had to get out of here before winter. When was Griff coming back? Tomorrow seemed like too late.

"So, Griff's coming back . . ." I prompted.

"Sure is, but you can never really tell when. Depends on the weather and what he's up to. Sometimes he visits a lady friend, and sometimes he gets melancholy for a few weeks, but eventually he always pours himself out of his bottle and comes back." Dad nodded as he talked. "Things don't run on a schedule the way they do in the city," he said. "Things happen when they're going to happen, and there's always more to do than you have time for. It's about priorities, not hours of the day."

My heart sank. It could be weeks, then. It could be winter.

No, it would be before that. Dad wouldn't want to build in the winter, right? He'd want the extension done before it snowed, so Griff would have to come back soon with supplies.

"Jess?" Dad said. He sounded hesitant, a question to my name; that was new. "You remember what Griff's plane looks like, right? The yellow one."

"Of course," I said, confused. Did he think I had memory problems? Was he going to start treating me like a baby, the way some people did? I'm pretty sure even if I did have brain damage, I wouldn't want people talking to me like I was a toddler.

"You see any other plane, come find me," Dad said.

"Why?" I asked, more confused than alarmed.

"It's just that . . . some of my friends, they're not as personable as I am," Dad said. "People this far out tend to be a little rough around the edges."

"Griff's rough around the edges."

"Griff would start a rehabilitation and rescue center for injured flies if he could get the funding," Dad said with a laugh. "The only thing you've got to worry about with Griff is making sure he doesn't swipe your beer. He's a good person. One of the best."

"But you've got friends who aren't good people?"

Dad rubbed his thumb along the side of his mouth. "Griff aside, I don't know that I believe people are good or bad all at once," he said. "We're all a collection of our choices. Good choices, bad choices, choices that don't look one way or another when you're making them. Anyway. Point stands. You see anyone but Griff coming, and you make sure to find me. How's that leg?" Dad asked suddenly.

I blinked at the sudden change of topic, putting my hand to

my leg automatically, kneading the meat of my thigh. "It's okay," I said. "A bit sore."

"You should rest, then," Dad said. He scratched at his neck, where stubble was bristling already. I wondered if he'd shaved for my arrival.

"Okay." I didn't move just yet. It seemed like he was going to say something more, but instead he shook his head. I walked back to the cabin. Bo started to follow until Dad whistled, and I walked the rest of the way alone. Step-drag, step-drag. I had worn myself out too much.

I sat on the bed and took out the picture of Mom. I wished I'd gotten a picture of Scott, too. He'd visited me in the hospital, and he'd called me once a week or so. He'd said he wished I could come stay with him, and I said I wished that, too, but I hadn't meant it, exactly. I hadn't wanted to live anywhere, then. I'd just wanted to sleep and wake up with my mom still there and everything just a dream.

DINNER WAS SMOKED fish and bread slathered in butter and honey. We ate in silence, but when I was licking crumbs and honey off my fingers, Dad finally spoke.

"I loved your mother very much," he said.

I looked at him blankly. It might sound weird, but I'd never really thought about the two of them being together. Mom never once said she loved him that I could remember. It was always, "I thought your father was so exciting," or "Your father wasn't quite like anyone I'd ever met."

"Do you know how we met?" Dad asked.

"You were in an airport," I said.

"She was heading back to Seattle from her cousin's wedding," he said. "And I was heading to Anchorage. I was going to drive tour buses around a glacier. She thought I was funny. We sat in the bar together because her flight was delayed and my connection wasn't for a couple of hours, and I liked her so much that I walked up to the counter and asked for a ticket on her flight instead."

"I didn't know that," I said. "I knew you met in an airport, but I didn't know that." I sounded stupid to my own ears.

"If you know what you want, don't let anything stand in your way," he said. "If you want something, you make it happen."

"I want to go home," I said.

His face fell. "You are home," he said, but it sounded hollow.

"I want to go back with Griff. It's okay, I won't tell anyone," I said. "I won't tell them you're here. I'll tell them . . . I don't know. I'll figure something out."

He shook his head. "Sorry, baby bear, but that's not possible."

"I'm supposed to be in school," I said.

"You'll learn plenty here," he countered. "Things that are a lot more useful than the names of a bunch of dead old white guys."

I pulled my foot up on the chair and curled my arms around my knee. I had to keep my bad leg on the ground. It didn't like to bend like that anymore. "I can't hunt. I can't fish. I can't even walk very well," I said. "How am I supposed to live out here?"

"I'll teach you all of that," he said. Then his face lit up. "Hey, now. What do you mean you don't hunt? Didn't your mom tell me you won some kind of medal?"

"For archery," I said. "When I was thirteen. And that's not hunting. It's shooting a target." My ears burned. I'd taken up archery because my mom told me that my dad was really into it. I'd stopped when she'd let slip that he was into bow *hunting*, and my vegetarian, animal-loving sensibilities had been wounded.

"It's not so different. The target just happens to be a deer or a rabbit. If you scare them into moving, you've lost half the battle. It's all about getting up close. Which means moving slow and steady, just like you've got to with your leg," he said.

"Too bad we don't have a bow."

He slapped his thigh, suddenly excited. "Come over here." He walked to the bench under the window. He lifted up the seat, revealing a storage area underneath. There were two rifles inside, both of them with gleaming wood stocks. And something wrapped in cloth.

Dad unwrapped it and held it out. It was a bow: compound, with pulleys and a sight. Not as fancy as some I'd seen in competitions but still much higher tech than the stick-and-string basics. It was dark green, mottled like camouflage. A hunting bow.

I turned it over in my hands. It wasn't the kind I was used to. Our bows were modern, but they were simple. This looked like complicated machinery compared to those, but really it was all the same concept. This would just be easier to pull and hold steady, and the sight would certainly make it easier to aim, once I got used to it.

"I don't want to shoot animals," I said. But I did really want to shoot that bow.

"You don't have to just yet," he said. "So long as you eat what I shoot. I should be able to bring in plenty for the two of us. Especially the way you eat."

"Are there arrows?" I asked, trying to sound disinterested and failing.

"Wouldn't be a very good bow without them," Dad said with a laugh. He rummaged in the storage space and came up with a quiver filled with about forty arrows. "That's all we've got, but if you want to keep using it, I can always have Griff buy you some more."

"Maybe . . . maybe I could go practice, tomorrow," I said.

"I know the perfect spot," Dad said. He was grinning so wide it made his cheeks round and red.

I plucked at the string with my fingernail. "Dad?" I said.

"What is it, baby bear?"

"Why'd you leave?" I asked.

He got quiet. "I never could sit still for long," he said. "Or stay too far from the stars. I'm not made for that life. A mortgage and neighbors and taxes to pay. Your mom was so pretty and so clever I could quiet down that part of me for a while. But eventually who I am caught up with who I was trying to be, and it wasn't exactly a fair fight. I figured I would go live on my own, have an adventure, just for a year. One year up in Alaska, I said, but your mom didn't understand. So we fought, and she said that if I left, I shouldn't come back. And I took her at her word."

"You didn't have to leave," I said.

"I did, baby bear," Dad said, shaking his head sadly. "Maybe you don't understand that, but I'm hoping that you will someday. When you get to know me. When you get to know this place and what it's like out here."

I don't remember what I said, but I know what I'd say now:

I will never understand it.

I will never understand why you would choose even a place as beautiful as this over your family. Over your child.

I will never understand why you couldn't at least come and visit.

I will never understand why you thought that it was a good idea to bring me out here.

I will never understand why you left.

I will never understand why you left me.

I will never understand why you left me here.

I will never

I don't

I THINK I am going to die here.

I THOUGHT THAT keeping this journal would make me feel less alone, less trapped inside my own head. That it would let me get my thoughts out, and that would be a good thing.

I was wrong. All it does is make me stuck on everything that happened, everything that went wrong. It makes me think about what I'm feeling, and I can't ignore it, can't focus on *what's next* and just get things done.

But I can't stop. Not now. Now that I've started the story I have to finish it, and I have to finish it soon.

I don't have much time left.

After

THAT SECOND NIGHT after my father's death, my thoughts are hazy and frantic at the same time. I keep thinking I hear footsteps. That those men are back for me. But it's really just the rain on the ground, on the leaves, or a bird or a mouse or even, once, a fat black beetle dragging itself over the ground, belly rasping against pine needles. Still I jump at every noise, and by morning Bo is wound up, too, snarling at shadows and walking everywhere bristle-backed.

Around midmorning I swallow another pill. One more, I tell myself, just one more so that I can get the work done to survive another night. I have to gather firewood.

As soon as the pain starts to let up I crawl out of the shelter. I move on hands and knees because it's all I can manage. I wear the backpack reversed, hanging down in front of me. It bumps and rubs at my chin and face, but it means when I find a stick, I can just tuck it into the backpack and keep moving.

I crawl all over the clearing, filling my backpack with the driest wood I can find. I know the sticks won't last long; I need something bigger to keep a fire going. But I don't have the strength to chop anything up. I have to get lucky, that's all.

But I don't have yesterday's luck. All I can feel is despair, wet and heavy and pressing down on me. I pull myself back under the overhang and sit panting for a while, clutching the bag to my chest. I can't put a solid thought together. Every time I try, my mind wrenches back to that moment. Dad shaking his head. Dad putting his hand out. Then—

I force the images away before I get to the end. It's easier not to think at all. Easier to lose myself in a task, and so I start sorting the sticks, separating out the ones that are a little bit drier. Sorting those by size. It's a pathetic, small pile. I need more.

Going back out hurts, but I move eagerly. If I'm moving, I'm not thinking. I do it again and again, gathering, sorting, heading out again. Five trips and the stack has grown enough that I trust it will last a little while. Long enough to dry myself out, to boil water. I hope. I'm relieved at how many thick branches I've found, some as big around as my wrist. They'll last longer. Maybe through the night.

I indulge myself with another few bites of salmon and three swallows of moose water, and then I realize that I don't have any tinder.

I reach for the notebook first. This notebook. But when I run my fingers over the pages they're slick, a little shiny, and I'm not sure they'll burn right. I set it aside—*useless*, I think. I grab the thriller instead. The paper is rougher, feels more like it will burn.

I open the book and tear out three pages: one with a bunch of quotes about how awesome the book is, one with copyright stuff, and one where the author thanks his writing group and his agent and some guy named Steve for "helping me along the way."

I'd like to thank that wilderness teacher in elementary school and Will and Dad for helping me along the way. So if you find this, can you figure out who that teacher was? And buy Will a candy bar, because he loves them but won't buy them for himself. He says the calories don't count if it's a present.

The thank-yous and copyright and the *A wild thrill ride like no other!* get crumpled up, and I make a little tent of sticks around them.

It takes me about a hundred tries to get the steel to strike sparks. The sparks hit the paper and glow a moment—and then fade. I try again. All I get are little black specks peppering the pages. I scrape at the flint and steel again and again, blow, pray, but every time the little orange-red dots fade out in a second or two.

I sit back. My eyes prickle with tears, but I clench my teeth and will them away. They won't help me. Thinking about what happened won't help me. The only thing that *will* help is figuring this out, and so that's what I'm going to do.

All right. I'm doing something wrong. What? The paper is thicker than the birch bark Dad used. And the bark—Dad had shredded it. So maybe if I shred the paper . . .

I grab the knife from the tackle box and smooth out the paper. I shred it as finely as I can with the knife. My hands shake; I keep missing where I mean to cut, and tension creeps up between my shoulder blades until I want to scream.

I stop, shake out my hands. I start to hum. Nothing in particular, just humming, giving my brain an extra tiny something to focus on so I stop obsessing over the exact path of the blade. Just cut and cut and cut, it doesn't have to be neat and pretty, and it's not, it's sloppy and there are chunks that are too big and bits that escape the pile, but then I have a raggedy stack of fine strips, and I fluff them all into a ball like a bird's nest.

I take a deep breath, then strike the sparks again. As soon as they hit, I bend and blow gently on them.

Smoke rises in a thin, curling line.

I do cry then, a wet, blubbery bunch of sobs that seize up my chest and make my back ache, and in the time it takes me to get myself under control the sparks have gone out again. But this time I know it will work.

It takes two more tries to get a small flame going, and I almost blow it out from puffing too hard. It takes an eternity to figure out how to blow enough air but not too much, to get the flames licking up, to get them to catch the sticks. But finally I have a little fire. I feed it very, very slowly, waiting until it's getting smaller before I give it more food. I open the tackle box and drape my clothes over it near the fire, hoping that will help them dry, and then I lie on my side. The rest of the wood is in arm's reach and so is the fire, and keeping it fed is about all I can do.

I can't sleep very well with the pain, but it's just as well. It keeps me awake to tend the fire when it's flagging, and I need the warmth more than the sleep. I set the jars of moose water I got from the lake snug up against the fire, building it around them to get them boiling. I don't have any way to hang them above the flames, and this is awkward, but eventually it works. When I think they've boiled enough, I use two sticks like tongs to pull them away and let them cool.

Bo's wandered off, but he comes back in the evening and lies down with me, and I'm properly warm for the first time in— well—two days, but it feels like longer. It feels like forever. It feels like a lifetime ago that I crouched in the woods, fitting an arrow against my bowstring, and my dad caught my eye. Shook his head.

Reached out his hand.

I reach behind me to stroke Bo's back, interrupting the memory. "Where you been, Bo?" I ask sleepily. My mouth is dry and I know I should have another swallow or two of moose water, but I'm too tired to even reach for it.

Bo answers with a blustery sigh and goes to sleep. I wonder if he's missing Dad. I wonder if I am. I can't be certain on either count.

Before

AFTER GRIFF LEFT, the days went by slowly. Dad took care of things by himself. I holed up in the cabin and read the thriller from the airport (again), and then the only three books Dad owned. Wildlife guides: one for birds; one for plants; and one for snakes, bugs, and anything that wants to bite you, basically.

I wish I had those books now. They had illustrations and photos and careful descriptions so you knew what would kill you and what would make you sick and what would feed you. At least I learned a little. Like about creeping snowberries—and wintergreen and cattails and wild cucumber and several different kinds of berries, some of which would kill you.

There are a lot of plants here I don't know if I can eat. There's one that looks like a blueberry, but it doesn't grow on a bush like I think that blueberries do. I don't know if I could eat it. Maybe someday I'll be hungry enough to try. But the berries are gone already. So on the plus side I won't be tempted to try eating something stupid. On the downside . . . Well. You know the downside.

On the fourth day in the cabin with Dad, I heard the sound of a plane, and I ran outside, forgetting for a moment how much it hurt to run. I was limping by the time I hit the pebbled path, but it was worth it for the moment I saw that dot of yellow coming close and knew it was Griff. I waved frantically long before he could probably see me, and kept on waving until the plane came down, chasing a ripple across the surface of the water and then making its own.

Griff yelled and waved when he hopped out of the cockpit. He brought the plane up close to shore and loaded up his dinghy with sacks before coming in.

"How you been, Jess?" he asked when he was on dry land.

I didn't know quite how to answer that. "I'm glad to see you," I said. "Griff, I need you to take me home." I said it like it was a done deal.

He looked puzzled and scratched his scalp. "Seems to me you are home, Miss Jess," he said.

"I mean back to Alaska," I said. "Or just as far as a bus that'll take me to Seattle. I can't stay here, Griff."

"Well," he said. He stopped and gave a kind of convulsive nod. "Well, I'll have to talk to your dad about that, won't I? But in the meantime, why don't you take a look at what I brought for you."

He reached back and picked out a sack that was tied off with a ragged red ribbon. He held the sack out to me with a sheepish smile.

It took some doing to get my fingers between the ribbon and the sack and work it up over the neck of the bag, since the knots had pulled themselves tight. I peered into the sack. Inside was a blue-and-pink backpack with a big cartoon kitten on it.

I looked up at Griff. He was ear-to-ear with one of those big grins, and he waved both his hands at the sack excitedly.

"Go on," he said. "Open it up. There's more."

I pulled the backpack free of the bag. It was a cheap kids' backpack, the kind that feels light and thin and has a kind of shiny vinyl on the front. Inside was a notebook.

This notebook, in case you couldn't guess.

It is the most out-of-place thing for miles. I mean, other than me. It's pink, the same pink as the ribbon on the backpack cat's head. It's spiral bound with eighty wide-ruled pages (I write two lines for every rule, to save space, and in the margins, too), and on every left-hand page there's a watercolor of a dancing pony smiling under the lines, and on the right-hand page there's a watercolor of the words YOU'RE AWESOME!

The cover has *three* dancing ponies, so you know it means business.

Also in the bag was a pack of gel pens in rainbow colors. So far I've bled the Brr Berry Blue one dry and I'm working on the Vivacious Violet. I figure that'll last another few pages, and then you get to experience the Princess Pink one. I'll probably never get to the Oh Wow! Orange. What the hell does Oh Wow! Orange mean? I have no idea.

The fox that haunts my campsite stole the Mmm Mint Green pen a while back, but I found it all chewed up. If I take it apart, I can put the little ink tube in one of the used-up ones, maybe. But like I said, I probably won't last that long.

I managed a "Thaaanks, Griff," and didn't even put a question mark at the end.

"I thought you'd like that better than the old duffel to keep things in," Griff said.

"That was really thoughtful, Griff," I said. He looked pleased.

Dad and Bo came out of the woods then, Dad with his rifle in hand. The rifles looked so much alike I couldn't tell one from the other, but I knew one was for hunting deer and one was for smaller animals, like birds and rabbits. He had a rabbit over his shoulder now, gripping it by its back paws. Its muzzle was rimmed with blood, its eyes wide and empty. I looked away.

We helped Griff haul the gear to the cabin, where it got stuffed in until there was hardly room to walk. The more winter wore on, the more space we'd have because we'd eat it up bit by bit. Bo was especially excited about a bag of doggy jerky treats, even though Dad grumbled about wasting jerky on a dog. I made Bo do tricks. Sit and stay, and shake. He didn't know shake before, but he caught on quick and soon he was following me around limping with one foot up in the hopes that I'd call him a good boy and give him another piece of jerky. I kept the treats in my pocket and tried not to smirk when my dad glared at Bo for being a suck-up.

"You should put your things in the bag," Griff said, and I smiled at him blandly. To make him happy, I shifted over a few things. My socks and my underwear and the thriller. The thriller's about a guy whose wife gets killed and so he goes around shooting people and staring in the mirror thinking about how hard his life is. Then he shoots all the people he wanted to shoot and the book ends.

Not as helpful as knowing what's edible and what's poisonous, but to be fair, it has been pretty useful. I've been using it as tinder when I don't have time to go by the birch trees and the grass is wet. I have gotten all the way up to the part where the man—his name is Jack, because all action heroes have names that start with J—finds out that the gangsters he's been shooting up to that point aren't actually the men who killed his wife. Then he gets to start shooting polished guys in suits instead. It is a terrible book and I have read it four times now. It's shorter every time, because I keep burning parts of it, but not any better.

Once I had the kitty bag packed I put it on the bed where Griff could see it through the doorway, propped up. If I wanted him to take me home, I had to make sure he was happy, but I also just liked making him smile.

"You staying long?" I asked Griff.

"Thought I'd stay a day," Griff said. "Tomorrow, that is. I'll take off Wednesday morning."

Wednesday. I'd forgotten what day it was. It startled me, how quickly I'd lost track. I felt unmoored in time.

This place does that to you. It feels eternal, until a plane flies over in the distance to rattle you into the modern world. The planes never come very close. They don't know that I'm here. And I don't know if I'd want them to. It could be *them* and then I definitely don't want them to know that I'm here.

Back then, of course, I hadn't heard any plane but Griff's. I was glad to hear he was staying another day. It meant that I would have time to convince him to take me with him. It also meant that my dad had more time to interfere with my plan, but I would deal with that when it came up.

The first thing we always did was eat. Or get ready to eat. To-day that meant skinning the rabbit, which Dad did out back and I didn't watch. I wish I had. I caught a rabbit once and skinned it, but this is the method I know how to use:

Stare at the rabbit. Pick up your knife. Stare at the rabbit some more.

Put the knife near the rabbit, then pull it back again.

Pick a spot. Maybe the back of the neck, the belly, something like that. Start cutting.

Realize that you are just slicing up the meat and the fur.

Go more carefully.

Realize that it is very hard to skin a small animal with all of its skin attached to all of its other skin.

Cut off the rabbit's head because that seems like something you have to do eventually anyway, and plus it keeps staring at you.

Start at the neck, sliding the knife in and sort of sawing under the skin.

Continue to mangle the rabbit until you reach the paws.

Stare at the paws.

Chop the paws off.

Finish mangling the rabbit. Pull away a rabbit skin that looks like an angry ex took scissors to a shirt and then dipped it in punch. And then glued meat to it.

Carefully scrape off all the meat. Pick fur off of it.

Keep the skin in case you can use it, even though it's all sliced to bits.

The end.

When Dad came back inside it looked like he'd just taken the rabbit's clothes off, so I know he couldn't have used my method. It was skinny without its fur, long and pink.

Griff and I got to talking while we waited for him. I learned that he had a daughter who was six years old and lived with his "lady friend" in Toronto, and he missed her something fierce.

"I bought that bag for her," he said. "But I figured she's got lots of bags. Being in a big city and all. But I got to thinking you've only got the one, and that's not right. Not for a girl. Right?"

I nodded. "A lot of girls like bags," I said. I didn't point out that I was ten years older than his daughter—and even when I was her age, I wasn't really the kittens-and-rainbows type.

"I think God was whispering to me to bring it to you," he said. My dad looked up, looked back down. Dad didn't seem to mind when Griff talked about God. Maybe because Griff's idea of God was very odd.

"I'm going down to see her, and I'll buy her another bag. Just like that one. And then you can have the same bag, and it'll be like you're friends," Griff said.

"When are you going down to see her?" I asked. Really I meant, how long are you going to be gone.

"'Bout a week," Griff said. "Found a job down there finally, so I'll get to see her a lot more."

"You're going permanently?" I said. My dad looked up in alarm.

"Job's for eight months," Griff said. "But if I do well, they'll keep me past that." He swept his cap off his head and held it in front of his chest, kneading it in both hands. "So I won't be coming up here anymore. At least not before the summer. Next summer. Maybe."

"Griff," Dad said. "You should have told me sooner."

"Wasn't sure until just yesterday," Griff said. "'S'why I came out early. To tell you, and to make sure I got to see you."

"We depend on you, Griff," Dad said. He was using me. *We* depend on you. To make Griff feel bad.

"I thought that you lived off the land," I said drily, wanting to defend Griff even as I wanted him to stay.

"A man should be with his family," Griff said forcefully, fiercely. "A man should be with his little girl." He looked at me when he said it, and my heart sank. He was never going to take me away from here, was he?

"We can talk about this after we're fed," Dad said firmly.

Over dinner, Dad and Griff told a story about one of their salmon-fishing trips, taking Griff's plane to a river where they thronged, and you had to shoulder your way past wolves and bears and eagles to get your turn. When we were down to licking grease off our fingers, Dad cleared his throat. "Our little bear's got something to show off," he said. "She's got a talent. Did you know that?"

"I figured," Griff said. "Didn't figure on what it was, though."

"I don't have a talent," I said.

"Archery!" Dad declared. "Show him the bow, Jess."

"It's your bow."

"Not anymore," Dad said. "I'm too damn lazy to bow hunt anymore. But that bow's about the most expensive thing I own,

and someone should get use out of it. Why don't you show Griff
how it's done?"

I hadn't shot the bow yet. I'd left it under the bed with the
duffel. I definitely didn't want to shoot for the first time in three
years with an audience. But Griff looked eager, and it was going
to take a hell of a lot of goodwill to talk him into to taking me. So
I slid off my chair and fetched the bow. Griff clapped his hands
together.

We traipsed outside. Dad picked out a target for me, a tree
that listed toward the lake. He was going to chop it down anyway, since a good storm would knock it over soon. It was a really
skinny tree, and it wasn't exactly close, either. I checked over the
bow to buy myself time. The arrows were nasty things, metal.
Made for punching through an animal's hide and bringing it
down. Not exactly meant for target practice.

"Show us how it's done," Dad said.

For one paralyzed moment I didn't remember how to shoot at
all. *Checklists*, I thought.

Take the proper stance: side to the target, feet spread for stability. Straight shoulders. Arrow to the bow. Check the target.
Distance. Wind. Raise the bow. Draw. Elbow bent straight back.
Think flat, flat like a single plane, like you're a sketch on a piece
of paper. Aim. Aim higher than the target; arrows arc. Breathe
in. Breathe out. Loose.

The arrow sailed past the tree and vanished into the woods
with a flurry of leaves and branches. Dad and Griff laughed. My
cheeks turned blazing hot, and I fumbled for another arrow.

"I haven't shot since I was thirteen," I said.

"That wasn't so long ago," Dad said.

"Three years." I didn't even know if he knew how old I was. Did he even know what year it was out here?

I tried to shoot again, but this time I was rushed and angry, and my hand jerked at the last minute, sending the arrow too high and too far right. Two arrows gone and I hadn't even come close. Griff and Dad started jawing about some hunter who'd accidentally shot his own dog, and I wondered where Bo was. I hoped he wasn't out behind the tree.

Arrow number three. I shut my eyes and counted to five, trying to block out Griff and Dad's voices. I could do this. I'd won a medal, hadn't I? I just had to get my arms to remember what my mind still knew.

Eyes still closed, I drew the arrow. I focused on the way it felt under my fingertips. Felt its weight. Heavier than I was used to, I remembered. And when I drew the bow, testing, it was much easier than I was used to. I'd gotten older, gotten stronger, and the pulley system was designed to make the draw easy. Too smooth. It was throwing me off.

I eased the bowstring again and lowered the bow before opening my eyes. There was the target. I raised the bow again. Drew. Released. All in one steady motion, one steady breath.

The arrow thunked into the tree. I wish I could say it was dead center, but it was a little to the side and higher than I'd meant it to be. But it hit.

"Nice work!" Dad declared, and clapped me on the shoulder. I flinched as his hand settled over scar tissue. It didn't hurt, but it made me feel the difference between us. "We'll find the frontier spirit in you yet."

"I don't think I have one," I said. I looked him in the eye. "I'm going back with Griff tomorrow."

Pause. Dad looked at Griff, who shuffled his feet. "You know about this?"

"She might have mentioned it, but I said that was up to you," Griff said.

"It is up to me," Dad said, irate, and Griff shrank away like a scared dog.

"It's illegal for me to be here!" I said.

Dad laughed. "Illegal? There's no laws can touch this place, Jess. This is nobody's country but the wild's and mine."

"I'll hate you," I said. "I'll hate you if you make me stay here. I'll never, ever forgive you, and I'll never, ever be the . . . the . . . the whatever you want me to be. I like movies and shopping and wasting time on the Internet and buying my food at the grocery store. Not this!" I waved a hand at the lake.

"Griff, can you give us a minute?" Dad said.

"Mhmm," Griff said. He ambled down the lake until he was out of earshot, or at least far enough away that we could pretend that he was.

"You have to stop saying you're not staying," Dad said. He crossed his arms, but he didn't look angry. Just like he was stating facts. "You are. That's all there is to it."

There were tears in my eyes, and I hated myself for it. "You can't keep me out here."

"Think of it like a vacation," Dad said.

I snorted. "A vacation where I'm cold and I have to eat nothing but rice and greasy meat and there's no one to talk to and nothing to do?"

"There's plenty to do. More to do than the two of us could get done in twice the time we have."

"You're making me into a prisoner," I said.

"You're a child. You do what your parents say." He was losing his temper now. His voice rose up, edging toward a shout.

"Mom never would have made me live out here!" I yelled. "She didn't even let you *see* me! She wanted me to live with Scott, not with you!" I didn't know if that was true, but I yelled it anyway.

"And who the hell is Scott?" Dad yelled back. He'd dropped his arms now.

I glared at him, my right hand in a fist and my left tight around the bow. "Scott's the guy who was really my dad," I said. I hadn't meant to say it. I wasn't even sure if it was true, or just what I wished had been true.

"What the hell does that mean?" The words came between his teeth. He'd tensed his jaw so much it bulged. I didn't back down.

"It means he was there. He made me waffles. And talked to me about school. And drove me to friends' houses. And went to parent-teacher conferences. And didn't kidnap me and make me live in the freaking wilderness!"

"How long?" Dad demanded.

I blinked at him. How long what? How long Scott. "Mom met him when I was eleven," I said evenly, making sure he heard every damn word. "He was going to ask her to marry him, and he was going to adopt me. And then I never would have had to come to the middle of nowhere with *you.*" Except they'd broken up. Three months before the accident. Not forever, I'd thought, they still loved each other. But then Mom died and forever was the only thing left. I didn't tell Dad that. I wanted him to be angry. Wanted him to hurt. Like I did.

"Christ," Dad said.

I grinned savagely at him. "Really, Dad?"

Dad took a deep breath and turned toward the lake. He was breathing weirdly, through his nose in sharp draws, and there was a tendon sticking out on his neck. I remember once when I was angry and my mom looked at me and said, real quiet, *Your dad had a temper, too.* Was he going to hurt me? I wished Bo was there. I didn't think Bo would let him hurt me.

But when Dad spoke again, his voice was quiet.

"What if it wasn't forever," Dad said.

I stared at him.

"What if it was just through the winter? Just one year. You'll be a bit behind in school, okay. But think about how amazing your college essays will be." He smiled a little, looking at a point in between him and me but not quite at my face. "In the summer we'll head back to the States, and I'll face the music for keeping you out of school. I'll get a regular job, at least until you're eighteen and you're in school and everything."

"Why can't we go now?" I asked.

"There's things I've got to do here," he said. "Things I've got to wait for. I've made some promises."

"To who? The moose?" I asked. "To those friends of yours who don't make good choices?"

He gave me a flat look. "I promise you I'll take care of you. And you'll learn how to take care of yourself. You'll get strong, and you'll get smart, and you will never, ever forget this year. It's not forever. Just until next summer."

It seemed like an eternity. And the thought of weathering a winter here was terrifying. But what was the alternative? The Wilkersons.

One year. One year in foster care or one year here.

He'd stayed one year for me, back when I was baby. So okay. I'd give him what he gave me, and not a day more. "Just until the summer?"

"Then I'll take you wherever you want to go," Dad said.

"Fine. Okay." Maybe I could handle a year here. There was hot chocolate in the cabin. Hot chocolate and campfires in a log cabin. People paid for that sort of thing. Besides, Dad was right. This would make an *amazing* college admissions essay. And I would always have the most interesting story to tell at parties.

"Shake on it?" Dad said. He reached out a hand.

I took it. It was the first time I'd touched my dad of my own accord since I was a kid. His hand was impossibly rough and callused, the creases packed with dirt. My hand felt tiny by comparison.

We shook, and I started counting down the days to next summer.

After

UNDER THE OVERHANG, sleeping fitfully between tending my small fire, I dream of Griff. We drive along a dark road toward a man standing on the median line, his back to us. "Don't worry about him," Griff says. He pumps the brake. "Look at him skeeedaddle."

But he doesn't. He turns. He raises his hand, and there's a gun in it. The gun roars with the sound of a fire, crackling and howling. Griff's head kicks back. The air fills with red blood like mist, and it's all over my clothes, it's all over my hands and my face and in my mouth.

I scream. The screaming wakes me. It wakes Bo, too, and he leaps up snarling into the dark. I sob, pulling myself into a little ball. The fire is out. I've slept too long. "Oh, Bo," I say. "I wish Dad was here."

It's not the same as missing him, exactly. I worry then that there's something wrong with me, that I want my dad's help but I don't know if I loved him enough to really miss him for his own sake.

Bo heads off to patrol the clearing. Does he even understand that Dad is dead? When he leaves, is he looking for him, roaming the woods to try to catch his scent? Does he go back to that spot, to the grave?

I hope he knows that Dad is dead, that he isn't coming back. Because it's awful, but worse would be waiting for him to come back.

With Bo gone there's no one to see the slow, awkward process by which I crawl out from under the overhang to pee. When I have my jeans buttoned again, my cheeks raked with tears more angry than sorrowful, I make my way around the clearing again. I think I can stand, but I stay on all fours for now, and keep going until my limbs start trembling.

I have twice as much to do as yesterday. I don't start the fire just yet. I drink the boiled water—flat-tasting but palatable—and eat a small meal. Only a few bites left of the salmon. It takes everything I have to screw the top back on instead of gobbling it down.

When I've cleaned my fingers on my jeans, I open the tackle box. I'm not ready to go fishing yet, but I should know what's in there. I start to inventory everything, setting things out carefully on a white T-shirt so I won't lose track of them.

All the expected gear is there, and a gift: a can opener. The compact camping kind, slightly rusted, but it means that I have a way to get the can of peaches open without using the knife. My mouth starts watering, imagining the sweet syrup, the slippery slices melting in my mouth. But I force myself to set the can opener aside. Not yet. Not yet.

Although—is there any point to denying myself? It assumes that eventually, I'll find other food. Maybe it would be better to enjoy it all now, one big meal, rather than just stretching out the time it takes to starve to death.

But if I think like that, I've got no chance.

I push to my feet before my willpower fails me. I sling the rifle over my shoulder. Building the shelter will have to wait—again. I need more food. Quickly. And more water.

I pack four of the moose jars, one full and three empty—one to drink along the way, since I'm sure I'm dehydrated, even if it's lost in the stew of other signals my body is sending me, pain and hunger and weariness and fear.

I bring the rest of the salmon, too, and then head out, walking stick in hand. I take my time. Every step takes conscious thought, and I lean on my walking stick heavily. If I wasn't so used to pain, after the last few months, I don't think I'd make it. If I weren't hurt before, I wouldn't be able to stand it now.

If I weren't hurt before, I wouldn't be here at all.

I stop to rest every hundred steps, leaning against my makeshift cane. I don't dare sit down. I don't know if I'll be able to get up again.

By the time the lake comes into view my breathing is tight and labored. I breathe through my teeth, hissing in with one step and out with the next. But I'm here.

The canoe has filled with rain. I shouldn't have tipped it over. Idiot. I was barely able to turn it when it was empty. No way I can empty it out now and still have the strength to—well, do anything.

Cursing myself, I walk toward the burnt buildings instead. I have to see what I can salvage.

I didn't look at the outhouse that first day, but I go there now, just to take stock. The structure was made of planks, not logs like the shed and the cabin, and the fire hasn't damaged it as much. It's taken off the roof and most of one of the walls, but the others are just scorched. I wiggle one of the planks of wood. It's loose.

Those planks are tall enough to fit my shelter wall, and even the ones burnt down to a foot or two will make good firewood. I start to tug harder, feel my back protest. My fingers scrape against the wood, bending a fingernail back painfully. I lose my grip and stumble back, barely catching myself.

Not strong. Smart, I remind myself. I step back and force myself to wait, to think it through. I take off the rifle strap once more and loop it over the plank. I start to pull, stepping back, but my leg almost buckles. No. I'm going to fall this way.

Smart. I tie the other end of the strap to my walking stick. This time instead of using my own weight, I brace the stick against the ground and face away from the outhouse—if I pull I'm worried I'll lose my balance. Pushing gives me more stability. I push the top of the stick, using it as a lever to haul against the strap. The plank cracks. I push harder. It creaks. I shove. It breaks, sending plank and walking stick to the ground. I jerk forward, but I catch myself before I fall. I nod, satisfied, and move to the next plank to repeat the trick.

I stop after three. No use wearing myself out and getting more than I can actually carry. I stack the planks and bind them together with my belt. Next time I'll bring the rope with me.

I'm still not ready to search inside the cabin. I walk past it and sit on the lakeshore, eating all but the last bite or two of salmon, sipping moose water like fine wine. The sun turns the water silver. A bird with a low, mournful voice sings out somewhere on the lake. It feels like I've been alone here forever. It feels like hardly an hour. Two nights.

It's strange sitting with my back to the cabin, not even the smell of smoke lingering to remind me that it's there. Looking out over the lake, there is not one sign of human habitation, not one footprint to suggest that Griff or Dad or I was ever here. The wild doesn't care and won't remember. However many days I hold on, claw my way through, at the end of them I will still die and my body will rot. It will feed the forest; moss and mushrooms will grow on me like on every other dead thing.

To survive you need to learn to hold contradictory things in your head at the same time. I am going to die; I am going to live. There is nothing to fear; be wary of everything. In this moment I find a new contradiction. The indifference of the wild is terrifying—I want to be remembered, to leave a mark. And it is freeing, knowing that the forest does not care, does not judge. My failure will go unmarked—no mourning, no mockery. For the first time in my life, there are no expectations of me at all. The only thing that matters is what I want, what I can do.

I decide, again, as I will every day, sometimes once and sometimes a dozen times, that I want to live. Someday, maybe, I'll decide I'm done. But this day, watching insects dance over the shallows of the lake, I'm still too stubborn and too fond of living.

I eye the last bite of salmon. Better save it. My belly feels caved in, but I'm getting used to this constant hunger. I know it'll only get worse.

If it was a few weeks earlier, there would be berries to eat. I've passed endless blackberry bushes, their berries long gone. Nothing but thorns for me there.

I think back to that day we went by the rock, my dad talking about the woods like it was his neighborhood, pointing out the landmarks, gossiping about the neighbors—in this case, wolverines and porcupines, hummingbirds and foxes. *Out that way, there's a field of snowberries*, he says. *You ever had a snowberry?*

I still haven't. But I remember the way he pointed, because I had to shade my hand against the sun. My left hand, and the sun was west, so I was looking north.

I screw the cap on the salmon, pack away my things, and stand, whistling for Bo. I can't be sure the berries will be there, or that I'll find them if they are, but I have to try. Berries, after all, have one major advantage as a food source: they can't run away.

Before

THE NIGHT OF Griff's second visit was the night Dad told the story about how he saved Griff's life. It was also the first time that I really laughed since coming out to the lake. Making the decision to stay had flipped something over in me, shifted the gravity. Before, it had felt like I was going to be on the lake forever. Now I had a date, or at least a season. Summer. I could make it until summer.

We stayed up late as Griff and Dad traded stories, and then it was just Dad, because he was the better storyteller by far. When he'd run out of stories and was getting hoarse, we went outside and sat against the cabin, leaning to look at the stars.

I fell asleep there, and when I woke up there was light on the horizon, very faint. I dragged myself inside, leaving Griff and Dad snoring. I collapsed into bed, and slept better than I'd slept since I got here. I felt at peace.

The next day we said good-bye to Griff and took Bo around to check Dad's traps. We walked slowly, and Dad pointed things out to me. He showed me where the snowberries were, and when

I asked about wild cucumber he showed one to me. He pulled one up from the grass by the traps and brushed off the dirt and I ate it. It was tiny. Not much food, but a few calories, and they were all over the place. You could walk and pick and walk and pick while you were doing something else.

The next day we gathered firewood. And split firewood. And stacked firewood. I thought we had so much we'd never run out, but Dad said it wasn't even enough to get us to winter, much less through it. The stack ran all along one side of the cabin, covered with a tarp to keep the rain off it.

When it got dark, we fled inside and sat by the fireplace. Dad wrapped a blanket around me and gave me a mug of something hot. I thought it was tea, but when I sipped it, alcohol scorched my throat and left me coughing.

"Hot toddy," he said with a grin. "Enjoy it while it lasts, because we won't have lemons again until Griff gets tired of his old lady and comes home."

"Don't say that."

He laughed. "Why not?"

"Because he's right. A man should be with his family," I said. "He's going back to them, and that's a good thing."

"Are you ever going to forgive me for that?" he asked, sounding annoyed.

"It's not like it's just a little thing you did one time," I said. "You were gone my whole life. Also, don't you know I'm too young to drink?"

"Well, give that on back, then," he said. I hugged the mug against my chest, and he laughed at me again. "You know, when you were a baby you grabbed at everything you could," he said. "Never could get your hands off my ring or your mom's necklaces or anyone's hair you could reach. I took you out hiking in one of those baby carriers, right? Strapped to my chest. And you bounced along and reached at the trees even though they were so far away. And then I stopped paying attention for one minute and you reached out and grabbed a bee right out of the air. It stung you good, and you wailed and wailed. Like a little siren out there in the woods. And there I am, bouncing and hushing you and singing Christmas carols 'cause that was all I could remember, and I get back to the car and your mom's sitting there with her book and she looks up and says, 'What did you do now, Carl?'"

He trailed off, smiling. It was a weird smile. Sad and maybe a bit angry.

"We never shoulda got married," he said. "Never shoulda."

"Why did you, then?" I asked.

"Because we were gonna have you."

I took a sip to hide my surprise. I hadn't known that. Mom always said she got pregnant right away, but I thought that meant after the wedding. "Sorry I messed everything up for you."

"You were perfect," he said. "I was so, so happy. Moira was the one who was worried. I thought, Everything's going to work out now. We're going to have a beautiful little baby and we're going to be a family, and we're going to be happy. But I was wrong. Moira knew better than me. I guess she always knew I'd leave, and that's why she couldn't love me the way I loved her." He stared into the fire. "I know I should have seen you more growing up.

There were a lot of things in my life that kept me from doing that, though. But it'll all be sorted soon. By next summer. And then I can be your dad for real."

"I'm almost an adult," I said. "I don't need a dad much longer. But I needed one when I was little. I needed one growing up."

"I wanted to be there for you," he said.

"What was stopping you?" I meant to sound detached and curious. I sounded angry. I was angry.

"I . . ." He hesitated. He wasn't a hesitant guy, but whenever he had trouble finding his words it felt like he was circling around the same subject, only I couldn't tell what it was. "When you were a baby, I got into a little trouble."

"What, like you got arrested?"

"No, not me," he said, shaking his head. "It was complicated, okay? But Moira didn't want me around while I was involved in all of that. Besides. You were probably better off. I mean, you had Scott, right?"

"For a while," I said. "Not long enough." I looked away.

"I'm glad he was there," he said. "Since I couldn't be."

"Wouldn't be," I countered.

He gave a low chuckle. It sounded like the smoke from the fire felt to breathe in. Like it stung a little. "You are just like me, aren't you, baby bear? You'll argue with a wall that it's a door, and walk on through to prove it."

"I don't argue that much," I objected, and then we both cracked up. "Okay, maybe I argue a little," I conceded. "But I wouldn't try to walk through a wall."

"Honey, a wall would be a fool not to open up for you," he said. His eyes twinkled in the firelight.

"Why do you call me baby bear?" I asked suddenly.

"Because you were so fat and roly-poly when you were a baby," he said. "And we'd bundle you up when it was cold so you were even fatter and rounder. And I called you my bear cub, and the first word you ever said was 'grrrrrrr.'"

"That is not a word," I objected.

"It's a bear word," he said sagely.

I hugged the blanket wrapped around my shoulders. "Well, I'm not a baby anymore."

"I can't just call you bear."

"You can call me Jess," I said. "It's my name."

"Your name is Sequoia," he said.

I rolled my eyes. "I hate that name. It's such a tree hugger name."

He scratched his neck. "Can't say as I've ever hugged a tree, but if you say so. Jess it is. Now tomorrow, you and I are going to go hunting, Jess. I know you don't like killing animals, but we won't survive the winter up here without it. I want you to learn. Take that bow of yours and I'll take a rifle, and I can show you around. At the very least you've got to learn to find your way around here. It's real easy to get lost, and real hard to find anyone that's gotten lost."

"I'll try," I said. I meant hunting. Even though it made me feel a little sick to think about killing something, I knew it wasn't that different from eating something that had been killed for me. It wasn't like the Wilkersons' meatloaf and frozen dinners, that looked nothing like the animal they used to be. When my dad brought in a rabbit, it was a *rabbit*, not just nondescript pieces of meat. Once I got over eating that, doing my own killing seemed like it couldn't be that hard.

I was right. I don't really care anymore. It's really, really hard to kill a thing quickly enough that you don't have to see it suffer. And that bothers me. But not the killing itself. Not anymore.

Now I just feel bad that I'm not better at it.

After

I DROP THE planks off at camp on my way to the snowberries. I stop just long enough to leave them by the rock and feed Bo a couple of jerky treats, since he's been eyeing my pocket the whole way. I know he hunts on his own, but Dad fed him, too, and I don't know if he can find enough food to survive by himself. Either I'm going to have to figure out how to feed us both or he's going to have to start hunting on his own more.

We set off north, Bo trotting along beside me. The sun trails spots over his dark coat and shimmers across lingering raindrops.

Bo freezes. Fear shoots through me, cold and sudden, but this isn't the stock-still almost-snarl of when danger is close by. He looks intent . . . and eager. I take the rifle in hand and point it in the direction he's looking. "What is it?" I whisper.

A rabbit bursts out of the bushes. I yank on the trigger, more out of instinct and surprise than on purpose. The rifle cracks and jerks in my hands, and I almost fall backward at the impact, my weight dropping back on my bad leg. I don't even come close to hitting the rabbit. Quickly I work the mechanism to feed another round into the chamber and sweep the gun after the fleeing rabbit. I pull the trigger again. Dirt sprays up a good eight feet from the rabbit's butt, and then it's gone.

Bo sits and looks up at me in mute disappointment. "I might need to do some target practice," I say with a sigh. I check the rifle. I have three shots left, and all the ammunition is back at the rock. How long will it last? The box is full, but I don't think I'll have much for target practice. I'll just have to make that practice useful, and pick a target that can feed me.

I'm imagining hunting with Bo, roasting rabbits over the fire, when I step out of the tree line and into the open air. Hilly land rolls out away from us, the trees resuming maybe a quarter mile away. And every one of those hills is spangled with low-growing bushes, every one of *those* bursting with pale berries.

I let out a whoop that comes out more like a whimper and hurry forward. I start up the crest of the first low hill—and a huge black shape comes trundling up the other side. Bear. I freeze. The bear freezes. I can see the fur on its muzzle, the bit of froth at the corner of its mouth. It has to weigh four times as much as I do. It starts to rise on its hind legs. I stumble back.

Bo gives me an irritated look and lunges forward, barking furiously. The bear drops to all fours and hightails it in the other direction quicker than I can blink. It has a rolling run, almost comical, and I stifle a laugh as it hoofs its way toward the far tree line.

"Rolly!" I declare. Bo gives me a *no, duh* look.

Look at him skeeedaddle, Griff says in my memory, and my

smile fades into a pang of loneliness. I bite my lip. No time for
that now, no room for it. The sun's slid past its peak. The days
are long, but the evenings cold, and I want to get that fire going
soon.

I kneel down to start picking berries, shuffling along from
bush to bush. I eat while I pick, but I make myself put three in
the bag for every one I pop in my mouth. Still, by the time my
back is aching so much I have to stop, I feel almost full for the
first time in days.

I push myself up with the help of the walking stick and start
back. I'm barely past the tree line when I spot a familiar cluster
of leaves. "Hey, I know that one," I say to Bo. "Wild cucumber.
Dad showed me."

Bo doesn't look impressed. I bend and pluck the cucumber. The root—the edible part—is just a little lightning bolt of
green, maybe an inch and a half long, but I shake the dirt off
and bite it clean off its stem. It's fresh and crisp and another few
calories to keep me from starving, but the flavor's faded before
I've gone two steps. There are more, though, everywhere now
that I know to look, and I stop here and there to pick them.
Save three, eat one.

As I tuck them into the smiling kitty backpack, I find myself
wishing Griff was here so I could give him a proper thank-you.
I hadn't exactly been grateful when he gave me the dumb thing,
but if it hadn't been for the backpack, I don't think I would have
thought to run back to the cabin before it burned to the ground.
I'd only gone back because I couldn't risk them finding it, and if
I hadn't gone back, I'd have nothing now.

Tomorrow, I decide, I'm going to get the rest of the planks pulled down, and then I'll go fishing. But I also have to make my shelter. I bite my lip. Which is more important? It hasn't been too cold at night, with Bo and the fire. And the sooner I figure out how to get food regularly, the better. So I'll go fishing.

Before

WE DIDN'T TALK much, the days after Griff left for the last time. I didn't imagine Dad did much talking before I got there, and the habit stuck. He'd get up before I woke up in the morning, and by the time I dragged myself out at what still felt too early for human activity he'd have breakfast ready. Corn cakes, mostly, drizzled with some honey, a little meat in gravy to bulk it up. Then he'd be off for most of the day working, and I had nothing to do but sit around the cabin. After not too long, I got bored enough that I organized and scrubbed and dusted everything I could get my hands on, and soon the cabin looked . . .

Well, it still looked like a dirty, tiny cabin in the middle of the woods, but it was at least fresh dirt now.

I woke one morning to the sound of Dad chopping wood outside. I shimmied into my jeans and fleece and boots and walked outside, standing in the doorway with the crisp morning air waking me up.

Dad had finished and was snapping the cover back on the hatchet, the wood already stacked. He cut wood every morning, assuring me that we'd never regret having too much wood, but we'd sure as hell regret not having enough.

"You're up early," he said.

"I can't tell." The light was so long that one day nearly bumped up against another, this time of year.

"Well, let's see." He pushed up his sleeve to look at the rugged analog watch that ticked away on his wrist. "Five forty-five. Early for you."

"Huh," I said, because I couldn't think of the right response to that information. I crossed my arms over my chest, tucking my hands in to keep them warm. "What are you doing today?"

"Hunting," he said. "With two of us to feed, I've got to step up the canning and smoking. Not that you eat much more than a bird. You should come."

"I'd just slow you down," I said.

"It'll be more exciting than staring at the lake all day again."

"I really shouldn't," I said. "My leg . . ."

"You're stronger than you think. Can't let a little limp hold you back," he said.

I thought about explaining to him that I wasn't holding myself back. I was pushing myself. I'd walked back and forth around the north side of the shore every day; I'd done my exercises and then some, knowing that I had to improve quickly if I was going to have any kind of mobility out here in this rough terrain.

"You can't just stay holed up here," he said. He braced a hand against his brow to shade it from the sun. "And I don't like you being here without knowing your way around, and knowing what's safe and what isn't. Being able to feed yourself."

"Fine," I said, frustrated. I didn't want to hurt myself, but I didn't want yet another fight, either. Not when we'd finally been getting along. "I'll go with you."

"You don't have to sound like I'm dragging you off to your funeral," he said.

"I said I'd go. I'm going." Maybe all we knew how to do was be mad at each other. By the time we were geared up, we were both in sour moods. I took too long getting ready for his liking, I was too slow following him, and Bo was off God-knew-where and that annoyed him, too.

"Stick close," he told me every time I lagged behind, as if it was because I was lazy that I couldn't keep up. I went as fast as I could without falling. Dead leaves and slick roots made it hard going, and every odd step made me grit my teeth in anticipation of pain, but I kept up. Mostly. And I didn't complain.

I was looking at the ground, picking out a path, when Dad threw his arm up to stop me. I opened my mouth to ask him what the deal was, but he pressed a finger to his lips, then pointed.

A rabbit crouched up ahead, pinned in a ray of sunshine, Hallmark-gorgeous and haloed in golden light. Dad started to lift his rifle to turn Hallmark into horror show, but then he lowered it, pointed at my bow instead.

A rabbit. Could I kill a rabbit? Did I want to?

Well, did I want to eat this winter? Because this was how Dad fed himself. *It's only a rabbit*, I thought, but that didn't feel convincing.

I'd probably miss anyway.

I still had to think about every action and motion of shooting; none of it was in my muscle memory anymore. I thought through it like a checklist. Finger position, arm position, aim, breath, draw. Release.

The sound of the release startled the rabbit, but it had only a fraction of a second to begin to move, to react, before the arrow struck, punched through. The rabbit's legs kick, kick, kicked, then slowed. I lowered the bow slowly, watching it die. I felt sick.

It's just a rabbit.

The sickness ebbed.

"Good," Dad said. He was grinning.

I nodded. Good.

He strode out to get the kill. I stepped out to join him, but my foot landed on a slick root and shot out sideways. I dropped, landing hard on my bad knee, my foot out to the side at an odd angle.

I hissed and grabbed my knee, biting my lip hard to keep from crying as tears sprung to my eyes. I wouldn't cry. Not in front of my dad.

I shifted until I was sitting, my leg out in front of me, and sucked in sharp breaths through my nose, blinking through the pain.

"Anything broken?" Dad called.

"No," I said through gritted teeth. The sharp pain was settling back into a throb. I didn't think I'd hurt it too badly.

"Then come on," Dad said. "There are some traps farther on I want to check, and we might be able to get a couple more of these little hoppers."

"No." My temper was flaring, or I would have tried for some nicer way to say it.

"You're fine. Just walk it off, that's the best way to handle a little bump," Dad said cheerfully.

"I can't just walk it off," I snapped. "Why can't you just believe me when I tell you I have to be careful? My doctors—"

"Doctors are really good at convincing you you're sick. That you're weak. They turn the body into diseases and problems. That's their job, and I don't blame them, but they're no good anymore at seeing what's strong and natural and good in your body. Trust me. I know what's best for you."

I twisted to glare at him. "You know what, Dad? I *am* weak. And no amount of believing otherwise is going to make my muscles suddenly stronger. And if you knew what was best for me, neither of us would be here, would we?" I pulled and pushed my way to my feet, standing unsteadily. "You can go check your traps and kill Thumper and Bambi and the rest of the forest friends, but I'm not going."

He grunted. His fingers tightened around the barrel of the rifle where he held it, a quick, reflexive motion. "Fine," he said. "Wait here, then."

He yanked the arrow free of the rabbit and stalked off into the trees. I watched him go, anger and pain throbbing in turn. A familiar sensation.

"He doesn't know what he's talking about," I said. There was no one to hear.

It began to rain. I didn't feel like sitting in the middle of the woods for however long it took my dad to decide to come collect me, so I started hobbling in the direction I'd come. It didn't take me long to find a stick that would work as a makeshift cane, and I moved along at a decent pace after that, spurred by the anger that had taken up residence in my ribs, making a nest of resentment and helplessness.

I knew I couldn't stay angry with him, not if I was going to have to survive months with him as my only company. I needed to find a way not to hate him, but it was hard. He was just *wrong*. He might love me, but he didn't know what was best for me. Not even close.

He was going to get me hurt.

Hurt worse.

I halted. I'd remembered the path up until now, but the sea of green in front of me all looked the same. Had we hooked south here, or kept straight? How far were we from the lake?

I started forward in the most familiar-looking direction, then forced myself to stop. I was being an idiot. I wanted to keep stalking off, nursing this anger, but I'd just get myself lost. And lost out here could be a death sentence, even with my dad looking for me.

I sat down against a tree and set the walking stick and the bow beside me, wrapping my arms around my knees. So I'd wait. In the rain, cold and damp, my leg aching, alone. I wanted to cry. I wanted to curl up and feel sorry for myself, but instead I set my jaw and stared straight ahead. I was sick of feeling like a kid throwing a tantrum. Dad made me feel like some snotty, spoiled teenager, whining about not getting candy or an Xbox or something.

I wasn't whining. I was trying to protect myself. And I was heartbroken to realize that my dad might be part of what I needed protecting from. The fact that he thought he was helping me made it worse, not better.

A sound rumbled under the rain. An engine. A plane engine, distant but drawing closer. Griff? I craned my neck up to peer at the sky, but the sliver the treetops allowed me to see was empty and gray.

"Sequoia?"

Dad's voice. *Not my name*, I thought, stubborn, and I didn't answer. I should, I knew, but I clamped my lips shut and leaned my head against the tree and stayed silent.

"Sequoia?"

The plane was getting closer and so was he, his footsteps crashing through the brush. "Jess!" I could feel his anger, even from this distance. What would he do once he found me? I didn't think he was violent, but what did I know?

Your dad had a temper, too.

He loved me.

Then again, Lily's mom loved her, too; George's dad adored him when he wasn't drunk and angry.

"Jess!" He barreled past the tree where I sat, striding forward. The plane sounded louder than ever, and he looked up toward the sound. I could see the side of his face.

He wasn't angry. He was afraid. Jaw tense, eyes wide. Afraid for me.

I shifted. He turned. His face crumpled into relief for only an instant before it settled back into a frown.

The plane flew overhead and farther. Passing over, nothing more.

"My name's not Sequoia," I said quietly.

He gave a short, convulsive nod. "Don't do that again," he said.

"I won't." I started to rise. A spasm of pain went through my knee; I steadied myself on the tree. He held out his hand. I ignored it, pushing myself up with the tree and the walking stick.

Wordlessly, we walked back together. Slowly this time.

At the cabin I hovered a moment, unsure where to go. Dad paced out to the shed, didn't seem to expect me to follow, so I went inside. My leg was feeling better. *No real damage*, I thought. Hoped.

The fire was already set up for the day; there were even matches next to the fireplace, so I didn't have to fuss with the flint. I got it going with only one wasted match, and when my dad came inside finally, I'd boiled water and set out two mugs of instant coffee. He set his pack by the door and sat across from me without a word. Didn't say anything until he'd taken a long sip.

"I can't remember the last time I was that scared," he said.

I bit my lip. "I'm sorry," I said. "I was fine. I just . . . I didn't want to sit there, and . . ."

"I know," he said. "Plus, you were pissed at me, and sitting still is the worst thing when you're pissed off. I know, believe me." He gave me a crooked grin and spun his mug idly in his hands. "I know you shouldn't be out here. You should be in school. Talking to boys. Going dancing. I mean, if you can . . ."

"I couldn't dance before the accident, so I doubt I can now," I said.

He laughed. "Take after me that way, then." He paused. "I'm sorry I told you that—I'm sorry I acted like your leg and all, that it didn't matter. I want you to be healthy."

"I am," I said. "I've just got a bad leg, that's all. I'm not sick. And I *will* get better. Maybe not all the way, but most of the way—and even if I don't, that's still got to be okay. My body's a bit broken, but it doesn't mean I'm a broken person."

"No, of course not," he said, shaking his head. "I never meant that."

"I know. But it felt like it, some. I think the same thing, a lot. I don't always use the right words or think about things right—there's a lot about having a disability that's new to me, too."

He flinched at the word. I didn't blame him—it had taken me a long time to come around to admitting it might apply to me, and I was the one with the scars to remind me. I wished now that I'd paid more attention to the websites and books Will had shown me, so I could explain things properly, but doing that had meant admitting the possibility that I wasn't going to get better.

"Maybe you're not going to be as strong as if you weren't hurt," he said. "If you can't be strong, you have to be smart. And smart is better than strong, out here."

"Smart?" I echoed.

"Careful. Thoughtful. Educated," he said. "Not letters and numbers educated, out-in-the-wild educated. I can teach you to be smart out here, and then it won't matter that you aren't so strong."

I bit my lip. "We could still go back, couldn't we?" I said. "Don't you have a radio or a satellite phone or something? Can't you call someone?"

"I'm afraid not," he said. "Too easy to track."

Too easy to track? "What kind of trouble did you get into when I was little?" I asked quietly.

He looked away. His weight settled back in his chair, and it creaked. For a moment I thought he wouldn't answer me. "I had these friends," he said. "Started out as a bunch of guys who liked the same things, that was all. Hunting, fishing, backpacking. We talked about living off the land. About living free, but most of it was just talk. Figured someday I'd have some land of my own somewhere with just a few neighbors and none that I could see from my front porch, but that was about it. That was it for all of us. And then things changed."

"Changed how?" I asked. I clutched my mug in both hands, hunched forward over the table.

"You know how it is sometimes, when you've got a group of friends and then one new person joins and suddenly the whole group seems different? It was like that. I mean, all of this—we were never political. I don't get along with rules too much and government's all about rules. I have a thirst for freedom and the firm belief there ought to be room for a man to find it in this world, that's all. But this new guy—Albert, was his name—he was intense, and he wasn't just talking about getting away from the government, he was talking about destroying it. I figured he was just kooky." He rubbed his face with his hand. "Probably shouldn't be telling you this."

"I want to know," I insisted. "I deserve to know."

"Guess you do," he said. "Anyway, some of the guys drifted away, some of them listened to what he had to say, and I just stuck around because I hadn't made up my mind to leave. And then it was too late to leave."

"Too late?"

His fingertips bounced on the table, a nervous tic I'd never seen from him before. He cleared his throat. "Something happened. Something bad." He held up a hand. "Nothing I did, I promise, but I'd have a hard time convincing a judge of that, and so when I said I wanted out, Albert had that on me. That and . . . I haven't always been good with money, Jess, and used to like to gamble quite a bit. I owed people money, and Albert covered for me. So he had the money and what happened on me. He said I could go, sure, but only if I kept doing a few favors for him."

"And you did?"

"What choice did I have?" He blew out a breath. "No. There's always a choice. You always have a choice and I made mine. I didn't want him even knowing where you were, so I stayed away."

I wasn't sure I wanted to know what favors he was talking about. And he didn't volunteer any details. "And what about now? Do you still . . . work for him, or whatever?"

"I told you, I've got promises to keep. Just one, really. One thing, and then we've agreed I'm done. He doesn't have much use for me, anyway."

"What one thing?" I pressed. "Dad, are you . . . you're not a criminal, are you?"

"No," he said, emphatically. "Oh, hell, kid, I've broken plenty of laws, but nothing that ever hurt anyone. It's nothing bad, this thing I'm doing for them. Not really. I'm just looking after some stuff. They'll be by in a few months to get it, and then that'll be that. We'll be free to go wherever we want, just as soon as Griff comes by to get us."

"What stuff?" I asked.

"Don't worry about that, baby bear," he said. "It's not important, and it'll be gone soon enough. Just . . . when a plane comes that isn't Griff's, you stay hidden. Stay out of sight, and I'll take care of everything. Okay?"

I wanted to argue. I could feel the fight in the air between us. All I needed to do was take hold of it. But we'd fought enough. And it wouldn't do any good. "Okay," I said.

"You trust me?" he asked.

I hesitated, nodded. "I trust you." Or I wanted to. Wanted to so much that maybe it was the same thing as really trusting him.

He sighed, shook his head. His eyes were fixed to his mug of coffee as he turned it slowly on the tabletop, like he was staring at it so he wouldn't have to look at me. For a few seconds, only the fire had anything to say, crackling in the hearth behind him.

"I wish I could've done better by you," he said finally.

"Me too." I didn't say it to be cruel or angry. It was just true. I didn't know him. I thought I might like him, with enough time. Mom did, after all, even if things didn't work out. I could see myself in him, in his temper, in the way we groused at each other, in our shared stubbornness. But even if we turned out to be the best of friends, he'd never have been there when I was five and broke my arm, or when I was ten and won the school spelling bee. I would always have grown up without him, and no amount of love or trust could change that.

Maybe, eventually, that won't matter as much, I thought. We'd know each other so long that I'd be able to forget the years he wasn't there. It hit me then that I had more years left with him than I would ever have with Mom, and suddenly thinking about the possibility that we might get along someday felt like a betrayal so keen it made me rock back in my chair, made my throat close up.

"I'm going to bed for a bit," I said. I couldn't stay here sitting across from him. I needed room to breathe.

"I'll let you rest, then," he said. I suspected he knew I wasn't tired. I was glad he let me go anyway.

I shut the curtain behind me and sat on the bed, thinking about the years we'd missed and the years we would have ahead. About what kind of relationship we'd have, what we'd do together. I imagined then that we'd have weeks and months and years; that we'd have decades together, the two of us, to figure out who we were to each other.

We had six more days.

After

THE FIRST FEW days by the rock, I think a lot about my last conversations with my dad. There weren't many of them. Not many times we got along. That day, the day I hid, was almost the last. Not quite, but close.

I keep replaying it, changing it. Imagining what conversations we might have had, if everything hadn't gone wrong.

I imagine him talking to me while I work, putting together makeshift fishing rods. I imagine him giving me advice, only I don't know a damn thing about making a fishing rod from scratch and I bet he would, so my imagined version of him mumbles a lot.

I start out with just fishing line attached to a stick. I don't have a good way to reel a fish if I hook it, so I keep the line short and hope it won't matter too much. I tie another bit of line to a short, fat stick; I figure I can twist the stick to wrap the line around it as a clumsy reel, see if that will work, but I'm guessing. Grasping at straws. I've eaten the last of the salmon and too many of the berries (*they'll go bad anyway*, I tell myself), and I'm out of time to figure something out.

I finish my work in the evening. I goad the fire to a little more warmth with extra fuel and hunker down, trying to sleep. It's not easy. The air is filled with humming, droning. Mosquitos. They've been around constantly, but tonight they're thick as a cloud. I feel them against my nostrils, against my lips. I pull my shirt over my nose to keep from breathing them in, wrap extra clothes around me to protect my skin, but they wriggle through and bite and bite and hum, and soon I'm itching everywhere a centimeter of skin has peeked through.

By morning I'm half-crazy with it, skin itching, no sleep, ready to scream. I dig the fleshy part of my fingertips into my arms to keep from scratching off the bites. And then I do scream, sending a pair of crows climbing, startled, into the sky, because there's no one to hear and no one cares and why shouldn't I scream?

And then Bo howls, flinging his head back, like he's joining in, and then, distantly, another howl comes, and Bo's hackles go up and he growls, and I remember that there are still things out here I don't care to bring into my camp.

I clamp my teeth over another shout. With all the pain I've dealt with, surely I can deal with *itching*. Right now, I have to focus on fishing.

I'm proud of my decision all morning, fishing instead of building up the shelter. I dig up some worms for bait and keep them in an empty jar. I empty out the canoe bit by bit, tipping it, scooping water out with the jars, and then finally rolling the whole thing over with the walking stick as a lever, and I hardly strain my back at all. *Smart, not strong,* I congratulate myself, not realizing that I'm neither.

Once Bo realizes I'm going out in the canoe, he takes off. I hope he's going to find something to eat; he's looking skinny. So am I.

Swarms of mosquitos buzz over the lake, but I'm too cheerful to care. I have my peaches to keep me fed for the day, and the sweetness is a welcome break from the salty salmon. As soon as I'm out on the lake with my lines in the water I drink some peach juice and then slurp down a whole slice of peach. The sun shines lazily down, and I drift.

A few hours in I realize I'm getting sunburned. It's hot out, so I've taken off my fleece and my rain shell. My arms are pink, getting pinker. My cheeks and the back of my neck are hot. My skin feels tight. I splash water on my face and my neck. I can't go back yet. I haven't caught anything.

I wait. Nothing bites. I start leaning over the side of the canoe to see if there are any fish under the water. Nothing.

Finally, fighting back tears, I awkwardly paddle to shore. The temperature drops as the sun dips. I've wasted the whole day. My muscles don't feel rested, they feel tight. I can barely put one foot in front of the other. I should have been stretching, moving to keep myself limber.

I hike back to the rock with new planks dragging behind me and despair crowding out my thoughts. If I can't fish, how can I get food? All I have are berries and a couple of tiny cucumbers. I'm moping, wishing for a cucumber plucked off a supermarket shelf—hell, wishing for the whole supermarket—when I spot a squirrel. A big, fat squirrel holding a nut, sitting ten feet away and he hasn't even noticed me.

I lower the planks slowly, letting them settle quietly on the ground. I sling the rifle around. I'm going to get that little bastard. I'm going to make him into squirrel stew.

I line up the sights. I try to think of it like the bow, except I don't have to aim *up* the same way; bullets travel faster, which means they cover more horizontal distance before they lose altitude. But the fundamentals are the same: steady hands, line up the shot, breathe steady, breathe out.

Instead of letting go, pull the trigger.

The gun jerks in my hand. The squirrel squirts off at top speed, bounding over the ground. My shot plunked into the ground a foot away. Only a foot!

An entire foot.

The squirrel freezes a few yards away. It flicks its tail and looks around, but it hasn't run up a tree or disappeared. It probably still wants its nut.

If I don't move too fast, maybe I can still shoot it. I start to lift the rifle. Then I frown. What did I do wrong? I aimed the sights right at it. My hands are pretty steady; I've basically been resting all day. Even if I am fried to a crisp.

I aimed. I pulled the trigger.

I pulled on it pretty hard, I realize. Hard enough that I pulled at the rifle, pulled the aim off as I shot. That's right. Isn't that what thrillers always say? *Squeeze* the trigger. Don't pull. Go slow, go gentle.

I aim at the squirrel again. Flick, flick goes his tail. Flick, flick. *Crack.*

I squeeze the trigger gently. The time between when I start to squeeze and when the rifle cracks feels like an eternity, but I know as soon as the shot goes off that I've hit. The squirrel flies up into the air with a jerk as the bullet hits and rips out the other side, embedding itself in the ground. The squirrel drops. I whoop. "I did it!" I yell. Birds burst out of a tree nearby, and I just about double over laughing. "I did it!"

I look around. It takes me a minute to realize I'm looking for someone to tell. I want to tell my dad so he'll be proud of me. I want to tell Griff so he'll get that dopey grin on his face. I want to tell my mom, too, though she was a vegetarian, so maybe I'd spare her the details.

A wave of sadness sweeps through me. I trudge over to the squirrel and nudge it with my toe. It looked sleek and fat but now it looks tiny, and I wonder how much meat I can really get from it. The bullet tore it open. The ammunition's supposed to be for bigger animals. I've basically pulverized the thing.

At least I know how to shoot now. A little better, anyway.

I pick up the squirrel gingerly, avoiding touching the big, ragged hole just behind its front leg. I carry it by the tail and walk the rest of the way back to the rock. And there I stop and stare.

All my gear and clothes are scattered across the clearing. My jars have been rolled out of place. Even the tackle box is gnawed on and knocked over. And on the far side of the clearing stands the culprit: a big red fox. He has a pair of my underwear—my dirty underwear—hanging from his jaws.

"Hey!" I yell, and jerk the rifle up, dropping the squirrel. I squeeze off a shot, hardly aiming, my anger making me wild.

He takes off in a red-gold streak. *With* my underwear. Grumbling, I start to gather up my clothes. It doesn't look like he's actually gotten into anything, so I stack everything back up the way it was and sit down to munch on berries, leaving just a handful for the next day.

My stomach growls petulantly. I have the squirrel, I remember. Time to figure out how to cook it.

It doesn't go well. I resort to hacking out pieces of meat and then picking tiny bones and bits of skin out of them. In the end there's no way to cook it on a spit like I envisioned, so I stick it in a jar with some moose water and boil it right on the hot coals of the fire. Squirrel stew.

It's disgusting. I almost wish Bo was back so he could steal some from me, but I know I need every calorie I can scrape out of the jar.

When I've choked down every bite and every drop of broth, I tuck myself into the space under the rock. Bo is nowhere to be seen, and the wind starts to pick up, along with a thin, cold rain. The wind howls through the trees—and straight into my face, carrying the rain with it.

I hunker in as far as I can, but it doesn't make much of a difference. I shiver. I feel sick. The squirrel was disgusting, even as hungry as I am, and the way it sloshed around in the water was sickening. The water itself is greasy and gamy and coats my throat.

I'm in a poor mood to begin with without the sky spitting in my face.

I pull my duffel up to my chest and pull out my photographs. I hold them in front of my face, hands cupped to protect them from the rain, studying them as the sun sets and the fire glimmers.

Mom is looking at the camera, but you can tell her attention is on me. She was gone a lot. Left me with friends. But I always knew she would come back, and she always had some little present for me. She called me every day, and she always missed me, but she never offered to get a different job and I never wanted her to. Maybe she was more like Dad than I'd realized. She couldn't sit still, and he couldn't stay away from the wilderness. Both of them got pulled away from me.

But Mom always came back.

Not anymore. Now neither of them will ever come back to me. So they're more alike than ever.

I fall asleep with that thought playing in my mind and the photos in my hand.

Mistake, mistake, mistake.

I SNAP AWAKE as the wind gusts, blowing a spray of water into my face—and a second later I jerk as the hot remnants of my fire skitter across the ground toward me. A smoldering ember hits my cheek. I scramble back toward my clothes, yanking the duffel with me.

The rain is astounding, the sound of it striking, hissing, and rolling against the treetops. The wind has shifted. And as it rages, it catches the photographs that still lay on the ground where I've dropped them in my sleep.

They flutter wildly, the wind sliding under them. I lunge forward, but I'm too slow. The wind catches them and throws them out of the shelter.

"No!" I yell. I run after them. It's pitch-black. The only light comes from the dying embers that have scorched my face, and I'm about two steps from the shelter when my foot catches something and I almost fall. I catch myself and stand, rain pelting my head and shoulders.

I can't see the photos. I can barely see my own hands. It's like a sack has been dropped over my head. The world seems suddenly impossibly huge. How can I find two little scraps of memory in all of that?

I can't. I crawl under the overhang. I'm soaked. My clothes are wet all the way through. My fire is out. Most of the clothes I've folded so carefully are now wet as the wind blasts the rain right under the overhang, into my face.

They're gone. The last picture I had of my mother, of my father. Gone. I already have trouble remembering her voice. How long until her face fades, too? Will I live long enough to forget her?

As I lie shivering, it seems impossible that I will. The wind will take me, too. Tear me free of my shelter. Of my body. Fling me up into the storm.

I huddle with my back to the storm, my face to the rock, my mouth tasting of rainwater. I don't sleep but somehow I dream, I dream that the wind has taken me, that I am flying, buffeted on the storm. I know that my mother is here with me, somewhere just out of sight and out of reach. If I can find her, we'll both be safe, but the night is too dark and the storm is too fierce.

And then I dream again of the road, of the man standing on the median line, of the gun. Griff looks at me, but it's not Griff, it's my dad, and he shakes his head, once, and he reaches out his hand and the gun cracks—*squeeze the trigger*—and I'm holding the rifle and there's a hole through him and I'm still in the sky, in the storm, and in the car with Mom and in the woods with Dad, and I'm huddled against the rock alone because both of them are gone, gone forever, and I will always be alone.

After

MORNING COMES, BUT the storm does not let up. The light is a weak, pale gray pressing through the cloud cover. It doesn't matter. I can't wait.

I am hollowed out. I have spent every ounce of sorrow and despair, every last drop of emotion that I have. I don't think. I don't feel. I just move. I lurch out into the wet, my belt-and-strap system ready. I slide it over the end of a birch log without bending over and use it to lift until I can get a hold of the log with only a slight bend of my back.

My back complains as I heft the log overhead. With the rain, I can't tell if I'm crying as I lean it against the overhang. It tries to roll away. I shove the end of the log into the ground, into the mud, and then stamp down the dirt around it to keep it in place.

I repeat the process again and again. Two birch logs, four planks, spaced across the shelter. Then I go around and gather evergreen branches. I strip low ones from trees and pick up some the wind has knocked down. All the while the rain funnels down my back, past my collar, sending a rivulet of cold down my spine.

Cold will kill you first, I keep thinking. But I can't get warm without shelter and a fire. I can't get warm without being dry, and I can't get dry unless I get this shelter finished. This is it; I know in my bones. I have been in danger before, but not since the fire has it come down to such a clear decision: succeed and live, fail and die.

I am not ready to die.

My stomach cramps. I need to eat. No, I don't. I *want* to eat. I don't need to eat for hours yet. I need the shelter, and I need more food, and then I can risk eating the last of what I have.

I start stacking the evergreen boughs on top of the boards, but they slide, leaving gaps. I yell in frustration. The sound barely rises above the driving rain.

THINK.

Throwing myself at something that isn't working is just wasting energy. Energy is food, and food is another thing I don't have.

So what do I have? I have the tackle box, my clothes, the jars. I have the canoe, down by the beach—at least I can hide under that if worse comes to worst, I realize, but I can't move it from the beach—no way.

The rope! I think of tying the branches individually, discard the idea—it would take too much rope and too much time. I shut my eyes, imagining ways to tie the rope. I could throw it over the side of the rock to dangle things over the planks. No. I need to somehow go across all of the planks side to side and top to bottom.

I open my eyes. I have it.

I get the rope out. It's still fairly dry, but I know it'll swell up with water pretty quickly, so I tuck it into my rain shell and feed it out of the neck a little bit at a time. I start at the bottom and weave the rope between the planks and the logs, making a zigzag net. I pull it tight but not too tight. The rope is long; it reaches all the way to the top. I'll miss that rope when I need to tie something later, but I keep thinking, *Cold kills you first.*

When I'm out of rope I tie it off around one of the birch logs. I have no idea how to tie a good knot, but I don't need it to hold too much. It just needs to stay in place. I start shoving the evergreen branches under the ropes. Then the evergreens are firm enough to sort of weave other branches with them, and they're all holding each other in place.

As I work, I warm up. I'm wet, but I've stopped shivering. Cold will still kill me, but not right now. Not until I'm done and have a chance to build a fire.

The whole time I'm working, I hardly notice how much my leg hurts. I do stop sometimes, checking. It's the good hurt, the you're-building-strength hurt, not the you're-making-it-worse hurt. So I keep going.

Soon I have a functional wall. It isn't perfect and I need more branches. A lot more branches, overlapping so that no rain can get in. And I need to stretch it out and bend it so that one whole side of the shelter is covered, except for an exit at the foot. Maybe I can even make myself a door. But for now, it will do. I crawl under and wrap my arms around myself. It will be cold very soon. I need to get the fire going.

I take a deep breath. And I turn to my wood.

Some of it is wet, but a lot of it has managed to stay relatively dry. And the thriller was tucked under my clothes in the duffel, so it's all right. A little damp at the edges. I tear out the title page and the first page of the prologue (in which a woman in a red dress gets murdered to show that the main bad guy is bad) and shred them up.

My hands are numb, but by now I have practice. It takes me only three tries to get the fire started, and I build it up just under the shelter of my wall. I still have a couple of chunks of chopped-up plank. They last a while if I keep the fire small, I've discovered, so I put one on when it's ready.

As soon as I can, I swap clothes, hanging the wet ones to dry. Bo chooses that moment to come home muddy and wet and plaster himself by my side. I look at him and sigh. I'll have to dry off that side of me, but at least Bo keeps me warm. At least he's here, and I'm not worrying about him being out in the storm anymore. I scrub his ears. He has blood on his muzzle, which he licks off idly. At least one of us is getting fed.

I eat the rest of the berries. It takes the edge off my hunger, but nothing more.

"When it stops raining, I'll get more," I say. "And I'll find Dad's traps. And then I'll finish the shelter. And when I finish the shelter, I'll gather more firewood. And if I gather more firewood, I'll go fishing again, but only for half the day. And if I catch a fish . . ."

If I catch a fish, I'll pick more berries, and check more traps, and catch more fish. I need to build up a surplus. Which means I need a way to store food.

There's no end to it. No end at all. I curl in over myself and bite my hand, hard, and then the grief is there again. Sharper and fiercer than it ever has been. My father is dead. My mother is dead. Even the photographs I had are gone, stolen by this place. By the wind and the storm. The cold is gnawing at me. The damp is everywhere.

All this work I've done, all this effort, is probably for nothing. Is definitely for nothing. Because everything is dead and gone even if I'm not. There's nothing to be alive for. I'm going to die eventually, and none of it will matter. No one will even know.

My tears are the only warm things in the storm, but they turn cold on my cheeks. I bury my face in my arms, and I sob and can barely hear it over the rain and the wind. There are no tricks to snap me out of it. No perky Will maxims. Just the storm, and me, and Bo.

And the stupid notebook.

It's so ridiculously out of place that glancing at it startles me for a moment. I pick it up and hold it for a long while. Once I'm dead, there will be no one to remember my parents. Not the way I remember them. There will be no one to tell what happened. I can't beat the wilderness. Not me, a city kid with a bad leg who's been camping a half dozen times in her life, and never without flushing toilets within a hundred yards.

But I can write it all down. That, I can do.

I tear open the pack of pens and grab one at random. I open the notebook to the first page. And I start to write.

I'VE CAUGHT UP to myself, then.

Of course, it's been days since the storm. Even writing every spare minute I've found, it's taken me a long time to get it all down. And I can tell you what's happened when I haven't been writing, how I've stayed alive these few extra days.

But I can't keep avoiding the one thing that made me start writing. It's time, now, to tell you about the moment when *before* became *after*. When everything fell apart.

This is how my father died.

Before

THE DAY DAWNED bright and clear. The sky was one big blanket of blue over the treetops, and the whole forest seemed to have come alive in celebration. Squirrels raced along the tree branches, chittering at one another.

"You can eat a squirrel," Dad told me. "But there's not much to them and they taste terrible. You gotta kill a few of them to make more than a morsel for yourself. I catch 'em for Bo sometimes," he said, nodding toward the dog, who ambled along beside us. "But mostly he catches them for himself."

Dad fed Bo whatever we were eating, but it wasn't enough to fill him up. Bo didn't seem to mind. He wandered off for hours at a time and came back sometimes with a bloody muzzle. But if my dad whistled, putting his fingers between his lips and letting it peal out over the lake and the woods, Bo always came running. Sometimes it took him a while, but Dad never had to whistle more than once. He just waited, and eventually Bo loped out of the woods.

I took my bow and my arrows, just like before. Dad took one

of the rifles and a handful of extra ammunition he put in the pocket of his big coat.

We moved along slow and quiet. Sometimes Dad stopped stock-still and listened, but Bo didn't do anything other than move along with us until midmorning. Then the dog froze, nose testing the air, trained on a patch of bushes.

Dad aimed his rifle down that way. "Shh," he said to me. We crept forward. Bo slunk alongside us. He moved like a cat, quiet and low to the ground, tensed to charge.

A deer bounded out of the bush. She was delicate and graceful, flowing like water over the ground. She raced past and into the woods, too fast for me to bring the bow up and try a shot. Dad didn't move.

Secretly, I was relieved. I started to ask him why he'd let her go, and then I realized that he was listening. I strained my ears to catch what he heard. An engine. A plane engine. They flew over every few days. None of them had stopped yet. But this one sounded different. Closer. Lower.

"Is that Griff?" I asked.

He shook his head. "Not Griff," he said. He lowered his rifle. We could see the plane now through the trees, angling for the lake. "Could still go by." But the plane was descending, coming toward us.

"Is that them?" I asked. "Those friends of yours?"

"They shouldn't be here yet. They're not supposed to be here until . . ." He scrubbed at his chin with his palm. "Listen, Jess. I need you to stay here, okay? Stay here with Bo and stay real quiet, and I'll come back and get you when it's safe."

"When it's safe?" I asked, alarmed. "Why isn't it safe now?"

"Just stay out of sight," he said. "Whatever you do, don't come down to the cabin until I come get you. Okay?"

"Okay," I said. He looked—not scared, exactly, but anxious. He gave Bo the command to stay and headed out.

If they were here now, did that mean we could leave soon, before next summer? Or did it mean that something was wrong?

Bo stared anxiously after Dad. I didn't like my dad keeping secrets from me, and I was worried about him. There was no way I could sit out here for—what, an hour? Five hours? A day? I knew I couldn't find my way back in the dark, and I had no shelter if I had to spend the night out here.

Dad said stay out of sight, so I'd stay out of sight. But I was going to go see who these people were, and what it was they'd left with Dad.

"Come on, Bo," I said, and snapped my fingers. Bo gave me a considering look. Probably trying to decide if my *come on* could override Dad's *stay*. But I think he was just as anxious to get back to the cabin as I was.

We moved along at a painfully slow pace. I'd pushed myself hard the last couple of days. My leg was sore. It dragged a lot more than usual, and eventually I grabbed a big fallen branch to use as a walking stick. Back in foster care I didn't like to use my cane too often, because I was worried that my body would get used to it and heal to match my cane-assisted walking. Right now I didn't care about any of that. I just cared about making good time.

By the time we got in sight of the tree line Dad was down by the lake. I could hear him talking; there aren't many secrets out here, with the way sound carries.

"—another month," Dad was saying.

Another voice, a man's voice I didn't know, answered him. "We were getting some unwanted attention. Couldn't risk waiting. You don't mind, though, right? It's not like it's extra work for you. One box is the same as another. You just keep doing whatever you do out here, and we'll be back when we're ready to pick it up."

My dad's voice dropped, and he said something quick and angry that I couldn't make out. The man answered in the same low tone. I crept closer. I couldn't see them yet, and it was hard to stay quiet. I was terrified that my foot would drag or I'd snap a branch and give myself away.

I crouched down behind a tree near the edge of the woods and peered around it. Bo hunkered down beside me, completely silent. It was eerie how he seemed to know that we had to hide.

Dad was talking to a white man with black hair; a sharp face; and long, thin limbs who stood with perfect calm. Even with Dad holding a rifle so tight it was like he was trying to crack it in two. Another man waited down by the water, next to a raft with an olive green crate on it. Their float plane, a big red one, was behind them on the water and in it I thought I could make out a third man. Pilot. His head was bowed like he was sleeping.

"Tell you what," the lanky man said. "Let's go inside, and we can talk it through."

Dad hesitated. Then he nodded. They turned and walked toward the cabin. I pulled myself in, hiding completely behind the tree trunk as they passed. Then I snuck a quick glance.

The man had a gun tucked into the back of his jeans. A handgun. Did my dad know it was there?

I squinted down at the man by the raft. He had a gun, too, this one in a holster at his hip. He rested his hand on it, his thumb idly snapping and unsnapping the bit of leather that kept it secure.

I shook. It was like I was the leaning tree in a windstorm, shuddering and shivering all over.

Leave, I thought. *Just do what you came here for and leave.*

It was a long time before my dad and the lanky man came out of the cabin, and when they did my dad was no longer carrying a rifle. The two of them walked down to the beach. Dad nodded to the man there. He didn't nod back. The two newcomers said something to each other, and then all three walked back up toward the woods, the second man carrying the metal crate.

I moved through the trees, staying low, crabbing along with my hands and hauling my bad leg with me as best as I could. I kept my bow on my back, but my arrows were rattling. I paused long enough to strip off my rain shell and stuff it down between the arrows, keeping them cushioned so they wouldn't rattle. Then I hurried, because they'd gotten out far ahead. We were deep in the woods now, out of sight of the cabin and the shore.

Bo didn't bark, didn't even look to the side when a rabbit burst out, racing through the brush. Soon we heard voices again.

"There was that girl, though," the lanky man said, and my heart gave a jerk in my chest like it was going to try to squeeze straight through my ribs. "What was her name? Sally?" They weren't talking about me. I relaxed a fraction.

"Sophia," the other man answered, voice slightly strained from carrying the heavy load. I still couldn't see them, but I followed the sound.

"Sophia," the lanky man confirmed. "She was something. She was—" He paused, and I thought he must be making a gesture. Probably having something to do with the size of some portion of her body. "Whatever happened to her?"

"Dunno. She wasn't exactly the bring-home-to-mama type," the other man replied. "Only stuck around for a couple weeks. Asked for gas money. Said she'd pay me back."

"Seems to me she already paid you back," the lanky man said, and gave a laugh that made my whole body clench up. "How about you, Carl? Don't suppose you get much tail around here. Not unless a moose stands still long enough."

Dad didn't answer.

"Come on now, Carl. Just being friendly," the lanky man said. Finally I crept up close enough to see them. There were beads of sweat on Dad's forehead, and he stared at the ground ahead of him instead of looking at them.

"Hold up," the lanky man said. "This'll do." They halted and set down the crate. They were standing in a little clearing where a big tree had fallen. The lanky man stamped on the ground. "Yep. Here."

The other man opened the crate and took out a pair of shovels before shutting it again. He tossed one to dad. "Start digging," he said.

The digging took a long time. The whole time, the lanky guy—Raph, I learned as they spoke—talked and talked. Mostly about women. Talking about women in ways that sex ed and prime time TV did not prepare me for. I hated him more and more with every word. The other man, Daniel, didn't say nearly as much, but he laughed at all of Raph's jokes and that was bad enough.

When the hole was really deep and as wide and long as the crate, Dad and Daniel climbed out. Daniel took the shovel from Dad, and Dad stood with his hands hanging by his sides.

"Well. Put the stuff in," Raph said. Dad looked at him for a long, flat moment. Cold fear snaked through my gut. Something was very wrong.

I took my bow off my back and slowly slid an arrow free. I set it to the string and eased out to where I could get a clear shot. Daniel had his back to me. Raph did, too. I had to shoot just right. I had to kill Raph right away, so he couldn't draw his gun. And then I had to kill Daniel, too.

Dad looked straight at me. I froze. Raph was looking over at Daniel, grumbling about something, and Dad fixed his gaze on me. *It's okay*, he mouthed. And then he shook his head, once. And he turned back to help Daniel. I hesitated. I could still shoot. They still weren't looking.

And what if I missed?

What if I wasn't fast enough to get another arrow out before Daniel pulled his gun?

What if I missed Daniel?

What if the pilot heard gunshots and came after us?

Dad said it was okay. So I had to believe that it was. They'd bury that box, whatever the hell it was. And then they'd leave us alone. I eased the arrow and sank back behind the tree.

Dad and Daniel hauled the crate over to the hole and lowered it in. When they were done they stood a moment and panted, wiping sweat from their brows. Dad turned to Raph. "There we go," he said. "Safe as houses until you need it. I'll make sure it stays that way."

"Still leaves us with a problem," Raph said.

"I told you. The money'll be here by the time you get back," Dad said. "I didn't steal it."

"Just borrowed it," Raph said. He smiled, nodded. "I believe you, Carl. I believe you'll get that money."

Dad reached out his hand. "I'll shake on it," he said. "My guarantee."

Raph kept smiling. And he took out his gun. And he shot my father in the head.

Before

I WROTE *BEFORE*, but that isn't right, not really. There's no more *before* after that moment; that's when the world split in two. It took less than a second. The time for a bullet to leave the chamber and travel a few feet.

My life has become a list of things that almost killed me. Ways I almost died. If the truck that hit us had been going just a little bit faster, I would have died. If I hadn't gotten up that morning on the shore, I would have died. If I hadn't gotten the fire started the day of the storm, I would have died.

If I had screamed when the back of my father's head burst open in a spray of blood and bone and brain, I would have died.

I tried to scream. The sound stuck in my throat, and I made a strangled, wounded noise. Raph's head jerked up. He looked toward where I was crouching. I held still, held my breath.

"I hate the woods," he muttered, and turned away.

I struggled to breathe. I fought a clutching sob that wanted to break free, and I stuffed my fist against my mouth to hold it in. My dad was dead. He was lying on the ground and the dirt was turning so dark with blood. He was dead. There was no moment of hope, of thinking maybe he would get up. That maybe I'd seen wrong.

"Jesus," Daniel said. He'd yanked his gun from its holster when Raph fired. Now he jammed it back in. "What'd you shoot him for? You think he was lying about the money?"

"He stole from us," Raph said. "You can't let something like that go. Now get him in the hole. Then we'll check the cabin. Could be he was lying, and the money's still here. If we find it, good. If not, fine. Either way we burn it all down. Make sure there's no reason for anyone to come here."

Daniel nodded. He dragged Dad's body by the shoulders, leaving a streak of blood across the ground. I closed my eyes as the body dropped into the hole. It hit the crate with a horrible thud.

Raph swore. "Make sure it's all in there," Raph said, and I squeezed my eyes shut tighter. Tears still managed to leak out, running down my cheeks as hot as blood. "And turn over the dirt where it's bloody, too. Don't want an animal digging him up or something."

I heard the patter of dirt, imagined it hitting dad's coat and his face and his open eyes. I felt paralyzed. I stared at Bo. The dog hadn't moved, but his lips were peeled back from his teeth. I wanted him to jump out and tear their throats out. But they'd kill him. They'd kill me. I couldn't even hit a tree consistently. How was I supposed to stop them? Three men with guns. One girl and a dog. There was no contest.

You probably already know that I couldn't have done anything, but I have to say it again and again because I still don't believe it. I still lie awake thinking of how I could have killed them before they killed my dad. Or how I could have stopped them after. Gotten to their plane somehow. Gotten rid of the pilot. Killed him. And then the plane—

I could have taken the plane. I could have flown it. It had a radio. I could call for help and help would come. The pilot was asleep. Maybe. I could have taken him. Maybe.

Except I would have had to get down to the water without anyone seeing me. I would have to get out to the plane and I would have to get the door open and *then* I would have to shoot him or stab him or whatever it was that I could possibly do to a man with a gun, a man whose friends had shot my father as he reached out his hand to shake.

Instead I just sat there and cried silently, hidden behind the tree. And then I remembered. The cabin. They'd said they were going to burn the cabin down.

They were going to burn the cabin down and then they were going to leave and then I was going to be alone out here, alone with no one and Griff wasn't coming back and my father was dead. Without the cabin I didn't have fifty pounds of flour and ten pounds of sugar and twenty-five pounds of rice and the sourdough starter and the smoked venison and the spices and the fishing rods and the rifles and the blankets and the nets and the snow shoes and the firewood and the tent and the salt—the salt, if I had the salt now I could keep the meat for more than two days. I could keep it from rotting, and instead the only time I have caught a rabbit I had to eat it all, stuff it in my mouth until my belly bulged and I was so full that I was almost sick into the dirt, because otherwise it would go bad in the summer heat—all of the things that had kept my dad alive were in the cabin.

Sorry.

I'm sorry, I'm sorry. It's just so hard to think about, so hard to remember.

And screw Will and his stupid trigger because I'm not moping, I'm pissed and I'm terrified and I'm going to die, so leave me alone.

The cabin. They were going to burn down the cabin, but first they were going to search it, and that was worse. Because on the bed in the cabin was a backpack that could only belong to a girl. There were clothes that could only belong to a girl, and a photo of that girl, and they would know that I was here and they would come for me.

I sat there, terrified, knowing that soon they would be done filling in the hole. I couldn't move through the fear. I breathed through my teeth. I knew I had to go to the cabin, but I couldn't make myself get up.

Bo saved me. He slunk over to my side and pressed his nose against my hand, looking up at me. I moved my hand first. I could manage that. I moved my hand over his nose and his eyes and found his big knobby head, and I sank my fingers into his fur. He was warm. He huffed a little breath. The fur on his shoulders and his neck stood straight up. He wanted to kill the men that had killed his master, but for some reason he stayed with me instead.

They would kill him, too, I thought. I had to save him.

I don't know if they really would have killed him. Maybe he

would have run away. But that was the thought that I clung to in that moment. I couldn't move for me, but I moved for him. At first all I could do was lean, shift my weight until I fell forward onto my hands. I pulled myself along more than walking, low to the ground. I got maybe fifty feet like that, and then Bo put his nose under my arm and shoved upward hard. I used him for leverage, pushing myself upright. I swayed a moment. The men were faster than me. I couldn't waste what little lead I had.

I ran. I heaved my bad foot with every step. It was a lopsided, ungainly run, and I grabbed at trees as I passed to launch myself forward faster and keep myself upright. Bo ran at my side. I could see the cabin through the trees. I could see the shining lake past that, and a flash of red. The plane. I was almost there.

I lurched forward another step. My foot caught against something. I pitched forward. My arms pinwheeled, but it was too late to catch my balance. I crashed to the ground. I got my arms in front of me just in time to catch myself with my forearms.

My breath went out of me instantly, and pain gnashed at my back. It felt like something tore, leaving hot agony in its wake. I did scream then, muffling it with my sleeve. Then Bo was there. Sticking his nose under my arm again, nudging me. I wrapped an arm around his neck and hauled myself upright that way. When I was on my knees I sank my fingers into the rough bark of a tree and pulled myself, shaking, to my feet.

I ached all over. I'd probably damaged something permanently, re-injured myself. But I couldn't afford to give in to the pain. I had to keep moving.

They'll hurt Bo, I kept thinking. A silly thought. Such a

ridiculous thing, but it was what I kept repeating over and over as I dragged my way to the cabin. Every step sent pain through me like the glass was going into my side all over again. And then I was at the back of the outhouse. From there I stumbled to the shed, and then to the cabin, keeping the buildings between me and the pilot. I clung to the wall, working my way around it, praying that the pilot was still asleep and wouldn't see me.

His head was still resting on his chest. I breathed out a sigh of relief, but I didn't let myself hesitate. I dashed for the front door.

I fumbled with the latch, and panic rose in my throat to choke me. Then it gave. I practically fell inside as it swung open.

Once I was inside, I froze. There was so much I needed. I couldn't even begin to think what I should take, and I only had a few seconds.

I had to get my bag. I lurched across the room to the bedroom. The curtain was shut. Raph hadn't seen my bag yet, then. I wrenched it open and grabbed the kitty bag, and then hooked one handle of my duffel and yanked.

I hadn't zipped it up the night before. Everything flew out, scattering across the floor. I dropped to the ground, clawing at my things. I stuffed everything back into the duffel. I didn't have time to check that I'd gotten it all.

I whipped back out to the main room. Dad's rifle was leaning next to the bookcase. I grabbed it, slung the strap over my shoulder. Ammunition; a rifle needed ammunition. There was a box on the shelf and I shoved the whole thing into the kitty backpack. *Thirty seconds*, I told myself. *Grab what you can in thirty seconds.*

I saw the hatchet and lunged for it. I shoved it in the duffel.

Food. I needed food. But everything I could see was in giant, heavy sacks. Rice, flour, beans. Meat. Where was the meat? I couldn't reach it.

A can of peaches (store-bought) and a jar of salmon (home-canned) were out on the table. I snatched them, and then I heard voices. Raph and Daniel were coming back.

I took one last look around the cabin. I can still see it all perfectly in my mind. All that food. I said I miss the people more than the food, but Christ, I miss that food, too.

I was out of time. I ran, hobbling along straight for the trees, not checking to see if Raph and Daniel were in sight, and I threw myself down on the ground among the bushes. Just in time. Raph and Daniel came around the opposite side of the cabin I'd run around. The door hung open. I held my breath. They'd know I'd been there. But they just walked right in.

Would they notice that the rifle was gone? Would they see that someone had been there? Had I remembered to let the curtain fall back into place?

I thought of a thousand ways it could go wrong. I waited for one of them to shout and for them to come charging out into the woods to look for me.

They rummaged in the cabin. Something crashed, shattered. Thumps and bangs echoed across the beach. They argued back and forth, and then finally Raph stepped out and walked a ways down toward the water. He put his hands in the pockets of his jacket and looked around slowly. He looked like I must have, the day we paddled across the lake. Taking in the water and the sky and the trees in a slow circuit. When his eyes passed over me, I hunched against the ground, shoving the bright backpack under me to hide it.

Then he spat. "Idiot," he said. "It's his own goddamn fault."

Daniel came out of the cabin, splashing gasoline behind him. I held my breath. He tossed the canister of gasoline inside. They must have found it in there or brought it with them. I hadn't seen it. I didn't know where Dad kept half his things. I hadn't been paying attention; I'd been complaining. I hadn't even known where the meat was. Then I remembered: the meat wasn't stored in the cabin, he hung it in the shed to dry it out. That was where he packed it in salt, too, to preserve it, and did the canning. The shed was just past the trees on the other side, where it was cooler and shadier the whole year.

For almost a minute, I hoped. I hoped that they would leave, and leave my meat, but instead Raph whistled. "Hold up," he said. "Don't forget the outbuildings."

Daniel gave a long, put-upon sigh and jogged down to the boat again. He came back with more gasoline and doused the outhouse and the shed. He struck a match, watching the burning point in his hand like it fascinated him.

"You sure we got to do this?" he asked. "Seems like a lot of effort for a guy that's already dead."

"Claimed he had documents," Raph said with a shrug. "Probably bluffing, but what if he's not? We burn it."

"Burn, burn, burn," Daniel crooned, and tossed the match inside the cabin door.

Air whooshed, and then an orange glow lit the windows. The fire snapped and crackled as Daniel walked around the side of the building and struck another match. Whoosh, and the out-house went up. A third match. The shed now, fire gnawing at it from the inside out, climbing the walls. It roiled, bright and hot even from where I stood, and the men retreated down the beach.

The flames claimed the walls, cracked the windows. They found the door and escaped, licking upward toward the roof, where they caught easily. I had never realized how loud fire could be, roaring and snapping and coughing. The fire destroyed everything, but it protected me. Hid the sound of my sobbing.

Raph and Daniel walked back down to the boat, their backs painted with light. They climbed in and pushed off just as the outhouse roof collapsed in a shower of sparks.

Beside me, Bo seemed to snap like a rubber band stretched too far. He charged.

"Bo, no!" My voice was hoarse, lost in the roar of the flames. He ignored me. He churned up pebbles all the way down to the shore until he hit the edge of the water, and there he whipped back and forth in a frenzy, growling and snarling.

Raph whistled. "See the size of that dog?"

Bo's jaws snapped, teeth pulled back to bare his teeth. Spittle flew in all directions. *No, no, no,* I thought, willing Bo to come back.

Raph pulled his gun. Aimed it at the snarling dog.

Daniel dug the paddle into the water, making the boat rock. Raph pulled the trigger, but his aim went wild, stinging out well over Bo's head and splatting into the pebbles farther up the slope.

"The hell, man?" Raph said.

"Just leave the dog alone," Daniel said. "I like dogs."

"You want to make friends with that dog, you go ahead," Raph said, but he sat back down and Daniel kept rowing. They rowed all the way out to the plane. Bo seemed to realize that they were too far gone to do anything, but he watched them with those pricked, wary ears.

And then he threw up his head and howled. The howl went on and on, the most horrible, sorrowful thing I'd ever heard. He howled and howled as the cabin burned, as the men got into their plane and lifted away into the sky.

When they were only a speck on the horizon I walked out of my hiding place. Bo sat by the shore. No longer howling, just whimpering and growling and pacing like he couldn't figure out what had happened and what he was supposed to do.

"Bo," I said. He whipped his head toward me with a snarl. His body vibrated with tension. I put out my hand, palm out. "Come on, Bo."

He snuck toward me step by step. His nose pressed against my palm. I slid my hand up over the side of his face to his ears, and dug my fingers into his fur. A shudder went through him. I sank to the ground, and he crawled up next to me, tucking his huge bulk against me. I wrapped my arms around his ruff.

We sat like that while the fire burned. It burned into the night, which this time of year was still light until its very core. When the sun finally set, I shut my eyes and lay down on the beach. Bo lay beside me, his warmth at my back. Somehow, I slept.

I HAVE BEEN on my own for more than a week now. Maybe more than two. I haven't kept track very well of the number of days, the number of nights. We're well into summer, and summer out here isn't long. I remember Dad saying that. Which means I have maybe a week, maybe three at most, before winter comes.

I am not prepared for winter. I almost did not survive these first days, but I know I will not survive the winter the way things are going right now. I have the same feeling now that I had when I woke up on the beach with everything burned down. A certainty that things have to change, and fast, or I will not make it to the next week.

I can fish a little. Not well. I've caught a couple of animals, mostly by accident. And I've lost some of those to the fox, creeping into my camp whenever Bo is away.

I've found a few more supplies—odds and ends scavenged from the cabin, when I could bear to go back there. Not much. It's not enough to get me through more than a day or two at a time, much less months of winter, of snow and ice.

I have a week, maybe three, to figure out how to survive. I don't think I can. But I'm sure as hell going to try.

FALL

I LEAVE THE notebook in the ashes of the cabin. I wrap it in a T-shirt and a plastic bag I found, tie it with rope, and weigh it down with a rock. Maybe someone will find it. Maybe not. Either way, some record of me will survive.

Longer than I will, probably, but I try not to think like that too much. I try not to think too much at all, but the habit's ingrained now. It's like I'm constantly writing in my head. Turning my day into a story, even if I'm not writing it down anymore.

There was frost on the ground when I woke up this morning, silvering the edges of fallen leaves and making the treetops glitter. That marks the end of summer, I suppose, and fall is short here. Winter's coming fast.

I've been thinking about that crate, and what could be in it. I doubt it's anything that could help me here. It's probably money or drugs. Worthless, in other words, unless it turns out there's a thriving cocaine trade among the squirrels. And to find out, I'd have to dig up the hole. Dig up the grave. It's bad enough going back to the cabin. I can't do that.

I remember once I overheard Mom talking to Scott about Dad. She said he used to have friends over that she didn't like. She called them *odd*. When Scott pressed her for more details, she said something like, "Oh, you know. Live off the land, hate the government types." She didn't sound too concerned. She couldn't have known the extent of it. I still don't.

I know enough, though. Everything I need to. Dad was involved with bad people. They blackmailed him into hiding money and something else for them, up here where no one would think to look. Only he didn't have the money for some reason— why? Did he gamble it away? Spend it? Give it to someone? It didn't matter—every explanation led to the same place. The same patch of forest floor, six feet long and five feet deep.

I doubt I'll find out all the details, the whole truth, before I die, and my curiosity is pretty blunted these days. The hunger doesn't leave much room for it.

From the cabin I go down to the water. Fishing again. Not that it's done me much good so far, but I have to figure it out.

I push out into the lake, picking a new spot this time. Farther east. I throw my line in. I've adapted it since the first clumsy attempt. Figured out I shouldn't be using dead wood for my rod, for one thing. It just snaps. Lost line and a hook like that. After, I cut it from a live branch, so it had more bend. I tried it out on land, pulling and tugging and yanking at the fishing line, and figured out I shouldn't just have it tied at the tip. Sometimes it slipped off, sometimes the stick broke. Finally I tied it near the base and wrapped it around the whole length of my rod, and tied it at the tip to keep it all in place. I still haven't seen much luck with it, but I'm hoping that luck will turn.

I get the pole in the water and then that's it. All I have to do is wait. I trail my fingertips on the surface of the water, watch a duck wing by. I spend a few minutes counting the trees along the shore. Got to do something to make the waiting go by.

The fishing pole lurches.

I grab for it, throwing myself toward it so quickly the whole canoe rocks side to side. It tugs and bounces against my grip. I haul on it. I pull it up, pull it over the boat, extending my arms all the way to get enough length to pull the end up out of the water.

I can see the dark back of the fish in the water. For a moment I doubt I can get it out—I made the line too long—but then with a thrash it flips itself out of the water and right into the bottom of the boat.

I squeal, half in surprise and half in delight.

It's a slippery, sloshy wrestling match to get the fish pinned, to club it, but then I have a fat fish—trout? Perch? I don't know the difference, but it looks tasty.

I want to paddle straight back to shore and roast it up, but where there's one, maybe there will be more. I spear a new worm on the hook and fling it back over.

A white shape a few feet away catches my eye as I settle the rod against the side of the canoe. Two white shapes, small and floating on the water. Too still to be birds. Some kind of trash? They look round and man-made, and anything man-made could be useful.

I paddle over, letting the line trail in the water. Closer up, the two white shapes resolve into small plastic floats. A cord runs between them. I lean out and snag one, drawing it in.

"Huh."

Six lengths of fishing line dangle from the cord. Two of them are broken off short, but four still have hooks on them—and one, the rotted remnants of a fish. I look at the cord, look back out at the water, and picture the floats spread apart, the six hooks dangling in a row between them.

Was this part of what Dad was doing when he went out to fish, those mornings I didn't go with him?

If this works, if I can dangle six lines at once without even having to be out on the water to do it . . . That's what I need. A passive way to bring in food. Hunting and fishing both take up so much time and energy. I don't earn back what I put into them. This could be a solution.

I pull the whole contraption into the boat to repair it. Now my hands have something to do. Working with fishing line, especially wet fishing line, is fiddly and frustrating, but after a while I have new lines threaded and all of them baited with bits of rotted fish. I push one float out from the canoe, letting it drift until the line is stretched to its limit, and set the other float into the water.

In the edge of my vision, the fishing rod dips.

I grin. Today is going to be a good day.

TWO FISH. TWO fish, and the promise of more tomorrow if things work out. I get back to land, and I feel like I'm soaring. Still no sign of Bo, but I can't blame him for ditching me. It's not like I've been able to keep him fed.

I gut the fish by the shore. I'm sloppy, but I watched Dad do it and can see where I went wrong—I'll be able to do it better next time.

I save the guts for Bo and wash the blood off my hands. Then I make my way back to the rock. The trip feels quicker than it ever has, and the whole way I'm imagining what it'll taste like when I put that first piece of flaky fish on my tongue. I'd be skipping if I weren't limping, and it's good to remember what a real smile feels like, stretching my cheeks.

I get my fire going and set up my "stove." It's not much—really just rocks I set around the fire, to prop up my pan. I found the pan in the cabin when I finally went to sort through the remains. Cast iron, so it didn't burn, though it's taken ages to get the ash and soot off it.

I get one fish cooking and sit staring at it as it sizzles, biting my thumb and jiggling my leg in anticipation. My stomach, silent all day, is rumbling up a storm, and the first whiff of cooked fish has my mouth watering. All the hunger my body has been working so hard to ignore comes roaring back, and it's all I can do not to gobble the fish down raw.

I don't have a real spatula, but I've bent a bit of flashing from the chimney into a tool that almost does the same job, and I get to work scraping up the fish to flip it. Out here, this qualifies as gourmet cooking. I'm glad now that I took the time to clean the pan, to make my little spatula, even if all I was really doing was killing time. It wasn't like I had any food to cook with it, but after trying to roast the rabbit over a spit I figured I needed something more sophisticated.

I'm so focused I don't notice the scrabbling at first. It's not until the flicker at the edge of my vision that I turn—and yelp in indignation.

The fox has wriggled between the pole wall and the rock, and grabbed my second fish by the tail. He's halfway back out by the time I spot him.

I lunge for him, yelling a garbled string of angry syllables. He books it, jaws clamped around the fish. The opening's too narrow for me. I have to scramble out the other way, past the fire, and by then he's halfway across the clearing and still running.

I grab a rock, huck it after the fox, but I miss by a mile.

I swear, watching the flip of his tail disappearing into the trees. "Asshole!"

Yeah, that'll show him.

I throw another rock after him for good measure, then take a sharp breath. There is not a single second to spare on regret out here. One fish is gone. The other is still here. I have a fish and it doesn't matter that ten seconds ago I had two. What I've got is what I've got.

That's what I tell myself, but I still mull creative ways to cook a fox as I finish frying up the remaining fish and eat my fill.

One fish and one rabbit every two weeks isn't going to keep me alive. I need to get better at fishing, and I need to get better at protecting what I've caught.

The light has that tired quality it has toward the end of the day, and the wind has a bitter edge. Frost again tonight, probably. How long do I have until the lake freezes over? That'll make fishing harder. That'll make everything harder. I can't rely on any one thing, which means I need to get good at hunting, too.

The only time I've ever killed anything with the bow was out with Dad, even though I've tried half a dozen times since. Beginner's luck. The rifle's easier. The only trouble with it is that I can't rescue the rounds like I can with the arrows—some of them get broken and bent, but so far I've only had to scrap two completely. Just like with the ammo, though, once I'm out I'm out. The bow is too strong for wooden arrows; they'd shatter. I'll have to make a new bow at some point, one that I can make my own arrows for.

But that's ages away. Right now I've still got both weapons, and a good amount of ammunition. Everything that's in the box, plus however much is in the rifle now.

I decide to check, since I'm not actually sure.

The answer is none.

No problem—I have the box of ammunition. I grab a round and go to load it, but it won't fit. I shove at it, but I can only cram it partway.

I look at the box. .30-30, it says. That doesn't mean anything to me. I have one of the spent casings. I hold it up against one of the bullets from the box.

They aren't the same size.

The bullets in the box are bigger. I have the wrong ammunition.

I almost throw the gun and the bullets away in frustration. Instead I shut my eyes and breathe long, deep breaths. Okay. Okay. I don't have a gun. I have a club that used to be a gun. And maybe there's ammunition left in the cabin.

When I went back for the rest of the jars, I poked around the edges of the cabin. Rooting around the chimney felt safe. That's where I found the flashing and the pan. But I haven't dug through the ash farther in, searched around the stubby remnants of the table, investigated the bedroom. I should. It's the smart thing to do.

There's still time for one more trip. I don't want to wear myself out, but the trip to and from the rock isn't that hard, now that I don't wander around along the way, and I'm never going to have more energy than when I've got a full belly. Besides, I don't like the idea of being out here without the rifle for protection.

Then it hits me: I've been carrying an empty rifle around for protection for days.

The thought stops me dead. I choke out a laugh, horrified. I haven't needed it, but what if I did? What if there was a wolf or a bear or a cougar or *Raph*?

I've been lucky. I haven't needed the rifle, which means that I'm still alive to learn this lesson: don't take anything for granted.

I bring the bow and the walking stick and set out, my nerves on edge. I feel exposed. I'm decent with the bow, but it's not great for protection, not if I get surprised. I have the hatchet, too, strapped to my hip, but if I have to use that, it's probably too late already.

The wind and the rain have cleared out a lot of the ash back at the wreck of the cabin, which makes it obvious that there's almost nothing left in it. I don't even pause before stepping over the threshold. If I pause, I'll chicken out and turn back.

So I walk through, sifting through the ash, kicking it. I find a few stray bits of metal. A few cans charred so badly they have chunks missing, their contents burned or spoiled. Jars cracked and blackened. I find metal drawer handles and another hatchet head, two blackened knives, a burlap sack that burned only halfway.

I gather up everything that looks even vaguely useful.

I find the rifles in the collapsed heap of the west wall. The ammunition burst in the heat of the fire, and even the few rounds that are still whole are blackened. I don't trust them one bit.

At least I can see what went wrong. There's a scrap of a box left unburned. It's a different color, and it has .223 stamped on it. I must have the rifle that takes .223 ammo. And the other rifles are ruined, which means the ammo I have is useless.

I take the rifles anyway. I don't know what use they'll have, but the barrels are straight and metal, and if nothing else I can use them to prop something up.

Movement at the far side of the clearing draws my eye. Something flaps and flutters against the ground. I make my way over, leaving my pile of scorched metal by the cabin.

The tarp that covered the woodpile is trapped against the roots of a tree, fluttering in the wind. It must have ripped free somehow. It's still in one piece, and only one edge is a little scorched, the plastic fibers melted.

I fold it up, grinning. It's big, and it's waterproof. Stay dry, stay warm. Stay warm, stay alive.

I almost miss the rumble. It's not the first plane to come by since Dad died, but every time I taste the same sour fear in the back of my mouth. Is it them? Raph and Daniel and the pilot, coming back for what they left? Have they found out I'm here? What if they're coming back to kill me?

I scramble back to where I left my finds. I spread the tarp enough to load them all on, then bundle everything up and make for the trees as fast as I can. I need to get out of sight before the plane gets close.

At the tree line I burrow deep among the trees, crouching out of sight. Probably it's nothing to do with me, just like the two that have gone by in the distance, never even coming in clear view.

Or maybe, traitorous hope suggests, it's rescue.

No one but Griff knows I'm out here. But maybe he's come back. Maybe he's sent someone to check on me.

I wait.

The plane comes closer. Closer. Then descending, and my breath catches in my throat. It turns and comes down on the surface of the lake, a smooth landing that sends ducks scattering.

It isn't Griff's yellow plane. It isn't Raph's red plane, either. This one is a dingy green, and there's only a single man in it. He hops down onto the float and stares at the burned cabin.

"Helloooo," he calls, hands cupped over his mouth.

Should I answer? I bite my lip.

"Helloooo," he calls again.

He waits, looks around. He climbs back into the cockpit and I think he might leave, but he seems to just be thinking, because he gets back out and comes to shore. *He can't be with Raph*, I think. If he is with Raph, he'd know Dad is dead.

But that doesn't mean he's a good person. I creep closer to watch as he walks up the beach, and my breath catches in my throat. He's armed. He has a gun just like Daniel's and Raph's, in a holster at his side. He comes up and stares at the burnt cabins, and he spits on the ground like Raph did.

He walks around all three wrecks. Cabin, shed, outhouse.

The notebook sits just inside what used to be the doorway of the cabin. If he finds it, he'll know I'm here. He'll know everything.

Isn't that what I wanted?

He crouches and picks up a handful of ash and lets it scatter. Then he stands, takes off his hat, rubs his scalp. Shoves the hat back on again.

He walks back to the water with a purposeful stride.

Call out to him, I think. *Call out. Call out.*

But my throat is squeezed shut.

He might shoot me.

The cold might kill me.

He might bury me in a grave like my father's.

I might starve to death.

He might let me into the plane and fly me to Raph and Daniel and tell them I saw.

I can't move. I want to, but I can't. I roll onto my back and squeeze my eyes shut and ball up my fists until the engines start.

Until the plane rises.

Until the sound fades.

Until I am alone again, in silence, the air gone brittle with frost.

THE FOX IS DEAD.

I find it ripped apart not far from my camp. My things have been mouthed at, torn up, scattered around. There's blood everywhere, smudging my clothes and staining the ground.

Some of the blood is the fox's. All of it? I don't know.

I cover the blood with dirt. Clean what I can. I carry the fox's carcass back into the clearing and lay it over a log. "I'm sorry," I tell it. I pet its fur. Even ripped, it's soft.

I should skin it. Use its meat and its fur. But for now I sit next to the log, feeling that much more alone.

I start to cry. I hate myself for it. It's stupid. Waste of energy, waste of water. But I cry because the fox at least was something I see every few days. I even gave it a name. I knew I shouldn't have, so I didn't write it down, but in my head I've always called him George.

Because George was an asshole, and so was the fox.

"I'm sorry," I tell the fox again. I knuckle away my tears and take in a gulping breath. I should have gone out to that man. I should have risked it. That was my chance at rescue, and I lost it.

Bo trots out of the woods. I let out a shuddering breath, more relieved than I realized. "Hey, boy. Where have you been?" I ask him. I put out a hand. He ignores me, goes stiff-legged to sniff the fox instead.

He doesn't look hurt. He also doesn't look like he expected to find a fox here. He whuffs and growls, then spins to face the trees, ears pricked.

I push myself to my feet, suddenly uneasy.

If Bo didn't kill the fox, what did?

I walk back to where I found the carcass. There are paw prints all over in the mud. The fox's are easy to pick out, but when Bo trots past, leaving a perfect imprint, I realize that the bigger prints aren't all his.

There's a third set. Canine. Bigger than Bo, and Bo's got to be a hundred pounds. "Somebody you know, Bo?" I ask. He growls, staring off into the trees.

I shiver. Rolly I'm not worried about, but I can easily imagine the jaws that tore the fox apart tearing into my flesh, too.

I keep the hatchet on me, and I take the fox well away from camp to butcher it. I shouldn't be cooking at camp, I decide. The food was what kept bringing the fox in, and there are clearly more dangerous things out here that I don't want nosing around my camp.

By the time I'm done working I have meat and I have a raggedy fox skin. It's still bloody, still stuck with bits of meat and fat, but I think I can scrape those off, and there's a good section that's still whole.

Fox fur mittens. I could use some of those.

Maybe I'll live longer because of whatever killed the fox. Or maybe it'll come back and kill me.

I split the meat with Bo. He's insistent, and I don't have any way to save it. Besides, I already had the fish today, and this won't last more than a day or two.

I lick grease off my fingers, watching the fire bank low. I have food. I will live another day. But to live longer, I can't keep doing whatever pops into my mind. I'm going to end up like the fox if I don't play this smart.

I need more firewood, for one thing. I've been hiking back and forth and fishing and hunting, and I've gotten behind on the dull work of chopping and gathering and splitting.

I know I need to get ahead of the firewood. I need giant piles of it, because some days will be too cold and too dark to go out during the winter. Or I might get sick or hurt and need to hole up for a few days. I do a little math in the dirt, guesswork and experience adding up to a number that's ten times as much as I've been managing.

It doesn't seem like it should be that hard to gather wood, but I'm slow and fire is greedy. Especially since I'm stuck gathering deadfall and branches, mostly—I can't bring down trees on my own with just the hatchet. Not that I didn't try—I made a handle for the ax, but I couldn't attach it securely. The first time I used it, the handle slipped and the weight was wrong and I swung it weirdly and if my leg hadn't buckled, I think I would have chopped right into it.

So I need wood, but wood isn't enough.

I need to check the floating fish lines. The fish don't do me any good if they hang there until they rot or if some other fish steals them.

I have to hunt.

I have to fetch water and boil it.

I take a stick and make a grid in the dirt, blocking the day. Walk to the lake. Check the lines. Go fishing, maybe, or go hunting. Go back to camp. Boil water and chop wood. Sleep. And morning again, and the lake again.

I can do it, I tell myself. It's not complicated, it's just hard.

Firewood, fish, water, hunting. What else?

Only one thing else: winter.

THERE'S ICE ON the edge of the lake today. Just a thin skin, like on a cup of milk that's been out too long. I break it with my toe. Soon that ice will stretch across the surface of the water. Too thick for the canoe, too thin for me.

When the ice comes over the lake, I'll have to break through it to fish. Once it gets thick enough, I can walk out onto it and chop a hole through the ice to fish, but for a while it'll be thin and crumbling and I won't be able to get out.

I don't know how long it'll be like that. A week? A month? Only the weatherman knows, and I don't have a radio. *Twenty degrees, chance of snow, and Jess can go out on the ice today without plunging to her watery doom.*

I wish.

At least soon it'll be cold enough for my meat to stay fresh longer. I can just pack it in snow. That assumes I have meat to save, which I don't.

The floating lines are empty. I get one bite, but I can't haul it up to the boat before it slips free and vanishes into the dark water.

I get back to the shore. Fill my jars with water. Trudge back to camp. I check the snares again. The bait's gone in some, but they're empty. The berries are gone, too, even the last rotten few of them. The wild cucumbers have died.

I trudge back, start chopping. Firewood today. Every day, firewood.

Maybe tomorrow I'll eat.

FOR ONCE, BO comes with me out on the lake even though he's usually wary of it. The jerky treats are almost gone. I've tried a couple of them myself, but Bo always gives me a betrayed look, and I figure I need him more than I need a few calories. They're in my pocket and maybe that's why he hops into the canoe when I shove it out onto the lake. He's looking thin, after all. Nearly as hungry as I am.

It's cold out on the lake. I don't mind his company, his warm body pressed up against my legs. I paddle out toward the floats. If there's nothing there, I don't know what I'm going to do. I'm so tired. Even swallowing makes me tired. It's been three days since I ate anything. I don't know how much longer I can go.

The cord between the floats is dragging down in the water, taut. Does that mean there's a fish on it?

My heart beats so loudly and so strongly in my thin chest I can feel my pulse in my teeth. I lean out and grab the nearest floater. I drag it toward me—and it jerks in my hand.

I let out a cry of relief and joy and pull it in faster. There—a big, fat fish, as long as my forearm, longer. It thrashes as I haul it up. Bo bounces up to his feet and backs away, giving me room, his tail wagging and his tongue lolling.

I drop the fish into the boat. Finally, finally. I pull the hook free so I can toss the floats back.

The fish arches. Thrashes. Flails its way up off the bottom of the boat. I dive for it so it can't flop itself out of the boat. I'm not thinking, I'm just so panicked at the thought of all that food getting away. The canoe rocks. My foot catches against the middle seat, and I sprawl forward.

My knee hits the side of the canoe with a *thwack* and pain shoots up my leg, but I only have a second to register it before the whole canoe jerks sideways under me, unbalanced by me, by the fish, by Bo barking and leaping backward out of my way, and then it flips and I'm in the water.

It's cold. Colder than anything I've felt. So cold it makes my chest seize, and I can't think or move.

I float—sink—for a moment, my limbs splayed out in the water, staring down into nothing but murky darkness.

The water churns above me. A paw hits my shoulder and shoves off, driving me deeper underwater, but it also snaps me out of my haze. I rake my limbs through the water. My clothes are dragging me down, making me move slowly. Especially my shoes, dragging at my feet.

I struggle to swim, but the weight is too much.

I grab one boot and pull. The laces are loose, or I would never be able to get it off fast enough. I force off one boot, then the other, stopping to sweep my arms through the water, trying not to sink too far.

It's only a few seconds, and then I struggle toward the surface.

Too far. It's taken too long, and now my lungs are burning. I reach for the shivering light above me, but I can't reach the air— and then my hand hits Bo's paw again, and this time I grab on.

He lurches against me, but I hold on fast. Pull. Use my feet and my other hand to try to swim upward, and I drag Bo under, but I break the surface.

I pull in a gasping breath and let go of Bo long enough to sling my arm over his neck. He snarls as he surfaces, turning his head, snapping at me. His teeth catch the sodden fabric over my shoulder.

He releases immediately. I don't think he realized it was me for a moment, but now the snarl fades.

We're breathing. But the water is frigid, and I know we can't survive in it for long. Maybe minutes.

The canoe is upside down. I swim toward it with one arm, trying to drag Bo with me. He gets the idea, and a moment later I'm close enough to grab hold of the canoe.

Without my weight on him, Bo swims more easily. But the cold is going to finish us both off quick.

"Sorry, Bo," I say, knowing I have to move fast. I grab him again, using him as stability so I can heave the canoe upright.

He yelps, but he doesn't bite me again. The canoe tips, hovers. I shove as hard as I can, dunking both of us underwater again— but the canoe rolls.

It settles upright. Now I just have to get back in without tipping it.

If I try to climb over the side, it'll just roll again. I tug Bo over to the bow. My teeth are chattering. I can't feel my fingers or my feet.

Everything in the periphery is starting to look hazy. Not good.

My paddle is floating near the bow. I grab it as we pass and toss it into the canoe. Won't do me any good to get back in only to be stuck floating in the middle of the lake, freezing to death.

The canoe sits low in the water. It's most of the way full of water itself, and I can't believe it's still managing to float. I grab hold of the stern. My fingers slip, but I stare at them and force them to close.

I push off of Bo and heave myself up. One try. I might only have one try, so I use all my strength, and then I'm lying on the bow of the boat with the end digging into my gut and my face a centimeter from the water filling the canoe.

The water is sinking the boat, but it provides ballast as I drag myself forward, flailing as I pull myself in. My whole body shudders. At least that means it's still got the energy to try to fight the cold.

The tackle box is gone. There's just the paddle. With my weight, the canoe is sinking even deeper in the water. I grab the paddle and use it to fling water out of the boat. It doesn't make a very good scoop, but the water is so high it doesn't matter.

I work frantically, as much to stay warm as to stay afloat, and

Bo paddles alongside, whimpering. When the paddle doesn't work anymore I use my hands. They're already so numb it doesn't matter when I dunk them back in the water.

I don't know how long I work. It seems like the water level isn't going down at all, and then I realize Bo isn't whimpering. He's quiet now, his movements slower, his head dipping halfway under the water.

If he gets back in the boat, it might tip.

If he doesn't, he'll drown.

There's no question of what to do.

I whistle for him at the bow. He swims around. I sit as firmly in the middle as I can and lean out to haul him up.

The canoe wobbles alarmingly. I pull Bo straight back, lying down and letting him claw his way over me to the center of the boat. I try to keep my weight as centered and spread as I can as we rock to and fro.

The canoe starts to roll. I throw myself toward the other side and so does Bo, and we start to go in the other direction, but I rock back the other way and the boat rolls into place, upright.

Bo scrambles up to the bow of the canoe and pulls himself onto the little seat there, sodden and shivering and panting. I huddle at the stern.

Cold will kill you first.

I don't have time to appreciate the fact that we are still alive. I have to start paddling.

I don't know how I make it back. I don't remember any of it, later, huddled by the fire. I remember gravel scraping against the bottom of the canoe, and then I remember being on my hands and knees on the same gravel.

I don't remember deciding to get up. I don't remember walking through the woods, except for flashes of green and a vague sense of pain.

I remember blowing on the embers of the morning's fire, watching a flame rise. I remember adding more and more wood. But then I don't remember getting out of my clothes, or getting into dry ones. Socks, underwear, T-shirt, jeans. No sweater, no jacket, no rain shell.

My memory keeps skipping. I remember Bo leaning up next to me. Thinking he shouldn't because he's wet and I'm getting wet again. Thinking at least we're getting warm.

Then I'm lying with my head on Bo's side, thinking how very, very warm it is, how nice.

Then Bo lurches upright. My head hits the ground, jerks me awake, and I realize the reason it's so warm is that the fire has jumped. I've built it too high. It snatches at the underside of the shelter, at the pine needles that have dried until they're the perfect tinder.

They spark and flare. Fire races along the shelter wall.

Bo backs up, snarling. The exit is blocked off, the fire grown too large, catching the stack of waiting logs behind it.

I stare dumbly as smoke fills the space. A spray of flaming needles drops as the branches burn. They hit the back of my hand and I yelp, shake them off, and finally move.

I throw my shoulder against the lattice I made to block off the head of the shelter, shoving it free. Bo lunges out, knocking me against the rock. I start to follow, stop.

Everything I have is in here.

I snatch my clothes, throwing them out of the shelter behind me. I grab my duffel and the bag and crawl out coughing, my eyes stinging with smoke. The fire is catching on the birch logs and the planks, now, devouring the entire shelter.

I have to save it, I think, except it isn't a coherent thought. Panic seizes me, and I grab at the nearest birch log. I yank, pulling it straight toward me so that it falls back from the rock.

The rope is still tying all the planks and logs together. When the log tumbles, it drags everything else with it.

The shelter collapses in a shower of sparks and embers. I scream, almost fall over, but I only stumble back. The fire rages at one end of the rock, still trying to devour everything, and I have no way to stop it.

I retreat, gather my things around me, and sink into a crouch.

Bo and I watch it burn.

I'M SO COLD. And so hungry. And I don't know what to do. The shelter's gone. My feet are bloody. I can't get warm.

The canoe is gone, too. It's floating off shore. I must not have pulled it up enough when I got back, and it floated free. It's only thirty feet away, but I can't swim after it.

No more fish.

No more bullets.

I am so hungry.

I REMEMBER WHEN I was little I had this bear, a stuffed bear. Not like a teddy bear, like a real-looking bear on four paws, with really soft fur. I think my dad bought it for me. Probably because I was his baby bear. It must have been. Mostly I think that because mom was always weird about it, about how much I loved it and I would sleep with it in my bed and everything, and she'd be sweet about it but also give me these weird looks like it meant something I didn't understand which I guess it did; it meant—I don't know, that I loved my dad or something, that I didn't hate him and maybe she wanted me to be mad at him for leaving her leaving us but that came later, I didn't know to be mad yet and he was like this story, this amazing story, this *dad* that was out there somewhere like Bigfoot. I don't know. It's just—

IT'S GETTING HARD to think and there's still no food.

Everything is gone and I have nothing. Except this morning I caught one tiny fish from the shore, and I ate all of it. Even the guts, most of them, cooked them up and ate them because otherwise there's nothing. I have to do something different, soon, today, or I have to get lucky. And I think my luck's all gone by now.

There was a storm last night, wind and sleet, and when I woke the whole world was covered in ice. Even my clothes were stiff. I haven't gotten any of the shelter back up so it's just the two of us huddled under the rock again, and it keeps most of the rain off but not all of it, and all those little droplets added up and froze together so I crackled when I sat up, and I had to get the fire going and huddle by it for an hour before I was dry enough to risk stepping outside. The ice was gone by afternoon, but there'll be more.

I had to cut up one of my T-shirts to bandage my feet. It's hard to keep them clean and dry and warm, but it's the only way they'll heal. And I need shoes to walk, but the best I've been able to do is to layer on the socks and then use what's left of the rope to tie tarp around them. It makes it even harder to walk, but at least they stay warm and they don't get torn up. But the knots slip as I walk, or the tarp shifts. I have to stop constantly and fix them, and every step hurts.

I have to find another shelter. I have to get food. I can't think it's over, not yet. Not while I can still think and I can still move. I have water and Bo and wood to burn, and it isn't winter yet. Not quite.

I have to keep trying.

COLD WILL KILL *you first*. I work on the shelter. Not much left. Two logs, one plank. So I take what's left of the rope and what's left of the tarp, and I stretch it out like a tent over the rock. It isn't big enough to reach the ground on both sides, and there's not enough rope to tie it down.

So I'll weigh it down instead.

I get a half dozen of my jars and fill them with rocks and water, then punch holes in the tarp and tie the jars to the holes with scraps of rope and strips of my T-shirt. That way they hang over the rock, and their weight is enough to keep the tarp in place.

It sounds clever until night comes and brings the wind with it, snatching up the side of the tarp. I've punched the holes too close to the edge of the tarp; it tears.

The edge flaps up, then it comes free at the bottom, where I've weighed it down against the ground, and seconds later it's tearing away and falling, and the glass jars tumble and shatter and I'm back to nothing.

It starts to rain.

It drums against the rock. It's not even raining that hard, but the noise of it makes my skin crawl. I cover my ears, squeeze my eyes shut, try to sleep, but I can't. The tarp flaps uselessly in the wind, the rain patters against the rock, and I pull Bo closer and whimper into his side.

I need to try something else, but I can't think of it. All I can think of is how much I need food.

I straighten up. Bo watches me with hungry, trusting, hopeful eyes. He looks lean. I can see his ribs. I know I must look worse. I can feel the bones of my face pressing against my skin. My ribs jut out, my belly caves in.

I'm starving. I've used that word so many times, casually, just tossing it off. *Let's get lunch, I'm starving.* I want to slap the old me. I want to do worse than that.

We've already split the last of the jerky. We've got a desperate, eager way of moving now, our chins twitching toward anything that might mean food. I wonder if he's going to leave me.

I wonder if I should kill him.

The thought makes me want to cry, and crying hurts now. It's always these wracking sobs that push up through my throat and make my back feel like it's tearing and sound like horrible, dying sounds. When I cry Bo crawls into my lap and licks my chin, which only makes it worse, and then I shove him away, which only makes him whimper and press against me harder, and then I feel terrible and I cry even more.

And then I think about all the energy I'm wasting, crying.

I've lost so much. I'm weaker. It's colder. I don't even have any bullets for the gun.

If I had bullets, maybe I could hunt. If I was smart, if I'd grabbed that other box, then . . . But instead I'm an idiot who didn't even check what she was taking.

I have nothing. The rifle is nothing. Just a club. A walking stick at best and even then it's too short to do any good.

Stop.

Enough. Stop.

I focus on breathing steadily. To shut out the sound of the rain, I listen to my breathing instead. To the beat of my heart. Every beat is a promise. I'm not dead yet. I'm not dead yet. I'm not dead yet.

I squeeze my eyes closed until the tears have nowhere to go. I'm not going to give up. I might die, but it's not going to be because I sat here crying like a useless lump. I can't let myself think I have nothing. That's what I thought that first day, and I was wrong.

I dig my fingers into Bo's fur and count breaths until they slow again.

It doesn't matter what I don't have. What matters is what I do have. Okay, the rifle's worthless without ammunition. Except.

Except there is ammunition.

I stare out into the night, the rain drumming unyieldingly against the rock. My heart's rhythm is quick and weak in my chest.

There's more ammunition. Not much more. But some. And I know exactly where it is.

In my father's pocket.

I remember watching him in the cabin. Remember the bullets clinking against one another as he shook them out of the box (the box he put back in the space under the bench, which I should have remembered that day, should have known not to grab the box that was sitting out). I remember their gleam in the morning light as he glanced at them once, and the rustle they made as he tucked them safely in his coat pocket.

And then—then the mist of blood. Then him falling, being dragged to the hole, then the rain of soil down on his body. Buried. With the crate and my father, buried.

They're still there. Under the dirt. Out of reach.

Unless I dig.

I can't. It's only a few bullets. Five, six. Or could it be more? How many did he take? I can't remember.

Enough to save me, maybe. Enough to get some food. Enough food while I get strong, while I find more. If I can only stay alive and fed for a few more days—for a week—

I don't know. Maybe I'll still die. Probably I'll still die, but I have to try, don't I?

I haven't been back there. To his grave. Not since the day he died. But I remember exactly where it is. I can still see that day every time I close my eyes. Crack, jerk, dead. I see it in my dreams when I don't see my mother's empty face.

I remember then the last time I saw my dad, before coming here. The last time he ever visited us. I used to wonder why he never came again, after that, but thinking about it now is like re-reading a book when you're older, all the jokes suddenly making sense.

My mom and I were decorating a Christmas tree. She would lift me up so I could reach the top branches, but most of the ornaments were still clumped down where I could reach, because I wanted to hang them all. She was only allowed to hand them to me. And then there was a knock on the door, and Mom went to open it. She told me to keep hanging ornaments, and I did, singing carols until suddenly the voices at the door weren't just talking, they were arguing.

I crept over to see what was happening. Mom didn't get angry very often; she was always so calm and reassuring. It was part of what made her a good pilot. It was part of what made us so different.

There was a man on the porch. I didn't know him. He had shopping bags sitting next to him, maybe a dozen of them, and he was gesturing and talking loudly, and my mother was almost shouting at him, but they both shut up the second they saw me.

"Who's that?" I asked, or something like that. I remember my mom not saying anything for a really long time, and then she smiled.

"Your dad's come for Christmas," she said. I recognized him then, or maybe I just convinced myself I did. I ran and gave him a hug, and he scooped me up into the air.

He came in, and he brought out present after present to put under the tree, more than I could count (not that I could count very high). He told me jokes and we drank hot cocoa with tiny marshmallows in it, and Mom set an extra place for dinner and didn't say much of anything at all. I thought it was a big Christmas surprise she'd arranged for me. Now I realize he showed up without permission. Without warning her at all. He was there for a day and then he vanished without saying good-bye to me. I cried for days. I think I'd gotten it into my head that he was home for good. That he was my Christmas present.

Mom didn't say anything about it. She never really said anything bad about him, or if she did, it would just be one short sentence and then she'd change the subject like she hadn't meant to. It meant I didn't grow up with her anger for him piled on top of my own, but it also means I don't know much about him at all. She didn't exactly trot out all the good stories, either.

Before I came here, that was my most recent memory of seeing him, touching him. And every year I thought about it and it got less cheerful, more messed up. But thinking about it now, my brain keeps trying to make it happy again. When I think about the time I spent here with him, it seems like the most amazing, wonderful time, even though I know it wasn't. Even though I know I was miserable.

I think I love my father more now that he's dead than I ever did when he was alive. Or maybe it's just that I miss him, and that's different. He's not the same in my mind anymore. I keep thinking that if he was here he'd protect me and love me and everything would be okay, and it's hard to care that we argued. In my fantasies, he's more like the father I imagined when I was little. He fusses over me. He brings me rabbits, he keeps the fire going. Sometimes I hear the stories he told with Griff that made me laugh so hard. It's like he's alive.

If I go back to the grave, he won't be. Going to the grave is like killing him all over again.

Not just going there. Digging him up.

I feel sick.

An acid taste burns in my mouth. My stomach lurches. What will I even find? A skeleton? My father, eyes closed but looking like he did, looking like when he died?

I have no idea. I don't want to think about it.

But I have to. I have to live. I have to stay alive. Dad would want me to. Wouldn't he?

I don't actually know what Dad would want. I don't know what he'd do for me. He was willing to give me up when I was small. He refused to give me up when it might have been better for me. It's his fault I'm here—but if he was here, I'd be okay. It's all a horrible, screwed-up mess and it'll never be sorted out, because I'll never really know him. He only got to be a person to me for a few days before he was a corpse.

A corpse doesn't get a vote—that's what he'd say. He's not here to make the decision for me. I have to make it on my own.

"Okay," I say. Bo jumps a little, sees it's only me, and settles back down. "I don't know what Dad would want, but I know what Mom would want. She would want me to live. She would want me to do anything at all to survive, and never mind anyone else."

I bite my thumbnail. I think Dad would want that, too.

The imaginary version of him in my head would.

I have to do it.

I have a shovel head. I got it from the shed ages ago. I even tied it to one of my walking sticks, and unlike the ax, it mostly works. I've just used it to dig temporary "outhouses." This'll be a lot harder. And the ground is hardening up with the frost, and I'm not very strong.

Which is all the more reason I have to do it now. If I wait, I won't be able to.

I have to try. Before I think about it too much more and talk myself out of it. Before I get any weaker. I don't think I'm strong enough, but I've surprised myself before.

"All right, Bo," I say. My voice shakes. "Let's go find Dad."

THE SHOVEL HISSES and scrapes on the ground as I drag it behind me. I keep my head bent, the sound of the rain against my hood constant and inescapable.

Bo walks with me. He can't possibly know why we're out here in the night, in the rain, but he looks at me with trust and hope I never earned.

I go to the cabin first; I don't know how to cut straight through to the grave. I have to orient myself in the ruins first. I glance at where the notebook still lies. When Griff comes back in the summer, he'll surely look around. He'll find it. He'll know.

I hope he won't be offended by anything I wrote. I almost go back to get it, to write him a note telling him how much I liked him, how none of this was his fault, but I didn't bring the pens with me and I don't have the time anyway.

The sound of the rain has muted, only a soft, shushing patter now. It takes me a moment to realize the silence is because it isn't rain anymore—it's snow, drifting down in fat, loosely spun clumps.

I brush the snow off my sleeve and set out for the grave as the sun comes up over the trees.

I count steps as I walk. A trick to keep myself from thinking about how far there is left to go. Not half a mile, just a hundred steps. And then a hundred steps after that, uneven, punctuated by the thump of my walking stick against the ground.

I don't know how many hundreds I count before I come to the place where my father is buried. I stop. This is it; I'm sure of it. A mound on the forest floor. And there's the wide tree I hid behind, the fallen log, its side ruptured by the rapid growth of a sapling.

This is where he has been, this whole time. And I never even came to say good-bye.

I can't do it. It's too much. Too hard.

A cold wind rises, raking my cheeks and pricking at my eyes. The winter is going to get deeper. This isn't even winter yet. This is fall, and early fall at that. It will get so much worse.

If I can shoot one deer, I can live for a week. A month. Long enough to catch a few fish. Long enough to catch another deer. A rabbit. A fox.

Long enough to survive.

Baby bear, I hear. Not a voice in my head; I *hear* it and I suck in a breath, cutting off a sob I don't have the energy for.

"You left me," I say. The voice doesn't answer.

I know it was my imagination. It was the wind, an animal, the hunger, the isolation. But still I tip my face up to the snow to listen for it.

"I left you," I say. "I left you here all alone."

I want to hear his voice again, even if I'm imagining it. I want his forgiveness. I want his apology. I want his permission.

Bo's nose bumps my hand, cold and dry. I look down at him. He pushes his head under my fingers, leans against my leg.

I dig.

It's slow, painful work. But I'm stronger than I've ever been. Even with the constant hunger, I've been working all the time, building muscle. Building strength. Just a little bit faster than I've lost it.

The damage I did to myself the day Dad died has almost healed. Even my leg is getting stronger. Instead of watching TV or reading books, I'm always moving, always working. There's no fat on my body. I haven't even had my period since getting to the lake. And when I strike the ground with my shovel, it slices right in.

But the ground is hard and the wind is cold. Soon I'm sweating. I've learned the danger of hard work: sweat makes you wet and hot, and then you rest and get wet and cold as the wind bites at you.

I keep working, afraid to stop and freeze. One load of dirt after another. There are no thoughts in my mind anymore, just the next strike of the shovel, the next thin scoop of dirt, my new strength fighting against my hunger-weakness.

My arms get tired and I keep going.

My legs get tired and I keep going.

The makeshift handle sinks splinters into my palms. I dig the shards out and keep going.

Bo paces, then lies down. He lifts his head from time to time to watch me. Waiting for me to do something that makes sense, maybe. He gives up and sleeps after a while.

Daylight comes. Strengthens, wavers, fails. I take a few breaks. I drink—I have water, at least, and I drink all of it. When I turn up a pair of squirming worms, I rinse them off and eat them whole.

I keep going.

By the time the sun has set again I am nearly four feet down. I cannot believe how hard, how long the work is. The ground resists when I strike it, but then once I've cleared a few inches the sides crumble in to erase my progress. I dig wide and deep, wide and deep. How deep do I need to go?

It was hard to see from where I'd hidden, but the hole had to be deep enough to fit the crate and the body and not have a fox or a wolf dig him up, so I think at least a few feet. And they had to clamber out, help each other out of the hole. How tall was Dad? I can't remember.

Can't remember, either, the color of his eyes. The way he walked. *He was a stranger, a stranger, a stranger,* the shovel says as it strikes the ground again and again. *Nothing to you, nothing to you.*

I wish it was true.

And then I dig deeper, deeper still. Darkness falls, but I keep digging because if I stop I will be killed. And cold kills you first.

So I dig.

Slower, slower. Weariness buzzes at me like flies. I can hardly see the shovel, it's so dark. I don't know how I'm still standing. How I'm still working. And then my shovel hits something. Something hard.

Bone, I think.

No. Not the crunch of metal on bone, but the scrape and clang of metal hitting metal. Shovel hitting box. Good. I don't want to hit my father with the shovel, to hurt him.

Stupid.

I scrape at the dirt with my hands, searching for his body. And I find it.

The stench hits me. It feels *alive*. Like a squelching, rippling creature moving over my skin, up over my lips, down my throat. My eyes water and I retch, but nothing comes up.

Choking, I pull my collar over my nose and mouth. It doesn't help. The smell is worse than rotting meat, worse than anything I've smelled before—a wet yellow smell.

I can't tell at first what part of him I've found. The skin is caked in dirt. It doesn't feel like skin anymore. It gives under my fingers, splits. Then my fingers brush through the dirt and catch in a clump of hair. It comes away in my fingers—and a chunk of scalp with it.

I scramble backward. I wrench my collar down just in time.

I vomit, a thin stream of water and bile. I heave again and again, throat scorched.

I press myself against the wall of the hole I've painstakingly dug, rest the side of my face against the dirt. I suck down the earthy scent, but the stink of decay won't let go. It seeps through every pore until my skin feels greasy.

"Move," I whisper to myself. "Move, move, move." But instead I stay crouched, shivering and shuddering.

The cold finds me quickly. I sweated while I worked and the moisture has cooled on my skin. The cold tries to burrow deeper, get into my joints and my bones and my lungs. I can't stand still. I can't get up.

It's not some great act of will or logic that gets me to my feet. I don't know what it is. I just suddenly stand. My mind is empty, like it's been shut off. My body is in charge, and that's better.

My body walks back to my father's corpse without me, foot dragging. It crouches. It rakes its hand through the earth by the corpse's side until it finds cloth—my father's coat—and pulls a flap up, dirt tumbling off it. It tries the pocket. No bullets. A plastic bag with a folded piece of paper in it, and something thick.

The girl who isn't me turns it over in her hands, testing the shape of it. It's something from a different life. An energy bar. Wrapped in its foil. Safe from decay and dirt.

The empty girl tucks it slowly in her own pocket with the plastic bag and the paper.

She moves to the other side of the body. She digs. She finds another lump of cloth, another pocket. And there they are: six bullets, gleaming, whole and untouched except for a few stray flecks of dirt.

I stare at them cupped in my palms and come back into myself, inch by inch. Six shots. It's nothing against months of winter.

Six shots. Nothing compared to the unknown stretch ahead.

I don't even know if Griff will ever be back. Maybe he'll stay with his daughter instead. Will he send word? Will anyone else know how to find us?

Find me. Not us. Just me.

And no, I think. No, that man who'd come—he was probably

my last chance. He'll tell people Dad is gone, is dead. Maybe Griff will come anyway, to check. But I can't be sure.

Suddenly I feel like a fool. All of my energy spent for a few bullets. And I'm not even that great a shot. I'll waste at least one bullet, maybe more. Maybe all of them. They were a talisman. A piece of magic I was searching for, but now I have them and I remember that magic isn't real.

I've killed myself, I think. *I've made my last mistake.*

I look at my father. I've managed not to look past his shoulders this entire time, but now my eyes drift to his head. It's still mostly covered in dirt. They dropped him facedown, and even with the dirt I can tell the back of his head is shaped wrong. The bullet punched through his skull and left a gaping hole.

I fight another wave of revulsion. The sight scrapes at me, like a knife dragged flat along my ribs, hollowing me out.

In that moment, I give up hope. I throw it into the hole with my father, and I finally understand it, deep in my bones.

I'm going to die.

No *if*. No *unless*.

Just certainty. I am going to die.

Those early days, I needed the *unless*. The plans. The future spooling out ahead of me, full of problems I could think my way through. But now, letting go of all of that, I can breathe again.

I don't need to figure it all out, *or else*. There is no *or else*, no happy ending if I try hard enough. This only ends one way.

It's like shrugging off a heavy backpack. It seems like giving up hope should mean despairing, but I feel light. Hope is a distraction. It makes you think about things that might happen to save you, instead of what's right in front of you. It makes you freeze up because you're so afraid of failing, because you don't understand yet that it doesn't matter.

In this moment, I am that empty girl, the girl who can do whatever she has to.

I smile. I feel focused. I don't have to worry about the big stuff; I'm already dead, after all.

I can sit down. I can rest. I can eat the energy bar, and I do, savoring every bite. Bo creeps into the hole next to me, panting, and I give him two small bites from my fingers that vanish so quickly I might have imagined them.

When we're done, I lick the wrapper and throw it away from me. I haven't thrown anything away in weeks, paranoid that I'll need it later.

That feels like freedom, too.

Knowing that I will die, winter doesn't seem so overwhelming. It can't do worse than kill me, can it?

Winter will bring cold. More hunger than ever. And it will bring Raph back.

I count the bullets with my fingertips, the cold metal numbing my skin. Yes, I decide. Yes, I am going to die; there is no unless. I will die and I will be with my father, be with my mother. I cannot make it to summer.

But maybe I can make it a little while longer.

Six bullets. Three men.

I don't even have to be a very good shot.

I DON'T HAVE the energy to pull myself out of the hole. I huddle against the dirt and close my eyes. Just a moment, I think. I'll rest just for a moment, and then I'll be strong enough. I won't even sleep.

And then I do.

A growl wakes me. In the haze of sleep, I think it must be Bo, but when I open my eyes, I know immediately that I'm wrong. Bo is beside me. He's taut as a bowstring. The shape pacing at the edge of the hole is wrong. Rangier than Bo, a little bigger but not by much.

The first pale light of dawn licks its fur, making the edges golden and making the dog—wolf?—stark against the sky. It paces back and forth, but it never stops looking at me.

I press myself against the edge of the hole and make myself think small, still thoughts.

It growls again.

Wolves don't attack people, I think. Haven't I heard that?

They're afraid of humans. But this wolf-dog doesn't look ready to run. He looks ready to attack.

The rifle is on the lip of the hole behind me. I reach up slowly, cautiously. The wolf-dog keeps up its pacing. My hand closes around the cold stock, and I tug it toward me.

The ammunition. Where is the ammunition?

It's scattered around me. I grope for it, not daring to take my eyes off the creature. I find one bullet. Pick it up with fumbling fingers. The growl rises, the wolf-dog going stock-still. Bo growls in answer.

I load the bullet as smoothly as I can with every muscle trembling. I barely learned to do it right with my dad watching and the sunlight streaming down; doing it in the dark, shaking in fear, I drop it twice. Still Bo and the wolf-dog don't move.

Then the bullet is in. I lift the rifle. The wolf-dog stares at me. It tenses.

Bo snarls as he flings himself up the side of the hole.

I whip the barrel of the rifle up as he slams into the wolf, teeth flashing white in the dark. They whirl together in a storm of snapping and snarling.

The wolf-dog springs away, runs. Bo runs after.

"Bo!" I shout. I don't want him to leave me. He slows to a trot and turns back to me, panting. "Please," I say.

He comes back reluctantly. I pull myself up the side of the hole as he approaches and slide my arms around him. His fur is wet. Warm-wet, not the wet of melted snow. Blood. I hope it isn't his.

He lets me hold on to him for a few seconds, then shakes me off and trots away. I call after him, but he ignores me. I hear him moving through the brush not far off. Circling. Keeping me safe.

I get to my feet. More scavengers will be coming. Or predators. I don't know if the wolf-dog is after me or the body, but either way I can't stay here.

My stomach cramps with hunger. Already the energy bar has burned through my system.

I get the shovel and start to lever myself out of the hole. And then I stop.

The crate. I should check the crate.

It isn't a big hole. His body lies on top of the crate, covering it. I'll have to move him to get at it. The thought makes my gut clench up, and I turn my face away.

What if I leave the crate, and whatever is in it could have saved me? What if there's food? Weapons? A *radio*?

Accepting that I will die is not the same as giving up. Leaving is giving up. I can't just leave.

I can see the edge of the crate under my dad. Under his body. *Under* the *body*, I tell myself. Just meat going bad, that's all. I can do this.

The longer I stand, the weaker I get. I grit my teeth. "Just a body," I whisper to myself, and grab the shovel.

I dig down beside the crate. Maybe I don't have to move the body. I dig until I find the bottom and clear all along the side. There isn't a lot of room to maneuver, but I get my hands around the handle of the crate and tug.

It moves. The body moves with it.

I yelp and jerk back, flattening against the side of the hole. The body moves wrong. It isn't solid, isn't whole. The stench of it hits me all over again, and I gag.

Just meat, I think, and press my tongue to the top of my mouth.

I take three deep breaths and yank harder, pulling up and over at the same time. This time the crate starts to slide free. Another few hard tugs and it's on its side, wedged between the body and the wall of the hole.

I settle back, panting. Spots dance in my vision.

Now I have to lift it. It isn't as heavy as I was expecting, and it only takes one huffing, puffing try to get it up to the lip of the hole. I scramble up after it without looking back, tossing the shovel up as I go. I lie at the edge of the hole until my heart slows down.

I sit up slowly. I'll hurt tomorrow, but I already knew that. I let out a sharp, angry breath. The crate is locked with a fat, dirt-packed padlock. I tug at it with a moan. No way am I getting that off, not with any tools I have. Useless. I'm useless. Spending all my energy on nothing.

"I bet you'd know what to do right now," I say to the body. The sun is coming up. It sparkles across the snow. "I bet you would have built a whole new cabin by now."

I don't know if I can even get back to the shelter, I'm so tired. So maybe . . . maybe this is a good place to be. Near my dad.

I look over at the rifle. It would be faster than starving to death, at least.

I try to pretend that I can do it. It seems so much easier than standing up. But I'm already getting to my feet, already reaching for the shovel. The wolf-dog could come back, and I don't want my dad unburied when it does.

If the forest is going to kill me, it's going to have to do it honestly. I'm not going to spare it the trouble.

It's pretty stupid, spending the time to fill the hole, but it's the task in front of me, and I have to keep moving or I'll stop. And if I stop, that's it. So I shovel dirt until I can feel the sun on the nape of my neck and sweat beads on my forehead.

Maybe I should wait for the wolf-dog to come back. I have the rifle now, after all. I could shoot it. Eat it.

I reach into my pocket to touch the last bullet, the only one I couldn't fit into the rifle, and my hand closes around something slick and plastic instead. That folded piece of paper, the one in the bag.

I pull it out and frown at it. I can't imagine that it's something that will help me—not like the energy bar—but it belonged to my father and suddenly there's nothing more important than knowing what's on it.

I nearly rip the bag getting it open. The paper slips through my fingers as I try to unfold it, and I force myself to slow down. I don't want to tear it.

It's a hand-drawn map, done in blue pen. I recognize the lake. A little house perches on the north end where the cabin used to stand. Spiky upside-down Vs mark the trees, and there are other landmarks scribbled in. Not labeled, but I think I can puzzle some out. There's a creek, the big lightning-scorched tree, the snowberries, the blackberries.

And there's another house. The shape is unmistakable. It

crouches on the other side of the lake, farther back from the shore. A short hike into the woods—not that the scale on the map is anything approaching accurate. It could be a hundred yards or two miles, for all I know.

I turn the map over. There's writing on the back, the letters all cramped together.

Sequoia: You'll learn your way around soon, but here's a map just in case.

I flip it again, stare at the map. At the second cabin.

Just in case.

My hand shakes. I nod once, swallow hard. There isn't any time to think and I don't have the energy for it anyway. I'm not sure I even register consciously what I'm doing, or why. I'm not thinking about how a cabin means shelter. Means food, maybe. It's just the thing in front of me. And so I start walking.

It isn't until I get to the shore that my brain starts up again, but I don't let myself start hoping. I left hope in the hole with my father, and it's better this way. It's easier. If there's no cabin, it won't mean anything. I'll just keep going.

I'll keep going until I can't anymore.

I CARRY ALMOST nothing with me. Either there will be shelter on the other side of the lake or I will die; either way, to get there I have to go unburdened. I take just the backpack with a single jar for water, the rifle, and the hatchet. Everything else I leave by the cabin.

I stare for a moment at the canoe, floating maybe twenty feet out from the shore. Thin sheets of ice have formed on the surface of the lake. There's no way I'll risk wading into that water again. I remember too vividly the shock of it. Much colder and I wouldn't have made it out.

Maybe I could figure out a way to get it, and God knows I wish I could paddle across the lake instead of walking all the way around. But I don't have the time to figure it out.

I whistle for Bo, but I don't wait for him. He'll catch up.

It's a few minutes later that he appears at the edge of the woods. Last night's fight has left him with a cut across his nose, but he doesn't seem bothered by it. He trots alongside me with his head hanging low, panting. He keeps up. I suspect he's eaten more than I have, but not much; his steps still have a draggy quality to them, and he looks constantly tired.

I keep my eyes on the ground, looking out for anything that might trip me up. I carry one of my walking sticks, a gnarled branch still studded with patches of bark and moss. I wrap my fingers around a knot in the wood and focus on the end where it strikes the ground with every step. If I stare at my feet and count paces, I don't think about how far I have to go.

I reach a hundred and start over again. Pebbles shift and crunch under my feet. Bo pants beside me. The shore bends to the left (sixty-three steps) and I follow.

My makeshift shoes slip, start to come apart; I can see red, raw flesh, but I don't dare stop. Another step, and another. I reach a downed tree, its trunk as high as my waist. It stretches into the water and back into the woods, and for a dumbfounded moment, my count still ticking up even with my feet standing still, I just stare at it (seventy, seventy-one).

I resent every extra step around the end of the tree (ninety-nine, one hundred, one), but I'm too tired to hold on to the emotion. Each step erases the one before it. We reach the easternmost edge of the lake and start curving around again, and the tree is now the faintest memory.

I realize I have no idea where to turn off. If there isn't a path, I could walk all the way around the lake and never find the right spot. But just as the thought floats hazily to the surface of my mind, Bo gives a soft bark and turns sharply away from the shore, trotting into the woods with his tail wagging. Like he knows where we're going. Like it's a good place to go.

The sun marches steadily along. Clouds shoot across the sky, looking like a clawed hand reaching up to drag the sun down below the horizon. We have to make it before dark. Have to.

Fifty steps, sixty steps, seventy steps. The trees grow too thick to see the sun at all.

The map is scarce on landmarks, but there are two along the path to the second cabin. A big rock, kind of heart-shaped, and a creek. I find both, and at both I stop. I rest my hand against the stone, dip my fingers into the creek. They're concrete signs that I'm going the right way.

My thoughts swim, blur. Touch is the only solid thing keeping me in the world.

Minutes slide by. I stop among the unfamiliar trees and turn in a circle, squinting for any sign of the cabin. Have we gone too far? It wouldn't be hard to miss it in the woods. I can't see very far. If I just go a little ways in the wrong direction to either side, I could walk right by it.

But Bo won't let me, will he? Bo knows where he's going, and, when I can, I spare half a second to look up from my feet and make sure he's still in front of me.

When I see the straight, stripped logs between the darker trees, I cry out in relief. I pick up my pace, stumbling along after Bo as he lopes up to the tiny cabin. It's half the size of the other one, if that's even possible, with another building behind it.

I stop at the steps, suddenly reluctant to step inside. I can't explain it, except that the thought that I might *not* die today is so huge, so overwhelming, that it feels like it will crush me. That it will ruin whatever mind-set has gotten me this far, a hundred steps after a hundred steps.

But I keep counting. Three more steps, and then I can reach out my hand to the door. I have the panicked thought that it will be locked, but when my hand hits the latch it gives easily. I laugh. Of course it isn't locked. Who would bother to lock a cabin out here?

I push it open and blink at the interior.

It takes several seconds for my eyes to adjust. The cabin is small, all right. It has a fireplace and a cot and some cupboards— that's it. But it has four walls and a roof, and even with the wind making the treetops shudder it doesn't get through. I have a bunker against the cold.

Tentatively, I step farther inside and reach for the nearest cupboard. It swings open with a creak and a stubborn drag of resistance from the rusty hinges. Inside . . .

Inside is food. Shelves of food. Glass jars labeled and lined up. Many of them empty, sure, but some of them full. There are pickled onions and fish and moose and deer and rabbit and carrots and potatoes and corn. There are two sacks of dry beans. Black beans, kidney beans. There's a big plastic container of vitamins.

I open the next cupboard. More of the same. And the next. I pull down the jars that still have something and line them up on the floor. Six. A dozen. I have sixteen full jars, about half of them meat and about half various jams and vegetables. The dates on the top are from before last winter. Dad must have been planning to do more canning in the weeks before winter, enough to see us through. Getting ready exactly the way I hadn't been.

In one of the lower cupboards I find a pair of heavy boots, a pair of metal things I finally realize are ice cleats, a box of tools, and a box of ammo. More .30-30. If I ever find a rifle, I'll be in great shape.

My stomach is starting to cramp up again, but I'm reluctant to open any of the food. It's beautiful, sitting there. It seems like if I open one of the jars, something will go wrong. It won't be real.

I sit there staring at the food, starving, and can't move.

Finally, tentatively, I reach for a jar of fish and a jar of carrots. Carrots are full of good vitamins, right? I open them both. The smell washes over me. My mouth floods with saliva. I breathe shallowly, my stomach lurching.

I break off a tiny piece of fish. I touch it to my tongue, but I don't close my mouth yet. I just let it sit there. The taste is so strong I moan. Bo makes a soft, eager noise, and I look over to see him sitting attentively, staring at me.

I give him a big chunk of fish and swallow my own. He wolfs his down and waits for more. I give him another piece and start in on my portion, eating slowly, afraid of getting sick.

It's so rich, so flavorful, it's hard to get down. Bit by bit I eat, trading off fish and carrots, but I make myself stop with my body still clamoring for more. I'll eat more later. Slowly. Slowly. If I throw up, the food is wasted. Gone.

Well. Bo would probably eat it. But still.

Then I close the door, and I climb into bed. It smells musty. The blankets are chilled. I peel my makeshift shoes from my feet, wincing at the raw, dirt-packed skin they reveal. I should clean them off, but I don't have the energy. I slide under the blankets, curling in on myself as tightly as possible.

It's a few minutes before reality catches up to me, before I realize what this means.

I've been saved. Now, with this food—now I can survive.

Now, when Raph comes back, I can be ready.

MY REALIZATION IS premature, of course. A few jars of food aren't going to save me. What they will give me, though, is time to figure out how to actually survive, and it's time I badly need.

I wake up with Bo on top of me. It takes a minute of shoving and grumbling to get him off—bony as he may be these days, he's still massive. As soon as I can move, I roll out of bed and stumble straight over to the food.

It takes every ounce of willpower I have not to scarf it all down, but when I screw the lid back on the fish, it's still half-full. I let Bo lick my fingers clean after giving him a few bites of his own, and then I look around.

I missed some things last night—like a mirror propped up against the wall, too grimy to see my reflection in, and the photos on the walls. There are three of them, set in wood frames that look handmade. Dirt clouds the glass. I swipe it clean.

Griff is in a couple. He's holding up a huge salmon in one. The other one is him with his arm around Dad and another guy, grinning as they stand behind a big bear they've clearly just shot. Once upon a time I would have been horrified, but I just think about how much I'd love a bearskin right about now.

The other guy in the photo looks familiar, which doesn't make sense. I don't know any of dad's friends other than Griff. It's zoomed out enough that I can't make out his features too well, but then the next photo is a close-up of the same guy and dad sharing a beer, and I recognize him all at once.

He was at the lake. He was the one who came after Dad died, who called out and then flew away.

I take down the photo and turn it over to pry the back panel off. The photo slides free. Sure enough, Dad's labeled it, the handwriting matching the writing from the map. *Jed & me, 2009.*

He was a friend once. *Didn't mean he meant well this time,* I tell myself, but I don't believe it and my throat seizes up. He was a friend. Someone who would have helped me. Who would have saved me. And I let him fly away.

I pace around, opening the cupboards, running my hands along the shelves. I find a couple of bottles of beer at the back of one cabinet, and a dented can full of rusty nuts and bolts. Mostly I find dust and more dust, but my hand catches against the edge of an envelope on the topmost cabinet, so far back I have to stand on my toes to reach it.

I tug at it and two more envelopes come with it, each one torn open with the letter still inside. Two of them just have *Carl Green* written on the outside, in two different kinds of handwriting. Griff must have brought them up.

The third is stamped, with the address printed neatly (the

address in Alaska where Dad never went), from the Washington State government. That one I open first, even though I figure I know what it's about: me. Informing Dad about Mom's death and that he now had custody of me.

The letter looks like it's been crumpled up and then smoothed out again. I imagine him balling it in his fist. I try to imagine what his face must have looked like when he found out, but I can't. I have to look at the photos again just to get his image fixed in my mind.

I sit cross-legged on the floor to read the two other letters. I can't tell which was older, so I open them in the order they were stacked.

Carl—

> *I can't thank you enough, you really saved my bacon or at least my kneecaps. I should be able to sell the house and get the money back before winter. You said that was plenty of time so I am hoping you weren't lying. I will be up again with the cash when I have it and some of that swill beer you like too. Don't get eaten by a grizzly or nothing before I get back up there*

> *Yours, Jed*

Some of the words are scribbled out, and the sentences are wobbly and differently sized. Jed is obviously not used to writing out his thoughts, but what's there is clear enough.

Raph's conversation with Dad comes back to me, clear as if they were talking just outside the door. Dad must have given Jed the money he was supposed to be holding on to for Raph. Kneecaps sounds like a loan shark, or whatever they're called. So that's what Dad meant when he said he'd have the money back; Jed was going to bring it. Had brought it, I'd bet, in that plane of his. That's why he came. He kept his word. He'd been a real friend. He could have helped me.

Too late to think about that now. I shake my head and open the other letter.

It isn't really a letter. Just a note. *Found these, thought you might like them.* The page is folded around two photographs.

The first is my dad and me. Christmas. That last Christmas. On the floor in front of the tree, surrounded by all those presents he shouldn't have bought. I'm grinning up at the camera, he's grinning at me.

And the other photo—

I shut my eyes, bite my lip, open them again, because it's hard to look. It hurts.

The other photo is of my mother. She's young. Standing at the edge of a trail, the woods behind her. Her hands cup her pregnant belly, framing it, and she's laughing. The sun is in her eyes. It casts the shadow of the photographer—my father—across the trail beside her.

I stare at the photo for a long time. Then I take down one of the photos from the wall, open up the frame, and tuck the photo inside. Griff and his salmon go on the counter; Mom and Dad's shadow go on the wall. I sit back down, lean my head against the wall, staring at the photo.

I sit like that for a long time.

THE REST OF the day I don't do anything at all. Once I've cleaned and bandaged my feet, I loaf around and play fetch with Bo and eat. Bo isn't great at fetch. When I throw a stick, he looks at me and sighs, then trots slowly across the cabin floor, and then looks back with the stick in his mouth like there's something wrong with me. Then he comes plodding back and thrusts it into my hand as if to say, *Here. Hold on to it this time. Sheesh.*

It's the most fun I've had in months.

The second day I do some math. Well, it's more like counting and guessing. I can stretch sixteen jars of food and the beans into maybe twenty days, I figure, and still manage decent meals. Any less than that I'll get weaker, and I'm as weak as I can be without just keeling over. No point in rationing myself to death. So say three weeks for the sake of neatness, and that leaves, oh, four or five months of winter without food?

I have no idea when in winter Raph and Daniel would be back. I have to be ready for them to arrive in a few weeks. I have to be ready for it to take months. And I don't have nearly enough to get me that far.

"Well," I say in a lofty tone, "this is quite the conundrum, Bo. We shall need to put our best minds on it."

Bo looks up from chewing on a stick, decides I'm not doing anything interesting, and gets back to it.

At least I have shoes I found under the bed, even if they're massive. I'll have to take them apart and remake them before I can wear them; for now, I wrap my feet back up and stump outside.

I haven't even looked at the shed out back yet, so I make my way over to it. I entertain fantasies of stacks and stacks of canned food, but force myself to keep reality firmly in mind. The door is crude: instead of a handle or a latch, it has a hole through the wood and the frame, a chain looping through both with nothing but a carabiner to hold it shut. I unhook the carabiner and pull the chain free, then fit three fingers through the hole and tug.

The door is stuck against its frame. I pull, my arm protesting, and then grit my teeth and yank. It pops open. I almost spill onto my butt, but I hang on grimly and get my feet under me.

The inside is dim and dry. Hooks descend from the rafters. Knives and tools hang from pegs on the walls. Something dark and brown stains the table against the back wall. Blood. This is where Dad did his butchering.

I walk around the room, touching my fingertips to the sharp objects Dad must have used again and again. Things for slicing and puncturing and cutting. I don't know what all the blades are for. I don't even know how to skin a rabbit properly.

I take one of the knives, a hunting knife with a leather sheath and a loop to string a belt through. I tuck it into my pocket. It'll do to replace the one I lost on the lake.

There's a single cupboard in the back corner. I crouch carefully, keeping my bad leg out straight, and open it. Inside is a basin, a pile of folded rags, and a water-swollen book. Thinking of tinder—my trusty thriller is about used up; I've already burned the scene where our hero makes manly love to the tough-but-vulnerable female cop—I pull it out.

A Guide to Field Dressing and Butchering Game.

Well. I'm not burning *that*. I flip through it and stop at the page about rabbits.

Rabbits are generally simple to skin, the book informs me. I snort and tuck it under my arm.

Maybe next time I kill a rabbit, I'll get a pair of gloves out of it. Not that I know how to sew gloves. But I'll need them soon. There are thick, rough gloves in the cupboard, but they aren't made for warmth. Protection, I figure, for when you're wielding all these knives and things.

When I'm done exploring I turn to go—and grin. Hanging on the back of the door is a matched set: a hat with wooly ear-flaps and a thick sheepskin coat. The coat is tan leather on the outside, soft wool on the inside. The tag at the collar has been clipped away, and the sleeves and collar are worn, like it's gotten a lot of use, but there's a tear along the bottom hem. Maybe my dad left it here meaning to fix it and never got around to it. I pull the coat on. It falls to my knees. The sleeves engulf my hands, and buttoned up it hangs loose as a tent.

It's perfect.

I roll the sleeves up and cinch the coat around my waist with a length of rope, and hang the knife I found on the makeshift belt. I jam the hat down over my head and step outside.

I haven't been this warm in weeks.

I'm sure I look ridiculous, but I'm long past caring about that. I tromp back to the cabin for another quick meal and a nap.

When I wake up, I use the back of the custody letter to make a list of absolutely everything I have, from thumbtacks to rope. It takes longer than I expected. It makes me feel wealthy beyond belief, but at the same time I start realizing the problems that come along with the cabin.

We're farther from the lake here, which means until there's good snow—and I'm not eager for that—I need a better way to transport water. And I need to get all my things over here. And above all else, I have to remember: food runs out. It's time to get hunting.

I look at the rifle. Six bullets. I make tallies on the page, one for each. Six bullets could be the difference between life and death.

The smart thing is to use them.

The smart thing is to let go of the idea of revenge.

But it isn't just revenge. It's rescue. Because when Raph comes back, he'll be in a plane. A plane that I can steal. A plane that I can fly.

Six bullets to kill the man that killed my father and escape.

Or I can hide. Wait. Let them come, let them go. Hope that Griff comes back. Wait through winter and spring. Hope that I don't get hurt. Don't get sick. Don't get caught out in a storm, or trampled by a moose, or drowned in the lake. That I don't run out of food.

No. I'm done with hope. I'll kill Raph and live.

Or I'll die.

I get up and walk to the mirror. I scrub at it with my sleeve, and it clears enough for me to see a face staring back at me. My face. Gaunt, now, my skin rough and darkened by the sun, making my scars stand out even more.

My hair is a snarl down to my shoulders. I tried braiding it for a while, but I gave up at some point. I have trouble now remembering exactly when. I take the knife from my belt and hesitate for less than five seconds before I grab a handful and saw through.

A minute later my hair is cut within two inches of my scalp, sticking out like a briar patch. It won't get into my face anymore, won't get tangled up. Without it, I don't even look female. With my livid red scars and dirt streaking my face, I look nothing like that photo of Mom and me. I look like a wild creature.

I'm not the same girl who crouched there shaking while Raph and Daniel buried my father. I'm not the same person who hid from Jed. If a strange man showed up today, armed or not, I'd step out of the woods with my rifle aimed at his heart and I wouldn't back down until I was sure I had a way home. Even if that meant I was the only one leaving alive.

I couldn't have stopped Raph, the day he killed Dad. I wasn't smart enough. I wasn't strong enough.

But I can do it now.

Of course, I'll need a plan. I'll need supplies. I'll need to be fit.

They'll be after the crate when they come back. That means they'll land at the head of the lake—on the opposite end from me. By the time I get up there, they could have the crate and be on their way. Especially since I went and dug it up for them.

But if I move it, they'll have to look for it. They'll know I'm here, but I know how to hide it. They can go off searching. And I can go after them.

Six bullets.

FINALLY IT'S TIME to go back around the lake.

I have to get the crate. The hatchet is there, too. The shovel, my clothes. I know I won't be able to carry them all by myself, and I don't want to waste energy tramping around again and again.

I find a grease pencil in one of the drawers, and write on the cabin wall.

TAKE IT SLOW, I write. And under it, SMART, NOT STRONG.

One trip. One trip for everything.

I sit down with the paper where I wrote my list, and I sketch. When I'm satisfied, I get to work.

I find two wooden poles in the tool shed—they look like the handles to brooms or some other tools. I find new rope, too. With the rope and the belt I make a harness for Bo. The belt will buckle around his big barrel chest if I punch a new hole for it. I use the strap for the rifle to make a collar, and attach it to the belt with the rope. Then I make loops so I can secure the poles to the harness.

I fit a crossbar across the bottom of the poles, and then build up a kind of shelf with sticks. Now it's a litter that I can strap things down to, and Bo can drag it. If I can convince him. Given the things he'll do for food, and given how hungry he is, I think we'll manage.

I train him with it empty for a good while, getting him used to the way it tugs on his shoulders. Then I load it up with random stuff from the cabin so he can get used to that. He's not happy about it, but since I toss bits of fish at him every few feet, he goes along with it.

It's only when I go to take it off that I realize how difficult it is—I practically have to disassemble the whole thing to get it off him. No good if I have to get it off in a hurry.

More rope, then, threaded up through the loops that secured the poles to the harness, held at the top with the carabiner. If I undo the carabiner, the rope slithers free, the poles drop off, and Bo is left with just the harness. I can get him free quickly if he gets stuck, if we have to run.

I take a long moment to look at what I've made. It's ungainly, ugly. But out here, good enough is fantastic.

And now it's time to go.

THE WALK SEEMS to take longer this time. Maybe because I'm actually conscious, instead of plodding along like a zombie. Maybe because the litter slows Bo down, gets stuck now and again.

After days of rest, my leg feels as good as it has in a long time.

My feet are still tender, but I've made better wraps for them, using the thick leather gloves from the shed as soles.

I feel like I could run a marathon, but I know it's an illusion. Adrenaline, relief. Overconfidence. One of my many enemies out here, one of the small voices I have to ignore. *Take it slow.* I mutter it to myself on repeat as we go. People would probably cross the street to avoid me in the city, but here there's only Bo to mind, and he already knows I'm crazy.

We go all the way to the rock, resting only once for a brief meal.

I step out into the clearing and halt. The rock stands as tall and unmoved as ever. It has stood here since it dropped from the belly of a glacier, and it will stand here long after I am dead and gone, but for a while it was home.

The remains of my shelter lie heaped beside it. Sooty. Rainlogged.

I gather what I can. So much is worthless. Still I clear it away, scattering it into the woods. No reason for Raph to come this far, but if he does I don't want to give him any information about me. My only advantage is that he has no idea who I am or that I'm here. Once I lose that, things get trickier.

I bundle up my clothes, the jars that survived, the remains of the tarp. I load them on the litter and give the clearing one last look.

"Thank you," I tell the rock, laying my hand on its damp flank. Funny the things you miss. Funny the things that keep you alive. I whistle to Bo.

Back to the cabin, then. Bo is getting anxious, so when we

break free of the trees I unclip the carabiner, let him run. He rockets down the shore, churning up pebbles and dirt, tongue lolling. I laugh, shake my head.

And then I look past him. Look to the canoe, still floating in the water. Not thirty feet out now but fifteen. Tantalizingly close.

I look south. It's a straight shot across the water. Hours less than plodding through the woods, along the shore, dodging roots and fallen logs.

I could swim out—if I went close—

No.

I sit on the shore, bad leg out in front of me, the other tucked up. *Take it slow. Smart, not strong.*

I'm not going to swim out. It's colder today than it was when I went in, and I barely survived then. I don't have a shelter to retreat to on this side of the lake. No swimming.

Okay, then. How do you get a canoe out of a lake without getting wet? It's like some twisted riddle. Either I need to get to it, or I need it to come to me. If only I were a cowboy, I could lasso the thing.

I hold on to that thought, silly as it is. Getting a rope out and hooked onto the bars seems like the obvious solution. A lasso, or a grappling hook. I don't have either, but "hook" isn't exactly high-tech. All I really need is something heavy. Something that I can toss into the canoe without damaging it, and drag the canoe onto the shore with.

A rock's too heavy. But a section of a wood plank might work.

I find one that's a foot long. Large enough to have some heft, small enough to throw easily. Tying the rope to the wood is quick work. I don't know knots, and I regret it for the fortieth time since getting here, but I work something out that's firm enough. Then I walk down to the water and throw it.

I was never exactly sporty, and I haven't miraculously learned to throw since my last embarrassing showing in gym class softball. My first throw lands short. I pull the plank back in, hand over hand, the rope spooling at my feet.

The next throw goes too far left. The next five are too short as well, the sixth hits the side of the canoe and bounces off.

Normally I would be frustrated. I'd be in tears by now. But it's actually kind of soothing. I try swinging the rope, try throwing the plank like a spear, try hucking it like my old enemy, the softball. And finally, finally, it hits square in the center of the canoe and stays there.

I yell in triumph, throwing both hands in the air. Bo barks excitedly and spins in a circle, but I'm pretty sure he's mocking me. I shake my head, hooting with joy, and get hold of the rope.

Pulling the canoe in is tricky. Pull too hard, and the plank starts to pull right out. But tug gently and it hooks under the edge of the canoe, first turning the canoe so it's facing me and then sliding it through the water. Inch by inch, I draw it in. Inch by inch and then it's two feet away and I lean out, drag it up on the rocks, and that's it.

There ought to be more drama, I think. A musical crescendo. Confetti. Instead, there's just more work to do.

Time to load up.

THE DIRT IS still heaped up over the grave, undisturbed, the crate lying alongside it. The wolf-dog hasn't been back, or hasn't bothered to try to dig. I keep myself from staring too long at the mound in the earth. Dad is gone; he isn't here. His body is buried for good.

No, not for good. When Raph comes back, they'll dig up the hole. They'll dig the body up all over again.

I wish I'd had the strength and foresight to move his body, to give him a proper grave somewhere else with a marker, someplace he wouldn't be disturbed. But I can't, of course. I can't even do that for him. Maybe if I live, if I get home, I can do something.

I stare at the crate, and not for the first time I wonder what kind of man my father was, to be mixed up with someone like Raph. He made it all sound like an accident, like none of it was his fault, but can that be true? He did favors for evil men. And he brought me out here knowing it would involve me, too, even if Raph never saw me, never knew I was here.

He put me in danger, and why?

Did he think he was protecting me, taking care of me?

Or was it more selfish than that? Did he just want me back, want me with him, and never mind what was best for me?

I tug at the padlock half-heartedly. If there are any answers about my father, who he was, they're locked away tight. Any chance of recovering them lies on the other side of the lake, with the tools from the shed.

Maybe it's guns. Automatic weaponry with ammo galore. I imagine myself going all action-hero on Raph, bullets flying, and

I smile faintly. Probably not guns. It doesn't seem like the right size for that, and it isn't heavy enough.

Whatever it is, though, it's something they needed to hide where no one would come looking for it.

I've worked up a sweat getting this far, and now that I'm not paddling or hiking I'm getting cold. I took it so slow around the lake, coddling my sore muscles, it's already sliding past midday. I need to hurry back if I don't want to be tramping through the woods in the dark.

I drag the crate down to the beach on my own—Bo has declined to assist—and load it into the canoe.

It's only then that I remember the notebook. If Raph finds that, I'm finished. I hurry up to the cabin, but I hesitate before taking the bundle from its spot. It feels wrong, like I'm betraying the me from days ago who left it there as a final testament—but I can't risk leaving it.

I put it in the canoe with the crate and most of the other gear. The litter won't fit—but it will float. I tie it to the back of the canoe and hope it won't destabilize the whole thing. I can't afford to take another dunking.

Bo won't get in. Too wary of what happened last time, I guess, and I can't blame him. I don't want to overload the canoe anyway, and he knows his way home, so I launch without him. He watches me from the shore for a few minutes as I make my tentative way out on the water. Then he sets off along the shore at a trot. He knows where I'm going. I'll see him there.

I take it slow all the way across the lake, and I stick close to the eastern shore until it bends away from my course.

It's getting dark by the time the canoe fetches up on the shore. No sign of Bo. I pull everything up out of the water, making doubly sure that the canoe is safely on land this time before abandoning it—I'll get it in the morning. Right now, I need to get back to shelter before I lose the way in the dark.

Bo catches up to me halfway there. "Wouldn't want to miss dinner, huh?" I ask him.

He's a pretty good conversationalist, once you learn his language. He's got three basic phrases:

And what does that have to do with me? (Disinterested gaze)

Well, that sounds brilliant, and you are the most amazing person on the whole planet! (Wagging tail, adoring eyes focused on the food in my hand, rather than my face)

What did you say? I was busy paying attention to something that's actually interesting. (Looking off into the distance)

Right now he's in the suck-up phase that rolls around right before a meal, and as soon as we get inside I indulge him. I get our fire going and settle in next to it, chewing a pickled pearl onion, savoring the flavor.

I wish I could actually have a conversation with Bo. I love him, but it's not like having people around. Especially here, back in a house with four walls and a roof, I feel achingly alone. I wonder if Will is having dinner. Maybe he's on a date with the nurse he was always sneaking looks at. Maybe he's hanging out with his cat, Brutus.

And Scott? Scott could be on a date, too, I guess. I mean, Mom is dead, I'm gone, he's got to be moving on with his life, right? I know he wasn't seeing anyone when the accident happened, but it's been months since then. He thinks I'm safe. He thinks I'm off with my dad getting started on a new life. If he thinks about me at all. I was just a kid that didn't end up being his, after all. He was just a guy that didn't end up being my father.

Or does he think that? Maybe not. Maybe he knows I'm missing.

The idea is startling. It hasn't really occurred to me that people must be worried about me. I mean, I was supposed to check in with my caseworker and Dad was supposed to do a bunch of stuff to get the custody sorted out completely.

Maybe they're looking for me. Not that they'd have a snowball's chance in hell of finding me, of course, but I do like the notion. Makes me feel not so . . . forgotten. I'm spending all this time thinking about other people, but I've never really expected that they're thinking about me. Forgotten is the most alone you can get.

So maybe I'm not that alone.

Bo rests his head in my lap. I scratch him behind the ears and he huffs contentedly. Night sounds shimmer outside; the fire hisses and pops.

I try to remember if this is what it feels like to be happy.

SIX BULLETS. I keep recounting them.

It isn't much, but it isn't all I have, either. I have secrecy and surprise. I know more about Raph than he knows about me. But I need to know more.

I bring all the gear up from the lake, along with as much water as I have containers to carry. As I walk I think about how to open the crate.

The knives are out—I need those intact, and it would be too easy to slip and cut myself. There are a few saws, a couple of hammers, and a chisel I think could probably work if I whack hard enough and get the right angle. It's not until I'm actually in the shed that I spot the holy grail, though: bolt cutters.

I prop the crate between my legs and set the bolt cutters against the padlock. I squeeze with all my might. The blades chop into the padlock and start to bite, but I have to let go before they're even halfway through. I shake my hands out, shift foot to foot, then try again.

It takes me four rounds before I finally clip through the metal.

I toss the bolt cutters aside and kneel. This is it. Whatever my dad died for is in this box.

I twist the padlock off and lift the crate lid.

A duffel is stuffed inside, crammed next to a cardboard box. I unzip the duffel first and blink. Money. Lots of money. Canadian and US dollars in neat, bound stacks. If they had all this money, why were they angry with my dad for not having *different* money?

I guess it wasn't that they needed it. Just that he'd taken it.

It doesn't do me a damn bit of good out here. I toss the duffel aside, not caring that some of the money spills out onto the ground. Maybe I can burn it later. The duffel will be useful, at least; I can finally replace the ripped one.

With the duffel gone, two round shapes are revealed in the bottom of the box. I blink at them a moment before I recognize them.

Grenades.

I almost throw myself backward, but I stop myself. They're just sitting there. I can see the pins in them—you have to pull those to make them explode, right?

They sit there so casually. Like they were tossed in as an afterthought.

I pick one up, hands shaking. I turn it over. I can't believe that it's safe, not really. I'm half-expecting it to go off in my hands and kill me.

I take the other one out, too, and walk slowly into the trees, to a white rock the height of my knee. Easy to spot. I settle them next to the rock and back away. I'll deal with them later. Right now I don't want them anywhere near me.

I pull the lid off the cardboard box next. A row of files stand on end, and a fat manila envelope has been wedged in with them. I pull the envelope out, and a bunch of little booklets slide onto the ground. Passports. I pick one up. Canadian, but it's blank. No name, no photo. The others are blank, too—and from all over. US, Germany, the UK. Mostly US.

However these guys started out, they weren't just hunting buddies anymore.

I go through the files one by one. They're a jumble of information. Old police files, including an autopsy report with photos of a dead man, shot three times in the chest. The file says he died in Alaska. It happened the year my dad came for Christmas. The year he disappeared for good.

There are pictures like surveillance photos. Names and dates I don't recognize. Some of them are just men talking to one another on the street. One set is a man in a business suit meeting a woman in a motel—and then losing the business suit over the course of ten or twelve photos. I don't need to be an expert in crime to recognize blackmail material.

At the end of the box is a slender book filled with names and numbers. I don't know if it's code or accounting. Either way, I don't understand it. I flip through—and stop.

Green, C.

My father's name and a string of numbers next to it. Money? Dates?

I flip through, desperate to find more details, but it's the only mention of him I can find. I don't recognize any of the other names. There are plenty of *R*s and *D*s that could be Raph and

Daniel, but I can't be sure. Some of the names are crossed out.

Would they cross out my dad's name next time they came looking for these files?

One of the other folders holds a bunch of bank statements. In another I discover a folded-up map and plans for a building. And there's a fat stack of paper in the back of the box with a binder clip and a rubber band on it. The first page is marked AGAINST TYRANNY.

The rest looks like a typewriter vomited onto the page— every line of text nestled up against the ones above and below it, to fit as many words as possible onto every page. Eerily like the way I wrote in my journal.

It gives the impression of an intense, manic mind—and one that really, really doesn't like the government. This must be their manifesto.

I think of Albert, wonder if he wrote it. Or if he's a follower of the man who did. I wonder how much of this my dad agreed with. How much he just went along with. Because he didn't stand up to them, didn't refuse to help them, didn't turn them in.

Not even when they put me in danger.

I lay the files and the slim book and the manifesto in front of me. I wait for meaning to come, for information to turn into understanding. I know what they are, these men. A militia. Criminals. Terrorists, even. And this is evidence. They needed to hide it; they hid it here.

I know all of that, but it holds no real meaning. Whatever this group wants, whatever they're doing back in civilization, it doesn't matter. It's too distant from me, from this place, for me to care. What matters is Raph. The man who killed my father.

Their plan was a good one. Hide this evidence where no one would think to look for it. Out here, you could be certain no one would disturb it. That it would be exactly where you left it.

Except it won't be, will it? These men, these dangerous men, will be so confused.

I pack everything back into the box. Everything but the grenades. I'm terrified to touch them, but they're the most lethal weaponry I have, and I might need them.

I drag the crate into the woods. I don't bother to bury it again, just cover it up with branches. It's as good as buried. There's so much forest, they'll never know where to look for it.

When they look for it, when they look for me, I'll have to be smart. I'll have to hide, and move quickly. I'll have to go after the pilot first. He'll be alone. And with him dead, they'll be stuck.

Then I have to get Raph alone.

When they come, I'll be ready.

WINTER

I LEAVE WITH Bo before dawn, my bow and the rifle both strapped over my shoulder. There's no choice any more, not with daylight so precious, but I've gotten used to the dark. I keep a lantern on my belt; I know how to navigate by the thin light of the stars, reflected off the ever-present blanket of snow.

I make little sound as I walk, stepping in yesterday's foot-prints. My feet are warm, wrapped in rabbit fur sewn to the trimmed-down soles from dad's boots, with the ice cleats lashed to them for better grip. The cleats are vital once I step out onto the lake.

I'm cautious every day, even though it's been weeks since the ice froze enough to hold my weight. My fishing hole is at least a foot deep by now, and every day I have to break through the ice that's formed overnight. But I've seen a crack appear after a windstorm, black water lazy and hungry beneath it.

Things can change in an instant. If you aren't ready, they won't give you the courtesy of a second chance. I'm out of those.

I stand on the lake and shut my eyes as the light comes up

over the eastern trees. The forest is never silent. Not even in winter. Sound carries across the ice. It has a thin echo to it; it will try to trick you. These are the lessons I've learned in the last few weeks, as the days have gotten colder and snows have fallen.

This morning I'm not listening for anything in particular, just listening. I like to do that as often as possible. It makes me feel like I'm keeping track of my little kingdom.

I know where branches fall from the weight of snow. I know that there's another fox around here somewhere, even though I haven't seen him. And I know that a moose crashed through the woods near the cabin last week. Luckily, he never came close enough to bother me.

I try to keep track of the days, but sometimes I forget. I don't know how long the winter will last. I think I am through the worst of it, though. The ice storms that made everything freeze into one solid sheet and kept us trapped inside the cabin for a week were the worst of it. Worse even than the days so brief they were barely a gray spot on the horizon. Worse than the windstorms, when I lay awake waiting for a tree to come crashing down on top of us.

But we haven't died. Not yet.

A delicate sound reaches my ears. Something moving through the trees. Big but nimble.

Bo's ears prick beside me. My heart thuds. A deer. I've seen them, of course. Does and bucks. Big and winter-lean, but even snow-starved they'll have meat on them—more meat than I can comprehend, living on fat little birds and stringy rabbits and an endless succession of fish hauled up from the ice-capped lake.

The field guide has become my bedtime story. I read the sections on skinning and dressing deer over and over, imagining having that much meat at once. I could store it now, pack it in ice; I could even smoke it.

A deer would feed us for a long time.

I move toward the sound. The snow on the ice makes it easier to find purchase, but I still take every step with care, remembering that crack. Winter is long, but not forever. Ice melts. And gaps in the ice can be hidden by snow, and by a film of ice that seems solid up until you trust it with your weight.

The wind blasts my face, thin and sharp. Good. It's carrying my scent away from whatever is in the woods.

The movement reaches the edge of the trees and I stop. My father's coat is gray. The snow has been falling all morning. My arms and legs are wrapped with pelts for warmth, rabbit and ermine; they are as pale as the ice. If I don't move, I might be missed.

The deer emerges. A doe. She's moving away from me, along the shore. She slows, picking her way over a gnarled, snow-shrouded log. I lift the bow.

Bo tenses against the ground, ready to run, but he holds for my command. I try to move like a tree would move, buffeted by the wind. Nothing to be concerned about.

The doe pauses, ears twitching and gaze rotating around her surroundings.

Please, I mouth. I loose.

The arrow strikes her side. She runs.

I follow. I jog, settling into a gait my leg can manage. The deer is out of sight, crashing through the trees, but the blood on the snow draws me a clear path to her, and Bo courses after her ahead of me.

The snow is dimpled where the deer collapsed on one knee. She thrashed her way back to her feet, scattering pink-tinged snow; her tracks continue forward.

Bo's crashing converges with the deer and he barks, a sound that shudders through the trees. He'll flush her back this way, wearing her out without letting her get too far away.

She doesn't charge straight back, but I abandon the blood trail to intercept her as she turns to run parallel to the lake. The crashing slows. Bo starts up an endless snarling, barking tirade that I know means the deer has stopped. I pick up my pace.

I find Bo and the deer in a little clearing. The deer has collapsed forward and is trying to rise. Blood bubbles from her nostrils in a pink froth. Her eyes roll back in her head, but the arrow has obviously pierced something vital. *A lung*, I think, looking at the froth on her muzzle.

"Shh," I say. I walk up with one hand out as if to calm her. She jerks, trying and failing to rise, and this time she falls to her side. Her legs thrash.

I walk behind her. She's weakening, but a hard kick from her would still hurt.

I draw another arrow. I don't want to get close enough to use my knife on her. I've killed rabbits and stoats in the snares that way, my hands protected by thick leather gloves, but if I stoop to slit her throat, I'm worried she'll find a last burst of energy and hurt me.

I steady my shot, breathe out, and end it.

The arrow goes in at the back of her head. She stills at once, limbs settling into a final, disjointed pose.

My breath fogs. I stare, not quite believing I've done it. She's small. Smaller than a buck, certainly. But I can get pounds and pounds of meat from her.

"Thank you," I whisper. "Thank you, thank you."

I sink down into the snow at her side, my hand on her ribs.

I'm not hungry the way I used to be. But there are bad-luck days and bad-luck weeks, and there are days I only have a bite or two, leaving my stomach growling and cramping.

I'm grateful for those days. They keep me smart.

Today, though, will keep me alive.

I've memorized every word and drawing in the field-dressing guide, but the process is harder and bloodier and more disgusting than I imagined. I can leave the skinning for later, when we're back at the cabin, but if I don't get the guts out quickly, the meat will spoil.

I've cleaned and gutted more small animals than I can count, but the deer is different. Her organs fill my hands and there's just . . . more of her than there is on a rabbit. It's hard, bloody work, and I don't think to strip my arms before I start. Soon my stoat-fur armbands are soaked with gore, my hands pure red. Bo sits hungrily by. I throw him scraps of organ meat as I work.

The day warms. Soon I've stripped off my coat, but still I work.

By the time I'm done, I'm exhausted. I clean my hands and arms with snow, getting as much blood off the armbands as I can, and drink water I've stored under my coat, where it won't freeze. I eat a few strips of smoked rabbit meat and consider my next step.

I don't have the litter with me, and I can't leave the carcass long enough to get it. That wolf-dog's still around, stealing food from my snares, trying to get into the shed at night.

So I'll have to drag it. No way around it.

I shrug into my coat, leaving it flapping open.

Bo whines. I stand. Time to move. As always, time to move.

I drag the deer by its feet at first, leaving its organs in a bloody, steaming puddle on the snow. It's harder work than the dressing, but different. At least now I can stand and move my legs. They're cramped from sitting and kneeling so long.

Soon my back aches with the weight. I head straight for the ice. The ice is flat and smooth; I won't have to worry about the deer snagging on anything. Once I'm back on the shore by the canoe, I'll have other supplies. A tarp, at least, to roll the carcass onto and drag.

I'm halfway across the ice when I realize we have company.

The wolf-dog. We've been leaving a wide red trail, and he's following behind. His coat is black with gray flecks, just like Bo, his eyes a watery yellow. Bo scents him and growls. I keep dragging and whistle for Bo to keep close.

I haven't given the wolf-dog a name because I'm pretty sure I'll have to kill him sooner or later. He's worse than the fox. The fox was afraid of me. The wolf-dog is afraid of Bo—maybe. He's definitely not worried about me.

I pause halfway across the lake, adjusting my grip. The wolf-dog draws closer. He pants, his breath fogging the air.

I glance at the rifle over my shoulder, next to the bow. I always have it with me. I haven't fired it yet. Every bullet spent is one less for Raph.

I could shoot the wolf-dog now. But I don't want to waste the bullet.

I shift to move again. The ice lurches under me. I register the crack only as I stumble.

Cold water gushes around my ankles. I yelp, hauling at the deer, and throw myself toward the still-solid stretch behind me. My foot hits solid ice—and my leg buckles like a hinge, the strength going out of it all at once.

I pitch forward, barely keeping my hold on the deer. My bad knee hits the ice with a crack, sending fresh pain shooting all the way up to my hip. The section of ice behind me is swamped with water. Not tilting, not sinking, but covered ankle-deep in frigid lake water.

Bo barks frantically. The wolf-dog charges.

He's across the ice in a flash. I pull and pull at the deer, but it's waterlogged and caught on the edge of the ice.

Bo lunges to meet the wolf-dog. It dodges past him, goes for the deer. For me. I'm on my butt hauling at the carcass. If I let go, I'm terrified the ice will give and the whole carcass will sink to the bottom of the lake. I can't let go.

I bring my good foot up. I slam it into the wolf-dog's face. His teeth close around my boot, but it doesn't hurt—with so many layers of leather and fur, I hardly feel the pressure. I hammer my other foot against his muzzle, but my leg is so weak it just slides across it.

Bo snaps at his flanks. The wolf-dog lets go and whirls on Bo. They're nearly the same size, both ferocious, but the wolf-dog is more desperate.

I haul uselessly at the deer. The wolf-dog gets a hold of Bo's shoulder, and Bo lets out an awful scream.

I give one last giant haul on the deer, pulling it farther onto the solid ice, and let go. I grab at the gun. It's slippery in my wet grip. The strap tangles around me. I bring it to my shoulder.

The wolf-dog lunges for me again. He's past the rifle barrel. His teeth rend the air in front of my face, and I fling myself backward away from him. He's on me again in an instant, Bo just behind him, all of us a tangle of bodies on the ice.

He goes for my throat. I jam my arm between us, and his teeth snap shut over it. Pain lances through my arm. I scream.

He's too close to get the barrel of the rifle between us. I grab for something, anything, and my fingers close around an arrow. I wrench it out and up as Bo's jaws close around the back of the wolf-dog's neck.

His teeth rip free of my arm. I thrust with the arrow.

I've never killed anything this close that wasn't halfway to dead already. The arrow goes in. It only punches through his skin. Blood gushes from the wound, but I haven't hit anything vital.

The dogs are off me suddenly, and the wolf-dog falls back. He crouches on the ice, bloodied, the snow growing red around him. He snarls and snaps but doesn't approach.

Rumbling, Bo circles to the side.

"Bo," I say, warning. He's bloodied, too. Favoring one leg. Bo might win, but there's no vet out here to help him after.

I grab for the gun, but the wolf-dog is backing away. Then running, limping, his pelt matted with blood.

Bo charges after him. "Bo!" He stops. Half-charges again. Halts.

Sobbing, I roll onto my side and then up to my knees. I can only kneel there, my arm throbbing. My legs are soaked. I need to move. Need to get warm.

I stand. The ice is crossed and crisscrossed with blood. Snow falls around us; in a few hours, you won't be able to tell that any of this happened.

If I don't move, the winter will swallow me, too.

"Come on, Bo."

WE MAKE IT to the shed alive. Well, Bo and I do. The deer's another matter. I get it hung through sheer stubbornness and then stumble back to the cabin. I have a little first aid kit. Not much—peroxide is the most useful thing in it.

Bo's neck is punctured. Gashes bleed sluggishly on his shoulder. With a small pair of scissors also in the first aid kit, I do my best to trim the fur away from his cuts. When I dab at his wounds with the peroxide he yelps and pulls away, but I put my arm around his neck. He could bite my face off if he wanted to, but he stiffens up instead and lets me treat his wounds. When I've dabbed peroxide everywhere, I wrap strips of T-shirt around them. They'll have to do for bandages.

It's only when I have him patched up that I turn to my own injuries.

I pull my arm out of my sleeve gingerly. The wolf-dog's teeth went right through my sheepskin coat and left a trio of deep punctures in my arm. I pour peroxide over them, terrified of infection. My arm is bruising in the shape of the dog's jaws. I flex my hand; it makes the bruises twinge, but I'm certain nothing is broken. It just hurts.

I've been out here long enough to recognize the difference between what's going to make me miserable and what's going to cause me real problems. This, thankfully, is the former.

Adrenaline fading, I indulge myself in a little bit of sulking and whining as I bandage myself up, using a strip off one of the blankets. I don't need the blankets as much as I need bandages, now that I have a patchwork of badly skinned furs that keeps me and Bo warm at night.

Still, it worries me to destroy anything. I can't get more out here. Everything that breaks, everything that gets lost, can't be replaced.

I get a fire going, piece by piece. I still have three pills left, and I take one to dull the full-body ache that's working through me. I wish I could give one to Bo. He's whining on his side, clearly in pain. But I don't know if it's safe for him. So I cap the bottle and crawl into bed. I curl around my arm and sleep.

THERE IS NO time to rest and recover in the morning. I get up before I quite realize I'm awake, before my body catches on and stops me. I move fast, as I do every morning, quickly pulling on my clothes, getting the fire started. Once you're out from under the furs, the cold provides all the motivation you need.

Breakfast is fish, a vitamin, and three thin spears of carrots. The carrots are almost gone, and that'll be the last of the vegetables. Just meat, meat, and more meat.

I would kill for a little salt.

Or cumin.

I spend the morning butchering the deer. Some of it I pack in snow. Some of it, I cut into thin sections and start to smoke. The smoking station is a tripod with a series of shelves made from branches, lashed together with twine and fishing line. I lay the meat out on the branches and wrap the tarp over the tripod before getting a low, smoky fire going beneath it. The smoke gets caught in the tarp, and as long as I keep the fire going, in a day the meat is cooked and preserved. I've only done it with fish and rabbit, but I'm hoping venison will smoke up the same.

I eye my fishing rods, knowing that I shouldn't savor this victory over the deer for too long. I have three of them; they even have reels—aluminum cans with a wooden dowel punched through them. The dowel is attached to the rod, and the can spins around it to wind the fishing line. It means I can cast farther, reel fish in faster. And it only took me about a week of staring and a half dozen failed experiments to make them work, too.

I can build the fire so that it lasts long enough for me to go fishing, but I don't want to go out on the ice again. Not after yesterday.

Instead I go to check my traps. Over time, I've gathered all of them that I can find, and I spent one entire evening sitting, figuring out how to set them properly. I have a dozen of them arranged in an easy loop behind the cabin, marked with strips of red cloth tied to nearby branches so I won't lose them.

Today I'm lucky. The first trap has a stoat in it, already dead.

I tie the stoat to my belt and reset the trap. They're not the best eating, but their fur is warm, and I've been wanting a new hat.

The next snare is missing its bait; the next three are untouched, but there's another stoat in the next one. It's still breathing, barely. I break its neck with barely a blink.

That's the last prize, but it's plenty. A strange concept: plenty. I have managed, from time to time, to be satisfied.

I have managed, from time to time, to be content.

Sometimes I think that Bo and I could live here forever.

And then my hand strays to my pocket, and my fingers close around the smooth, cold metal of the sixth bullet.

My mother is dead. My father is dead. I don't have anything to go home to, but I have things left undone. The bullet reminds me. I am not merely surviving. I am waiting. I am preparing.

I roast the first of the venison that night, on a spit above the pan to catch the grease. I eat my fill and more; I let Bo have as much as he wants and a bone to gnaw on after. I look at the wall, where those first words—SMART, NOT STRONG—have been joined by dozens more.

Pay attention to the wind.

Steep drop west of the snag.

Say something out loud at least once a day.

Remember they're coming.

The notebook lies on the shelf. I have filled in every last page by now, and added more, pages scavenged from the end of the thriller, from the field guide. I have written on the backs of the photographs and the files in the crate. I have made a record of my days.

I will not vanish. I will not fade. I was here. I've made it through another day.

I sleep fitfully, with the wind as a poor lullaby.

The wind is like a living thing to me now. It paces around my cabin and tries to find a way in. It lashes out and leaves destruction scattered everywhere when it can't get its way.

But the wind is also protection, in a way. The days the wind is the worst, I know Raph won't come; the weather's too dangerous for flying. I both crave the wind and dread it. The wind means *not yet, not today.*

The wind makes its way into my dreams. It flings me into the air. I rise and then I fall, and when I crash down to earth I'm in the car again. My whole side hurts and I can't figure out why, until I realize that the side of the car is crushed in, that pieces of it are lodged in my leg, pieces of it are grinding pebbles of glass into my skin. The pain is strange and distant, a disconnected fact. Then I look over. Then I see my mother. And—

And then we are driving again, and she's turning to say something to me, and then her arm flies out across me as if she can hold me back, as if she can shield me from what's coming, and there's a roar in my ears.

But that roar is only the wind, and my mother is dead, and I'm lying alone in the cabin, trying not to cry because I don't cry anymore.

When I wake like this, the firelight low, I squint to see the words I've written across from the bed, unsteady letters on the wall.

This is not enough.

I need something more. More than existence, more than survival.

Some days, I hold on to Bo. Keeping myself alive means keeping him alive, and I love him more fiercely than any living being.

Other days, I think about my old life. Friends. Food. Television. Takeout.

But Bo can live without me, and my old life doesn't feel real, and without my mother in it I'm not sure I even want it back.

And so I always come back to one thing. One reason to keep going. To beat the winter. One reason to survive the cold, the hunger, the loneliness: revenge.

I wake to sunlight and sit up, startled. I've slept in. I never sleep in, but the sun is streaming through the window. It's late, and the wind is howling.

Except—that's not the wind. The wind stopped long ago.

That's an engine.

That's a plane.

They're here.

I'VE IMAGINED THIS day a thousand times, but it still takes me a few seconds to truly realize what's happening, to start to move.

I grab my shoes, my coat. I sleep in everything else. It's too cold not to. I take the rifle and head out the door, hobbling as the cold stiffens my leg.

A whistle to Bo keeps him at my side, but he seems to know what's up. He has the tight gait he gets on a hunt; his ears are pricked.

The trees are too thick to see the sky. The plane is still coming; I can hear it, but I can't see it. I can't be sure it's them.

Some part of me has never quite believed they would come. Even now I'm sure it's just another traveler passing overhead, nothing to do with me. It doesn't seem possible that the end could be here. Everything has been leading to this, but until I break free of the thickest trees and spot the plane, I don't believe it's truly happening.

It's risky, landing on the lake. My own scrape with the wolf-dog proved that. But they're not the sort to be scared off by risk,

I suppose. I take note of that, remember it. They will take risks. I can use that.

The plane draws closer and closer. I crouch at the tree line, still as I can be. I have nothing bright enough to stand out against the snow and give me away, but they might spot movement.

The plane dips. It roars over the ice, touches down for a brief moment, flies up again. The air hums and shivers with the sound of the engine. It works its way down into my breastbone and speeds up my heart until it beats like a hummingbird's wings.

The plane circles around. They were testing the ice, found it solid, and this time their glide down is smooth and final.

It might not be them. It could be rescue. Another friend, like the man who came before. It's not the same plane—but that doesn't mean anything; they couldn't land the float plane from before on the ice.

The plane taxis over the ice toward the north end of the lake. It comes to a halt. I squint. It's too far away to make out any detail.

Rescue or not, Raph or not, it's time to go.

I stumble back to the cabin. I've planned for this, I've practiced this, and still fear makes my blood like acid and my breath so cold it feels like I'm being strangled. I stop myself at the door of the cabin, taking steadying breaths. I have time. The ground is frozen; it will take them time to dig through it.

I make myself slow down, running through my preparations over and over so I'm sure I haven't forgotten anything. The rifle. A two-day supply of food and a pack with enough gear to keep me alive in the open for at least that long. A hunting knife at my belt, another, smaller knife strapped to my leg. The fight with the wolf-dog taught me the importance of having extra weapons.

And now it's time to go.

The shortest route is across the ice, but I'll be spotted if I go that way. Instead I hook to the east until the rest of the shore hides me from the plane, then bolt across the lower section of the lake and into the woods again.

There's a deer trail most of the way, thin but easily navigated. I follow it, breathing through my teeth, the air making my lips sting. Bo is silent as ever.

At my pace—much faster than that first trip down, half-starved and newly shorn of hope—it takes maybe an hour and a half to get to the north end of the lake, to the spot I've chosen. It's near the wreck of the cabin, but far enough back that no one can see me from there, and well away from the path you'd take to anywhere interesting. *It will take a long time to dig,* I tell myself. Longer with the ground frozen; they'll need pickaxes, I bet, and plenty of strength to break up the icy ground. I have time.

I crouch low. The plane sits on the ice twenty feet from the shore. The wind has cleared the snow, making it smooth and easy to land on. I squint. Is the plane empty? No. Movement inside; the pilot is still there. Just like last time.

Bo growls so softly it's barely a vibration in the air. I put my hand on his shoulder to quiet him.

I wonder if it's the same pilot. At least one of the men who came before has to be back—no way they'd rely on directions to get to that patch of ground and dig it up again.

Raph is here, I know it. And maybe Daniel, too.

This is where I make my first gamble. The pilot is alone, but if I go after him now, I don't know how much time I have before Raph and Daniel come back. I have to decide now: do I attack now, or do I wait, and hope they don't just leave? I've got no guarantees once they find out the crate is gone. They might split up. They might group together. They might take off and leave me behind, wasting all my preparation.

I tighten my grip on the rifle. I have a chance. I have to take it. I start to rise.

And then: a shout. Raph comes striding out of the woods, and my decision is made for me. With Raph here now, there's no chance to pick off the pilot on his own. I drop back into my hiding place, breathing fast.

The door of the plane pops open as Raph approaches. The wind carries Raph's voice to me over the ice. The words are muffled, but I piece them together. "—else dug up the hole," he says, and my skin prickles. I made the hole bigger when I dug it up. Raph must suspect someone's been messing with it. "Can't be sure . . . got the heater . . . while longer . . ." I can't hear the rest, but it sounds like they haven't gotten through the soil yet. That's good. That gives me more time.

"—waited for spring," the pilot replies, the beginning of his sentence too muffled to hear. Raph snaps something back, and the pilot laughs.

I grip the rifle tight. At this range I couldn't hit a mammoth, much less a strip of jerky like Raph, but that doesn't stop me from wishing I could pull the trigger and end him. The me I used to be might flinch at killing someone, but the me I am now thinks, *It's just Raph,* the way I used to think, *It's just a fish.*

The conversation ends in a few more angry, indistinct words, and then Raph stalks back into the woods. My breath leaves me in a rush of steam.

Raph vanishes into the trees. I lower the rifle for a moment, hands suddenly shaking. *It would have been a mistake to shoot him,* I tell myself. *The pilot would come after me. I need to get them isolated. Away from one another.*

The pilot doesn't move. *Good,* I think. *Split up.* The plane door closes.

I'm shaking as I rise from my hiding spot. The plane's rear is to me. I snap for Bo to follow and scurry across the ice, staying low, staying out of sight, hoping the pilot doesn't glance toward me.

The ice creaks under my feet. It makes only thin, pale sounds, but I hear them, and I'm sure he does, too. I'm sure he'll look, and he'll get his gun.

But the stretch of ice between us shrinks and shrinks again, and then I'm close enough to reach out a hand and touch the plane, to slide forward on the ice toward the door.

And then I'm by the door and the rifle is in my hands and I reach up toward the cold metal skin of the plane and knock three times. It's a tinny, sharp sound with a hollow space behind it.

There's a pause. Then the door opens, the pilot leans out, and I aim the rifle at his face.

Time goes slack for a moment as we take each other in. He's a big man, with muscles turned soft and a gut poking out in front. He wears a brown coat with a patch on one sleeve. He looks friendly. Like the kind of guy who could get work as a mall Santa this time of year.

Or is it too late for that? I haven't thought about Christmas all winter, but suddenly seeing him I'm punched right back into the flow of time without any sense of where I am in it, like stepping out of an airport into an unfamiliar city when you've gotten used to empty sky.

"Hello," he says. His weight shifts. I can tell he's reaching for something. His gun.

Shoot him, I think. I swallow. "Stop," I say, and Bo's growl echoes my rough voice. "Get out." My voice is rough as tree bark after weeks of disuse.

"Hold on there," he says, lifting his palms. "I don't mean you any harm, sweetheart. You all alone out here?"

Shoot him.

"Out," I say. In a movie I'd cock it dramatically, but of course I've already made sure there's a round ready to fire, because I'm not an idiot. At least not about that.

"You wouldn't shoot me, would you?" he says with a halfway grin.

I bare my teeth at him. "Wanna bet?"

He doesn't. He slides himself off the seat and down onto the ice, keeping his hands nice and peaceful at his sides. His gun is in a holster under his armpit. I can see it when he raises his hands, his jacket pulling out to the sides.

Shoot him.

But I don't have to. I can take the plane. I can leave; leave Raph, leave Daniel, leave the woods. I can fly and get help. Let the forest kill Raph, or let the police find him.

I can't. I can't let Raph go.

But to kill Raph, I have to shoot this man, standing here with his hands up.

It wasn't supposed to be like this. He wasn't even there when my father died. Couldn't have said a word to stop it. He'd just sat in the plane, that was all.

"Take that out," I tell him, nodding my chin toward his gun. "Throw it away."

He obeys slowly and carefully, pinching the gun between his thumb and index finger so it won't look like he's grabbing it. I have my finger so snug against the trigger that if I twitch, I'll shoot. I ease it off a little. If I'm going to kill him, I should do it intentionally.

Am I going to kill him?

"Key," I say, tilting my head toward the plane to make it clear what I know. He flicks a keychain to me, two keys on it. Door and engine. "Walk to shore," I say. My voice shakes.

"What are you going to do?" he asks. He's still trying to sound friendly. He still has that kind of smile that's probably supposed to make me feel at ease.

"Walk to shore," I say again, and he shrugs like it's no big deal.

"You took our stuff, didn't you?" he asks. "Little girl like you. And here I was expecting . . ."

"Walk. To. Shore," I say. Finally he starts to obey. He backs away, step by leisurely step. Finally he turns. Starts walking. Still taking his time. Twenty feet away. Twenty-five.

This is it. Shoot him now, or get in the plane.

The barrel wavers for a moment. And then I make my decision.

"Bo, up," I say. Bo looks at me skeptically, but when I snap and point, he jumps in. I reach to heave myself up, letting the rifle dangle from its strap.

A few seconds of inattention and everything falls apart. The pilot's footsteps hammer on the ice. I whip back around.

He barrels toward me, head down. I fumble with the rifle. I get it up, my aim wild. He's almost across the ice to me. My hand clenches. The rifle bucks before I realize I've fired a shot.

Then he's on me, his hands closing over the rifle barrel, yanking it out of my grip. He swings it up, hard, and the butt smacks my jaw.

I fall. The strap, a makeshift bit of rope, is still around my shoulder. It pulls against my back, jarring me. I crash to the ice, my fall wrenching the barrel free of the pilot's grip. My head cracks against the ground and the breath goes out of me.

Bo growls and launches himself from the plane.

For a few seconds, I can't make sense of the chaos. My vision swims. I can't move, can't pull in a breath. The pilot is yelling, Bo is snarling, and the sky wheels overhead, a too-perfect blue, a vast forever.

And then: a gunshot. Not mine, the rifle slack across my chest. Not the pilot's, still on the ice.

Bo leaps away from the pilot and lands half-crouched. Raph sprints across the ice. The first shot has gone over our heads.

Bo charges. I scream at him to stop. It's too far across the ice, too much distance between them and Raph is aiming the gun right at him.

I push to my knees and fumble with the rifle, bringing it up, but the pilot grabs the barrel and twists. His foot lashes out, catches me in the ribs.

Bo courses across the ice. Raph levels the gun. Bo keeps running. A few feet now.

The pilot and I grapple over the rifle. I claw at his wrist. He punches me hard under my arm, driving the air out of my lungs.

And then another shot. Bo jerks sideways. He falls, collapsing forward onto the ice. Tries to rise. Falls again.

I think I scream again, scream for Bo. Scream for Raph not to kill him. But I'm not sure. The pilot tears the rifle out of my grasp. His eyes are wide and wild, his lips curled in a snarl. Blood stains the front of his coat. My blood? No, his. My shot—I hit him and he doesn't even seem to have noticed.

He slams the butt of the rifle against my jaw. I jerk away, but it still hits with the edge, sending pain exploding through my skull. The taste of blood floods my mouth. I fall flat on my back.

I can't see Bo.

The pilot wrenches the strap over my head. I grab it weakly, my hand closing over empty air.

Now Raph is shouting. Shouting at the pilot. Telling him not to hurt me, not to kill me.

Is Raph helping me?

I start to laugh. It makes my ribs pop and burst with pain, but I can't stop. He can't let the pilot kill me. Because I know where his goddamn crate is.

I'm still laughing as darkness closes around me like a fist. The pain is gone. I float.

And then I'm not in the darkness anymore. I'm nowhere. Nowhere at all.

I'M CONSCIOUS WHEN they tie me up, but my memory stutters, erasing itself except for flashes here and there. I know someone lifts me off the ground. I'm aware, briefly, of being dropped again, and then my memories fall apart. The next time they knit themselves together, my eyes are closed tight. I must have fallen asleep.

My whole body throbs with pain, and I know it'll get worse as soon as I open my eyes.

The first thing I smell is wood smoke. My left side is warm, my right side a block of cold, and my ribs ache in time with the throbbing of my jaw.

I picked a fight and lost, and now I'm probably going to die. It's a good thing I'm used to that by now, or I might just lie on the ground and give up. It still takes me a long moment to get up the courage to open my eyes and look around.

We're near the burnt remains of the cabin. A small fire crackles to my left. Judging by the state of the branches, it's been burning for quite a while. I don't think I lost consciousness completely for long, but unconscious even for a few seconds means a concussion. Not good.

My hands are tied in front of me. It's not like I feel like running anyway, but if I try it, I won't get far without my hands for balance.

Where are Raph and Daniel and the pilot? I look to my right slowly, because if I do it any faster, my head swims and I feel like puking. Definitely a concussion. It's getting better second by second, though, so I hope it's a mild one.

Raph and Daniel are together some ways away, and the pilot sits near them, his back against a rock. His coat is off, his midsection bandaged. He looks pasty and sweaty, his hair sticking to his forehead. When he shifts, he winces. My bag lies a few feet away from him. My hunting knife is on the ground next to it. I flex my foot, trying to feel if the smaller blade is still there, but then I see it. Raph's holding it. Flipping it idly around his thumb.

He has something yellow in his other hand, held up to the side of his face. It takes a moment of squinting to recognize it. A satellite phone. He mutters something into it, then scowls and listens. He doesn't seem happy. Reporting progress, I guess. Or lack of it.

I look toward the lake. No sign of Bo, but the ice is red near the plane. The streaks move toward the woods. I can't see if they reach the trees.

I tell myself he got away. He has to have gotten away. *Run*, I think. *Run, survive, forget about me.* And then I hope for him to come back. To somehow rescue me.

But I know he's probably dead.

Raph approaches me. He crouches and looks down at me. I don't have a good way to push myself up with my hands tied, so I'm forced to stare up at him.

"You're awake," he says, and smiles. It's not like the pilot's smile, fake and falsely reassuring. This smile is not pretending to be friendly; it's all sharp edges like an arrowhead. It punches right through you. "I take it you're the enterprising individual who took our crate. Pretty rude of you. Especially since Daniel and me had to spend all that time digging up an empty hole while you napped, just to be sure."

I just stare back at him. No point in answering. He already knows.

"What are you doing out here? Last I checked, Carl lived alone. You his little piece of jailbait, then?"

My face twists in disgust. "I'm his daughter," I say.

"He never mentioned you," he says with vague disinterest. "So, let me guess. You were going to use the radio to call for help."

"I was going to steal your plane," I say. I don't know why I'm telling him the truth about anything, except his smug expression made me want to scratch his face off and I don't want him thinking he's right about anything.

"A little wild girl flying a plane? How entertaining," he says. "Tell you what. You take me to my crate, and I'll let you hitch a ride."

"Like you'd let me go."

He shrugs. "I don't kill little girls. The way I see it, there's nothing you can do to us. So we'll drop you someplace out of the way with fifty cents in your pocket, and by the time you find a pay phone we'll be long gone. Everybody parts as friends, right?"

Every word coming out of his mouth sounds completely reasonable, but he's lying.

I haven't seen a human being in weeks—months—but I've gotten good at watching. At knowing when an animal sees you or when it's ready to run, based on the tiny tremors of its muscles. And the way he's talking, he's suddenly gotten a little more tense, the tendons of his neck shifting minutely, the corner of his eye twitching once.

He doesn't care if I can do anything to him. I've already done it, by moving the crate. By shooting the pilot. He's got plenty of reason to kill me.

"Okay," I say. "I'll take you to it."

"Good," he says. "Very good." That smile again, with bare, blunt teeth that scare me more than the wolf-dog's fangs. But I don't know what else to do. If I refuse, he'll hurt me. If I agree, I'll survive a little while longer.

I shiver. I should have let them come and go. I'd take the winter over this.

But I haven't ever given up yet, and it isn't time to start now. A plan is the first thing you need. I don't have one, but it starts to form like a frost bloom.

"I'll take you to it," I say again, and try to think.

HE'LL KILL ME like he killed my father, standing by the crate. If I take him to it, I'll die. If I don't take him to it, he'll hurt me, but he won't kill me. Not yet. These things I'm sure of. I'm not sure of anything else, but it's enough to start with.

I take him around the east side of the lake. To the blackberry patch, now just a snarl of dormant vines capped with snow. Daniel has to carry the tools—shovels and picks and a bag with a big propane heater to thaw the ground—and the pilot stays behind.

Daniel hasn't said anything except to agree with Raph's orders, and he watches me with a hangdog look. Raph said he doesn't kill little girls. If Daniel said it, I'd believe him, but I also don't think he'll do anything to protect me.

No, Raph will kill me and Daniel will stand by and tell himself there was nothing he could have done, it wasn't him that did it anyway, it wasn't his fault.

It's weird, though. There's a part of me that finds them comforting. People. Human beings. I'm not alone. I'd be safer if I was, but some stupid part of my brain doesn't understand that. It's doing cartwheels at the notion that I have company.

Next thing you know I'll be wanting to put out the fine china.

We move along slowly. Mostly because of me. I stumble a lot, but at least my head has stopped spinning, and Raph even gave me a couple of painkillers. I only took one. It's dulled the edge without making me loopy. I hid the other in my palm and snuck it into my pocket when Raph wasn't looking.

"This is it," I say at last, when we've reached a flat, empty patch that could plausibly hold the crate.

Raph inspects the ground. It's snowed a few times since I was here last and the only thing that has come through is a deer, judging by the tracks.

"Doesn't look like you've been out here," he says.

"I don't exactly make a daily pilgrimage," I say. "I buried it before the ground froze. You really think I could have managed it otherwise?"

He looks at me. Sees a scrawny girl with scars on her cheeks and a bad leg. Doesn't see the muscle on that scrawny frame. Sure, I don't have any fat on me, but I surprise myself every day with my strength. Especially now that I have food, good protein-rich food, filling me up three meals most days.

"All right," he says. "We dig."

I'm worried for a moment that he's going to make me do it, but apparently thinking I'm a weak little girl extends to his opinion of my current usefulness. On that score he's probably right. I'm banged up enough I couldn't swing the pickax to break the ground. And I'm not about to complain.

He situates me to the side, my back against a tree trunk and my legs out in front of me. He and Daniel set up the heater, but Raph's impatient; he makes Daniel get to work swinging the pickax before the heater's been running more than a few minutes, hacking at the hard-packed, frozen earth.

Daniel has my rifle slung over his back, and he positions himself so he can keep an eye on me. No sneaking off.

I figure it'll take them at least an hour to dig even a foot down, and they won't get suspicious until they hit four feet without finding anything. Or if they find a giant rock or something that I obviously didn't shovel back into place.

I have to get away from them before then.

I have to get them to split up, and I have to get my hands free.

No way Raph will untie me, but Daniel? I can get him to do any-thing short of letting me go, I bet.

I give it twenty minutes before I speak up.

"I've got to pee," I say, loudly. They stop their digging. Raph looks at me. Daniel looks at Raph.

"Then pee," Raph says.

"Seriously?" I arch an eyebrow. I have to think about the right facial expression to make, it's been so long since I interacted with a human being.

He laughs. "Fine, then. You can have a little privacy."

I try not to look hopeful and anxious. I figure I have even odds of either man accompanying me. If it's Raph, I'm screwed.

"Don't take her too far," he says to Daniel. "And turn your back while the lady relieves herself." He looks at me. "Happy?"

I glare at him. Daniel nods. He rests his pick on the ground and comes over to help me to my feet.

He avoids my eyes. I try to catch his gaze, but he stares stub-bornly to the side.

I walk beside him into the trees. I can still hear Raph swing-ing away at the hard ground. *Thunk. Thunk. Thunk. Scrape.* But soon I can't see him through the trees, and Daniel stops.

"I'll, um, turn around," he says, repeating Raph's instructions like they're his own idea.

"You have to untie my hands," I say. I keep my voice matter-of-fact, even attempt to sound a little shy.

"What?" he sounds alarmed.

"Um. Girls have to squat," I say. "I can't exactly balance with my hands tied. Basic biology and center-of-gravity stuff. Plus it'd be hard to pull my pants down, and unless you want to do that—"

"No, no, all right," Daniel says, his cheeks turning red.

Behind him, something moves in the woods. Something low and dark and four-legged. Bo? Or, more likely, the wolf-dog. It slinks toward us step by step.

Daniel steps up to me. He tugs at the knots a moment, curses as he catches the side of his nail, fumbles a bit more, and then gives up.

He looks really young close up. Early twenties, maybe. I feel older than he is, even at sixteen. Or am I seventeen now?

"What day is it?" I ask.

"Huh?"

"I've lost track," I say. "What day is it?"

"Uh. February sixth," he says. "Monday."

"Guess I missed Christmas," I say. And my birthday is in November, so I've missed that, too.

It's weird, realizing I'm seventeen. That I've been seventeen for months. I should be waiting on college admissions and feeling the effects of senioritis. I can barely remember what school was like. It's so surreal to think about it's almost funny. A day dictated by bells and classes, hallways crowded with other people my age.

I always liked school. I can't remember why, now.

Daniel flicks open a knife and sets it against the ropes. *Wait*, I tell myself. *Wait, and then move.*

There's a rock at my feet. Small enough to lift. Large enough to hurt.

Daniel cuts through the rope. It takes some sawing to get through, but then I unwrap my hands quickly.

"Thanks," I say. I want to add, *Sorry.*

He gives me a tentative smile and turns away.

I lunge. He must hear the movement, because he starts to whip back around, but I bring the rock up in both hands and swing it as hard as I can at the side of his head.

Something crunches at the impact. Daniel's hand seizes up, squeezing a shot off into the ground. He drops to his knees. I don't wait to see if he gets back up.

I run.

I RUN DEEPER into the woods. I have seconds before Raph follows, and the snow means I'll leave tracks, but it's the only hope I have.

Get away. Get armed. Get to the plane.

Branches whip past my face. Pain stabs through my ribs, but it isn't the worst I've felt, not close. Just bruises, and the painkiller is still blunting the sharp edges of it.

Footsteps crash behind me. I don't dare turn around.

A shot rings out. Then another. A bullet strikes the tree to the right of me, bark and splinters of wood exploding from the impact point. But Raph is firing blind; I had a decent head start on him.

I know the woods, know where there's a creek I can run up, ice that won't leave tracks.

I know where the snow will be patchy on the ground because the trees make a thick canopy above, and where the deer trails drive furrows through the underbrush.

I just have to go faster.

Snow starts to fall, pelting down out of the sky to cover up my tracks. The sound of Raph's crashing through the woods fades behind me. I halt a moment, taking stock of my surroundings.

I could switch back here and cover my tracks. I don't want to lead him straight to the cabin.

I set out again, picking my route carefully. Raph yells, cursing at me. Hard to tell how close he is. The trees should keep him from spotting me, but I stay low just in case.

I hook back for a few minutes, then loop around behind where I think Raph is. I'll go wide, and come back into the cabin from the far side; it's the best way to be sure I've lost him.

I slow to a jog, then a walk. My breath is sharp in my throat. I've started limping, and deep breaths make my ribs scream. I don't know how much damage I've done to Daniel.

Head wounds are fickle. I know that. Sometimes you can take a spike to the brain and live forty years. Sometimes you get tapped and die.

I didn't tap him, that's for sure. I knocked him out. Maybe cracked his skull.

Definitely cracked his skull. I felt it give.

Maybe I killed him.

I'd set out to kill him, but now I'm worried I've done it. I remember him digging his paddle into the water, throwing Raph's aim off as Bo barked on the shore.

He saved Bo, and I might have killed him.

The pilot might die, too. I might have killed two men, and I didn't really mean to. Except that I did. Except . . . except that I pictured it like killing a rabbit, like killing a deer. I never admitted that I'd have to look in their eyes. I never thought they might talk to me.

It didn't occur to me until now to wonder if Daniel has parents, has a family or a girlfriend. If he regrets getting involved with Raph. If the pilot has a daughter.

But maybe they aren't dead. Maybe I haven't killed anyone. Not yet.

I'm glad, and angry at myself for it. I want to be empty. But I'm filling up again with fear and with guilt and with feelings I can't even name.

I stagger up to the cabin. I half-expect Raph to step around the side with his gun aimed at me, but it's as still and silent as ever. I walk around the side of the cabin and halt, breath caught in my throat.

The snow is red with blood, leading up to the front steps.

Bo lies sprawled at the door, his head on his paws. He lifts his head weakly when I appear. His tail thumps against the stoop.

I rush forward. "Oh, honey," I coo at him. He licks my fingers. His fur is matted with blood, and I don't want to touch his side in case I hurt him, but I run my fingertips lightly over his fur.

He snaps when my fingers find the bullet hole, but he pulls his head away from me when he does. I'm not afraid he'll bite me. It's been a long time since I was afraid of that.

The bullet went in at the back of his neck, by his shoulder, half-obscured by the bite from the wolf-dog. There's a lot of blood, but he's breathing and he's alive.

I tell myself he'll be all right. He's too tough to die.

I step over him to open the cabin door and then coax him

inside. Even though I can feel the time I have left before Raph finds me slipping away, I pause to give him a whole heap of rabbit meat while I wash off the blood. I tear up blankets and tie them around the wound.

It's hard to get the bandage to stay in place, hard to convince Bo to let me wrap him up. I have to loop long strips around his neck and his chest, over and over again, and by the time I'm done the bandage is bleeding through and I have to change it. And all the while I'm waiting for footsteps outside.

It feels dangerous to be there. Exposed. Easy to stumble across, even though I know how hard it is to find anything, even something the size of the cabin, in these woods.

I tell myself we're safe. That Bo will be all right.

I don't believe any of it.

I don't have a plan. A goal, sure, but that's not a plan. Of all of the scenarios I imagined, none of them ended with me leaving Bo behind. The bullet's still lodged somewhere inside him, and he's still bleeding. He whimpers every few seconds. His breathing is shallow. He's lying on his side, watching me like he expects me to fix it, but I can't.

This is all my fault. If I'd just shot the pilot, we could have gotten in the plane. We could have left. Bo would be fine. I'd be sipping hot cocoa by now.

Raph is coming for us.

He could just leave. Maybe he should. But he won't. He'll come after me. And I'm not even sure he'll care about getting the crate at this point. I've lied to him once. He's not going to let me do it again.

He's going to come for me, and he's going to kill me. Unless I kill him first. Or unless I get away.

Until now, I've had a choice. Revenge was a choice. I could have left the crate, stayed hidden, waited for summer and Griff. Taken my chances with the wild. But it's not a matter anymore of choosing between Raph and the winter. Raph isn't going to leave me to the elements and hope the forest kills me before someone comes to save me. He's going to hunt me down and kill me.

It's getting dark. My eyes are good at night and the sky is clear, which means light from the moon and the stars. Raph's eyesight won't be that good. He hasn't been out in the wild like I have. He'll need light, and that will make him easy prey.

Prey. Like a rabbit or a fox or a deer. That's all.

Prey that can bite back.

I can do this. I can kill him. I can get us home. Get us help. And if I don't, then—

Then I made it this far.

I PACK A fresh bag, since Raph took the one I had. I bring a little food. A knife, fishing line, things that might be useful. I take my bow and my quiver of arrows, and then, after a long debate in perfect silence, I walk outside and find the grenades.

When I stored them, I wrapped them in cloth and plastic to keep them dry. Now I unwrap them, two round, dark blotches. Deadly fruit.

I put them in my bag slowly, take them out again, consider. I have seen enough movies to understand the general principle of how they work, but there are still unknowns. I can't be certain how far I'll have to throw one, how much damage it would do. But Raph has a gun and all I have is a bow. I need some kind of advantage.

In the end I only take one. I feel safer that way, like there's less of a chance I can screw something up.

Bo drags himself out of the cabin. I send him back in with a snap of my fingers and a scowl. I can't shut the door. If I don't come back, he'll be trapped in here. But he can't come with me, not in his condition.

I have to do this by myself.

He keeps trying to follow me. Finally I sit in the doorway, Bo stretched out next to me, and stroke his side until he drifts into a fitful sleep. Then I creep away.

This time, he doesn't follow.

My fingertips are gummy with blood from his fur. I rub them off in the snow, hands shaking. He can't die. He can't leave me alone. He wouldn't. He won't.

I don't know exactly where I'm going yet. To find Raph, that's all. Before he can find me.

I walk without much purpose and realize I'm heading back to the blackberry patch, where I saw him last. As good a place as any. I keep low and go slowly. Keep my ears trained for any rustle or sigh, but it's like the whole forest has hushed up for the night. Tonight belongs to us, the human interlopers.

It's the first time in weeks I've felt like something that doesn't belong out here, that isn't part of the forest, at least in some small way. The forest doesn't care that I've been here for so long, that I've become part of its every day. It won't help me just because I'm less of a stranger than the men with their plane and their guns.

I creep closer to the edge of the clearing and spot the remains of Raph's search for the crate. The heater still pumping out warm air. The hole, barely more than a few inches scraped in the hard ground. And Daniel, lying on his side with one arm twisted awkwardly under him. I watch for a long time, but he doesn't move. He doesn't breathe. Dead. My fault.

The uncertainty, not knowing if I killed him or not, was sickening. This is nothing. A pang of regret, less for killing him than for the fact that he's here at all. If anything, I'm relieved to have the answer.

I killed him. And now I know that I can kill a person. A human being.

I walk toward the north end of the lake. Out on the ice, the plane crouched, waiting. Maybe Raph is there. Guarding it from me. Maybe he's searching for me, and the forest will take care of him. It takes back what it can. Daniel's dead body or Raph's living one, it won't care.

But I won't be that lucky.

When I get close to the old cabin I make a wide circle, searching for signs of Raph. The only thing out of place is a fire down by the shore. In its light, the pilot sits leaning against the same rock as before. His eyes are closed. My rifle is across his lap.

I unsling my bow from my back and put an arrow to it. He's too far away for a good shot, and I don't trust him not to wake up if I try to creep closer, but I can't just leave him there. Not if I want to go for the plane or go after Raph.

I lick my lips. I have to risk it.

Then I see a shape across the clearing. Bone-thin, slinking through the trees. The wolf-dog, hungrier and more desperate than ever after a desolate winter. He tests the air with his nose. The moonlight glints off his eyes, a horror-movie effect that sets my hair on end.

The pilot jerks. Not asleep, then. And he's seen.

"Git," he says. He lifts the rifle, but it shakes and dips in his hand. Even his voice is weak.

He squeezes off a shot. The wolf-dog flattens itself into the ground but doesn't retreat. A second shot goes wide and splats into the snow and dirt. The wolf-dog advances.

You have two bullets left, I think.

The pilot shoves to his feet. The wolf-dog is mad, crazy. The pilot's got to put one through its head or its heart, and fast. It advances, moving swiftly over the snow. The next shot catches its flank and it howls in pain—and flings itself forward.

The pilot swears loudly. He whips the barrel of the rifle up, trying to track the wolf-dog's movement, and the fourth shot rings out. Snow bursts behind the wolf-dog.

It keeps coming.

The pilot's finger tightens.

Click.

I look away, but I can't block out the sound. The pilot doesn't scream, at least, but he fights, and I hear the blows of his fists against the wolf-dog's side, the wolf-dog's barking, the sound of cloth and skin tearing.

Then there is silence, and I look up again. The wolf-dog stands over the pilot's body. Blood splashes out over the snow and stains the wolf-dog, muzzle to shoulders. His breath hisses out in clouds of steam, and the blood steams, too, thickening in the air.

A growl rattles between the creature's teeth, and it looks at me like I might try to take the meat it's won.

I draw my arrow back, aiming carefully. The wolf-dog comes forward. Gravel scrapes under its paws.

It charges. I release.

My aim is better than the pilot's. The arrow catches the wolf-dog in the chest. Its momentum carries it forward, but it's already dead or dying, and its legs collapse. It falls, bleeding, its blood mixing with the pilot's. By the time I reach it, it's stopped breathing.

I glance at the pilot, look away quickly. But not before his empty eyes catch mine. I start to move away, but I stop. Force myself to turn back. I swallow against the sour taste in my throat and approach the torn-up corpse.

The rifle lies on the ground, half under him. I grab the strap and pull. The body rocks toward me, then back as the rifle slides free. I swallow. Not done yet. I reach into the pocket of his coat, and I'm relieved when my fingers touch cold metal right away. The keys. I pull them out and back away two steps, staggering with my eagerness to get away from the body.

"I didn't kill you," I say. "This isn't my fault."

His gray-blue eyes stare sightlessly at me. I turn away.

My hands are shaking as I drop the keys into my pocket. And then my fingers close around the cold metal of the last bullet. Wherever Raph is, he'll be coming here now, drawn by the gunfire. I have minutes. Seconds.

The plane is unprotected. I hesitate, indecision clutching at me as it did before. I can stay and hide and fight, or I can run for the plane and hope I get to it before Raph catches up to me.

I look at the pilot, at the wolf-dog. Standing your ground gets you killed.

The faster I get help, the faster Bo gets help.

I run for the plane. My bag slaps against my back. I load my rifle as I run. One shot. The one I've been saving. I hook the strap over my shoulder opposite the bow.

I see him coming down from the tree line when I'm halfway across, but it's too late to stop now. Out here in the open I'm too vulnerable.

I fling myself across the ice and haul at the plane door. *Unlocked unlocked unlocked*, yes—it opens.

I pull myself into the seat, slinging my bow into the seat beside me so I'll have room. I stare at the instruments and dials. I've practiced everything about getting to the plane, but I haven't actually practiced taking off, and suddenly everything I know rushes out of my head.

Checklists, I think. But I don't have time for safety.

I can do this. Put the key in. Turn everything on. Nav. Radio. What else? My mind is blank. *Steering lock.* I pull the pin, hands shaking. And everything else is gone, and it doesn't matter because I'm out of time.

All I can do is start the engine. Start the engine and *move* because there's no time for anything else.

It growls to life and I reach to close the door, but Raph is here. I yank on the door, but he jams his shoulder in the way and grabs at me. I twist, trying to bring the rifle up.

He grabs fistfuls of my jacket, pulling me out of the seat. We spill onto the ice. The strap of my bag digs into my shoulder. The contents spill, scattering.

He drags me toward him. The rifle skitters on the ice after me. I yank, scrabbling for it, and grab hold just as he flips me onto my back.

He twists the rifle neatly out of my hands, yanks the strap from my shoulder.

I plant a boot between his legs and shove off hard. He stumbles back with an *oof* of breath and pain, and I grab for my bag, for the thing that didn't fall out, for the bundle of cloth that unwraps easily.

The grenade. Cold in my hand.

He's raising the rifle, he's aiming, and I lie flat on my back on the ice and raise the grenade above me, my fingers wrapped tight around the pin, ready to pull.

He freezes. We stand there and pant for a couple of seconds before he speaks.

"The hell do you think you're doing?" he says.

"Keeping you from shooting me." I pull the pin out, mashing my hand hard around the grenade, keeping the lever depressed so it won't go off. "See? Shoot me and we go boom." I can't believe how calm I sound, given that my heart is trying to climb its way out of my throat and plop onto the ice.

It takes five seconds for Raph to decide what to do, and in that time I'm trying to see a way out of here and failing.

He makes a choice for me. He dives for me, for the grenade, letting the rifle fall.

I roll out of the way. My elbows bark against the ice.

I'm still holding the grenade with both hands, terrified it will slip free. I can't push myself up. His hands close around mine with crushing pressure. We struggle, his weight and strength against mine.

He hauls at me and I come halfway upright, flailing to get at least my good leg under me.

All I can think is that I have to hold on, have to get away, but my fingers are numb with cold and they slip. I slip. My hands loosen at the same moment as my weight suddenly jerks against his grip.

He fumbles. The grenade flies out from between our fingers.

We each act on instinct. His says, *Catch it.*

Mine says, *Run.*

Only I can't run, just fling myself on all fours across the ice away from it, parallel to the plane as the grenade strikes, bounces, rolls, and by the time Raph has taken one step toward it he's realized what he's done and he heaves back around.

One second.

Two seconds.

Three seconds.

Boom.

THE SOUND IS so immense it isn't even sound. It's pain and pressure and the air ripping apart around me.

I flatten myself against the ice, covering my head with my hands like that's going to help. My leg flares with pain.

My ears ring and roar. My vision blurs, and I feel like a giant's foot has crushed me into the ground.

But I'm alive. Is he?

I can't see.

I need to. I need to move.

But instead I see—my mother, still, blood on the side of her face, looking at me, looking and not looking, empty.

My father, head going back with a jerk, blood a mist in the air.

Wolf's teeth, wolf's jaws clamping shut over my arm, cold water sluicing up the ice.

And I can't move. My hollow self has filled up. All that emptiness just left room for fear, and now I'm choking on it.

I can't hear anything except the roar, but I feel the ice crack under me. Feel it heave.

There has to be something more than fear, and I find it. I find it in the frozen image of a photograph, my mother's arm around mine, wind whipping our hair across our faces.

I find it in the look my father gave me, the one that said maybe if we'd had more time, I would have realized how much we could be to each other.

I find it in Will's voice, his idiot grin as I inch my way across the floor and don't give up.

And in Griff, and Scott, and Lily who told me she wanted to be brave like me.

It isn't the food and work that make me strong in that moment. I'm still injured. Still weak.

But I'm not alone. I've never been alone. They are, every one of them, reaching out to me with the words they spoke and the things they did for me.

They made me strong.

Move.

That's enough. Enough. ENOUGH.

MOVE.

I get my hands under me. Push upright. I brace one foot against the ice, then two—and pain stabs through my calf.

It's my bad leg. Worse, now. I crane my neck back to look. Blood soaks through my pants. But that isn't what my eye tracks to. Black water. The blast broke up the ice. There's a hole where the explosion was centered. Shattered, cracked ice reaches out from it with still-stretching claws.

Raph is on his side on the ice. His face is pointed away from me, and I can't tell if he's alive, but he isn't moving.

The cracks reach out under the plane.

I have to get to it.

The rifle is between me and Raph. I crawl over the ice to it, weaving as the world tilts and spins around me. I use the rifle to push myself upright.

I lock my leg and grit my teeth and get upright, barely, leaning heavily on the rifle, and limp toward the plane. The ice lurches alarmingly under me. Water sluices up here and there, sloshing over the fractured sheets.

I hear Raph grunt behind me as he pushes himself up. I hurry forward. I step over a crack that's gushing water like blood from an artery and reach the plane. I pull myself up into the seat and reach for the controls.

The engine is still going. It's only been, what, thirty seconds, a minute? It seems like an hour. A day.

I fumble at the controls.

The plane heaves. Nonononono—the ice is breaking up under me. I have to move, but the plane only tips with a shudder, the front wheel sinking forward.

For more heartbeats than I can spare, I somehow believe that I can do something. Get away, take off. Enough heartbeats for the ice to give still more, the weight unbalancing and the plane nodding forward into the black.

And then there isn't even time to grab the radio, to get a message out that will tell someone—if they're even listening—how to find me.

A scream of fear and frustration rips out of my throat, felt but not heard.

I throw myself out the other door, the far side of the plane, onto the still-solid ice beyond. The plane is beginning to sink. The water clutches at it greedily, pulling it down into the dark, and I can only drag myself away and farther away as the ice shifts and cracks and settles.

Raph is on his feet, reeling away from the spreading hole. He nearly makes it to shore before he collapses on his knees. I watch him instead of watching the plane's slow surrender to the water, and I don't move until I feel the ice twitch under me again.

I drag myself toward shore. My chest hurts. It's hard to breathe. I realize I'm sobbing, my whole body clutching up with it. I move forward on my elbows, pushing weakly with one leg and dragging the other behind me. I leave a streak of red on the ice.

The shore is close and miles away, and it only seems to get farther, but the ice under me is solid now. Solid enough to rest.

I check Raph again. Not moving. I shut my eyes.

The world contracts to the steady roaring in my ears. The ground seems to pitch under me, but I know it isn't the ice. Just whatever damage I've done.

I don't sleep, exactly, but I drift. I half-dream, and in the dream I'm flying. Bo is beside me on the seat, and home is ahead. I've made it. I'm safe.

I don't ever want to wake up.

I DON'T KNOW how long I'm on the ice. When I come back to myself, back to the ground, the first thing I notice is that I can hear again—sort of. One ear is still full of the ocean-roar sound, but from the other I can make out the muffled sounds of the wind and the creaking ice and my own breathing.

My leg has stopped bleeding. I hurt, but that's nothing new. I push myself cautiously upright, touching my head—tender— and my chest and my limbs, checking that everything is in one piece.

When I'm certain that I'm not dead, I look around. The plane has vanished. The hole is ragged, twice as big across as the plane, and still only a fraction of the lake's surface.

Raph lies on his back maybe twenty yards away, his head rolled to the side away from me. I squint, trying to tell if he's breathing, but I can't see. I pull the rifle against my body. I still have the last shot.

Getting to my feet takes a full minute. Even then I wobble, but I take one step after another and draw close to Raph. By the time I'm ten steps away I can see he's breathing—uneven, shallow breaths.

Five steps away and I have enough of an angle to see his face. His eyes are closed, his face oddly swollen. A bubble of blood forms at the corner of his mouth. It expands slowly, turning pinkish as it thins, then pops, splattering his face with tiny red droplets.

I lift the rifle and step forward. Two more steps. I'm close enough that he could grab me, if he moves, but he's not moving.

One of his hands is on his chest, the other flung out away from me. He's on his back, but his legs are twisted to the side, and the stray, strange thought floats through my mind that it can't be very comfortable.

One bullet. One bullet I've been saving for him, and here's my chance.

"Hey," I say. He doesn't move.

I inch forward and nudge his shoulder with the rifle. He still doesn't move.

He isn't going to wake up. I'm not going to get to look him in the eye. And even if I did, he would never have felt sorry for what he's done. Never felt guilt or shame or regret. He'd just have hated me. I can't make him hurt like I hurt.

But I can kill him.

I level the gun at his chest and wrap my finger around the trigger. One tug and I'll be done. Put a bullet through his heart. Or maybe his head.

I hold there. Seconds drag past. My breath comes out in quick, sharp puffs of fog. Just one little pull, hardly a twitch. A few muscles, one finger. Boom, dead. Easy.

And yet I don't pull the trigger. I lower the gun. Raph's breath hitches, then resumes.

He's nothing. Less than nothing. Killing him won't do anything. It won't bring my dad back.

I sit down. I put the rifle over my lap, and I watch his chest rise and fall and rise and fall. The pauses between his breaths get longer, the rasping louder. But it goes on. And I watch. I'm too tired to move. Too wounded. And I need to know that he's dead. I need to be sure.

It's an hour, maybe two, before it finally stops. It happens suddenly and quietly. A ceasing. No death rattle, no dramatic last collapse of his chest. The stillness creeps up on me. I only realize it's there long seconds after it's begun.

I wait longer, to be sure. I touch his cheek. It's already cold, like he's been dead all along, even though I know it's just from the frigid air.

I feel like I should say something. Something fierce or forgiving, angry or aloof. But I don't feel anything toward him now, and I have nothing to say.

I look up at the sky. It's clear as glass and vast as heartbreak, and endlessly, endlessly empty. But it doesn't have to stay that way. The plane is gone, but I'm not lost. The satellite phone is on Raph's belt.

I take it from him carefully, trying not to touch him. I clutch it against my chest. It's safety. It's rescue. I'm saved, but I've thought that before and been wrong.

The call is a blur, barely registering. There's a number on the phone for emergencies, but it's some emergency center in Alaska. Nowhere close. They still talk to me, though. Say calm, soothing things I can barely hear, even with the volume turned all the way up and the phone pressed against my ear, as I try to explain brokenly, haltingly, who I am and where I am.

Eventually they say people are coming. They tell me to stay by the lake, to make a signal so they can see me.

But I can't stay here. If we're going to be rescued, we're going to be rescued together. Bo and me.

THE WALK BACK takes a long time. My leg drags. I pause to rest here and there, and melt snow in my mouth for water. I'm not cold, at least. The movement keeps me warm, the pain keeps me alert.

Bo is in front of the cabin, his chin resting on his paws. He lifts it weakly when I approach and whuffs softly in my direction. I sink down and scrub his head and ears.

"Good boy," I say. "Come on, good boy. We're going home."

But he won't get up. Can't get up. He tries and falls and tries again, and finally lies in the pink-tinged snow with his eyes full of failure and apology.

"It's okay," I tell him. I rub his side, stroke his nose. "Shh, it's okay." Tears well in my eyes. I have to move him. I have to get him to where help can come. I can't leave him here.

I put him on the litter. He's almost too big for the platform of sticks and planks. I put a blanket over them and another over him to keep him warm, and I hold tight to the harness. I have to walk backward to drag him.

Even with the path we've worn over the weeks, it's slow, the litter catching on rocks and roots and chunks of snow, Bo whimpering with every jolt. I talk to him the whole time, nonsense words. But he's so heavy, and I'm so tired. I can only make it a few steps before I have to let him down and rest.

We're only a couple hundred yards from the cabin when my leg gives out. I drop the litter and collapse on the ground. Bo lets out a strangled whine. He's drooling, blood mixing with the drool, and his whole body trembles.

I crawl over to him. "I'm sorry, I'm sorry," I say, stroking his neck. He moans. I look behind me. We've hardly made any progress at all. "Hold on," I say. "Help's coming, you just have to hold on a little while."

I force myself to my feet. I lock my leg, hip, knee, and ankle, and bend over to grab the litter. I heave. The litter lifts six inches off the ground.

My fingers slip.

The litter falls back to the ground, and I drop down beside it, tears choking me. *Get up*, I tell myself, but it's no use. I'm not strong enough. Bo is too heavy.

His ears are flat against his head, his eyes so narrow they're almost closed. He pants, his breath heavy and uneven, and every few seconds his whole body shivers. He doesn't seem to notice when I put my hand on his ruff.

I can't leave him like this. I can't get him to the lake. Maybe when they come, they'll be able to come help me get him, and take both of us—

I shut my eyes and bury my face against Bo's fur. Bo isn't going to live long enough for that.

I can't save him. I can't keep him alive.

All I can do is sit beside him while he shudders and whimpers in pain.

He seems to go still. I lift my head. He's looking at me, his mouth open. Blood tinges his teeth red; his tongue lolls out. His side rises with a wheeze, and then collapses. He lets out a slow, pleading whine.

I can't let him stay like this, in this much pain. I don't leave the animals I hunt in pain like this. Raph didn't die in pain like this, awake and aware. I have to do something.

I have to. I can't. I have to.

I stroke his face. "I'm sorry," I whisper. "I know it hurts. I'll make it stop. I'll make it stop."

I get to my knees and move around to the other side of the litter. I touch Bo's cheek again. He whines and licks my hand, but it's all he can do.

I pull the rifle around to the front of my body. One bullet left. I can't.

Bo looks at me steadily.

I have to.

I aim the rifle between his eyes. He doesn't flinch out of the way, only pants.

Tears blur my vision. I blink them away.

"Thank you, Bo."

I BUILD A FIRE where the old cabin stood, throwing on every downed branch and plank I can find. And then I sit by the lake, my arms around my good knee, my bad leg stretched out in front of me, and wait with an empty rifle on my back.

Snow falls over me, and I don't shake it away. It settles on me until the chest-rattling sound of a helicopter draws close; it lands near to us on the shore, and the wind of the helicopter's landing scatters the snow.

Two figures come across the ice toward me, heads and bodies bent.

"We did it," I whisper, imagining Bo beside me. "You did it. You saved us."

They speak to me, but I only shake my head. I don't understand; I can hardly hear.

They lift me up. They take the bodies, too. Raph and the pilot. Not Daniel, somewhere out in the woods, not Bo.

I want to tell them about Bo, want them to take him home, too, but he's already home, already in his right place here where the sky stretches, empty, to the horizon and there are no human voices to stir the shadows.

I almost tell them to leave me. *I've made a mistake. Leave me here where I belong.* But it's the hollow me that still stands beneath the trees, and another me that lets them carry me across the ice.

The two of us lock eyes, a winter ghost and a living girl. And then I rise into the sky and she turns back with a four-legged ghost at her side, into the woods to face the winter, and I wonder which one of us is real.

SPRING

THERE ARE TWO ways the story gets told. In one of them, there's a girl all alone in the wild. She's brave and resourceful. It's an adventure story, a triumph. And there's a footnote at the end, a mention of a paramilitary group, of three deaths—or four, if they count my father—and not much explanation. That story is inspirational. People want books about that story, they want TV specials. They still call sometimes. I've stopped answering.

The second story is about a group of bad men. Domestic terrorists, the story calls them. Men with guns and bombs and plans for mayhem, who dodged the FBI by moving north and going quiet and hiding evidence where no one would look. It's a story of thirty-nine arrests, of two separate manhunts, of FBI agents and cops and politicians taking credit for *dismantling a criminal network*. In that story, I'm the footnote. Rarely even mentioned. I'm just a source of information.

I'm glad. The stories overlap, but few people realize it. Which means that few people ask too many questions about those last days on the ice. Everyone who had to know agreed it would be best for me—quiet, strange, traumatized me—to keep the whole story of what happened and of what I did out of the media. They didn't bother asking me one way or another.

That second story fills in some of the gaps in what I knew. The way it was explained to me is this:

When my dad was younger, before he had me, he got involved with a group of men all high on the same ideas. They wanted to be self-sufficient; they wanted to be left alone. At the beginning there were only a few of them, and mostly they just hunted and fished and drank and talked.

Then a new man joined them, a man who didn't just want to talk. Albert. He started to take charge. He had a warrant out on him for something boring—dodging taxes, I think. They got stopped on a trip, out on a road in the middle of nowhere with a cop who'd just meant to let them know they had a busted taillight. There were three guys in the truck, and my father was one of them. The cop ended up dead. Dad was just in the car, that was all, but years later when they had a hundred members and more murders to their name, when they had pipe bombs and automatic weapons hidden under floorboards and were blackmailing people for money, they still had that day to hold over him. That dead cop whom he hadn't even said a word to.

So they used him to hide things, when the FBI was tearing apart every piece of property they'd ever set foot on. At first it was just money he was supposed to hold on to. Then there was a raid on Albert's house, and they basically dumped everything that was in his safe into a box and ran like hell.

That was the way it was explained to me, sitting in a cold gray room with a can of perfectly chilled Coke cupped in both hands, which I couldn't get down but was as good a thing as any to stare at so that I wouldn't have to look at the woman explaining it all. She was a federal prosecutor. She was polished, from her smooth brown hair to her buffed fingernails to her slim-but-practical heels. I had trouble meeting her eye. She had this look I was getting used to but still hated, balanced between pity and horror. It came with whispers. *Did she really . . . ?*

Sometimes I looked down and for a moment I was startled that there wasn't blood under my fingernails, still. Not even dirt.

I had a funeral for my father. Not a funeral, really, since there wasn't a body. A memorial. The social worker's idea, taken up by my new foster parents. They bought me a black dress with sleeves that went down to my wrists, and black tights. I slicked back my hair to show the scars on my face and I stood in an empty chapel while a preacher said kind words about a man he didn't know, a man who would have hated every mention of God and heaven in the service.

They think I'm wounded, but there is a difference between a wound and a scar. I'm done bleeding. I'm tougher now. And if these scars sometimes make things stiff, make it a little harder to move smoothly through a conversation or the routines of normal life, they just keep me from forgetting.

I have friends again. My old friends, Michelle and Ronnie, even though it took weeks for them to learn not to ask questions, and a few new ones. I see Scott every few weeks, and Will sends me emails with jokes and pictures of cats. I even managed to track down Griff (took a lot of dead-end calls to small Alaskan towns before I got a lead), and not long after, I got a lumpy package in the mail from him with yellow snow boots and a souvenir shot glass and a box of smoked salmon in it, clearly all bought in a panic at the same shop. I went to visit him and his daughter and told him it wasn't his fault, but he didn't believe me.

My life is full of people now, and even if I'm not the girl I was before the lake, before the accident, I'm alive and almost whole. I am where I belong, and most days I feel it.

Although sometimes—

Sometimes when I turn my head a certain way, so my deafened ear blots out the noise of city streets and babbling voices, when I find a moment of sudden silence, I shut my eyes. And in that moment I am back in the woods, back in the lake. My forest around me, a kingdom that I understand. A place that does not love me and that I do not love. But we don't expect love from each other, the wild and me. We only want to survive.

And I did. And I will.

My name is Jess Cooper, and I am still alive.

acknowledgments

This book began on a camping trip with my husband, Mike, who let me chatter at him and nodded in all the right places until I had something resembling a plot. My agent, Lisa Rodgers, was the first one to read that outline and tell me I had something worth writing on my hands, and through every step of the process (as always) she brought a keen editorial eye, boundless enthusiasm, and the business savvy I'm fortunate to be able to outsource.

The actual writing began on a mountain surrounded by a brilliant crew of writers, who provided their expertise on details like the right ammunition to use and what a fox would taste like, while helping me come up with trouble to throw at Jess (so much that we accidentally killed her a few times and had to walk it back). So thank you to Scott Andrews, Andrea Pawley, Mike DeLuca, Susan Sielinski, Erin Hoffman, Al Bogdan, and Rita Oakes, as well as the cows, the turkeys, the deer, and the bear who kept us company. And special thanks to my son, our retreat stowaway.

Many other people provided support, feedback, and consultation along the way. My parents were wonderful as always, and my mom, Alice, helped bring fresh eyes to the manuscript when the text started to swim. I don't know where I'd be without the No Name Writing Group, so thank you, Rhiannon Held, Corry L. Lee, Shanna Germain, Susan J. Morris, and Erin M. Evans—you guys are the best. Day Al-Mohamed provided immeasurable insight, particularly with regards to Jess's disabilities, and was generally an excellent human being whom I'm privileged to know. Sylvia Spruck Wrigley and Gwen Hill helped turn my woefully inadequate knowledge of airplanes into something vaguely plausible—any remaining errors are entirely mine. The Class of 2k18, thank you for all of your hard work and support, and I can't wait for us all to finish out our debut year in triumph.

To my editors, Kendra Levin and Maggie Rosenthal— thank you for your hard work and your editorial guidance; the book wouldn't be the same without you. The design of this book is absolutely beautiful from cover to cover, so I'd especially like to thank Dana Li for creating a cover that made me gasp and Jim Hoover for an interior design that so perfectly complements the text. And of course I don't know where I'd be without the meticulous eye of copyeditors like Janet Pascal, Abigail Powers, and Jody Corbett to fix my hyphenation and rampant comma abuse.

The whole crew at Viking has done a fantastic job, as has the JABberwocky team. I'm lucky to have so many immensely talented people behind this book.

Finally, thank you to Vonnegut, who grew up alongside this book and without whom my feet would have been much colder. Who's a good boy? You are.

Kate Alice Marshall lives in the Pacific Northwest with her family. She works in the gaming industry as a writer and designer, most recently focusing on educational games for kids of all ages. She spends her winters cheerfully avoiding the rain, and during the summer ventures out to kayak and camp along Puget Sound. Her short fiction has appeared in venues such as *Beneath Ceaseless Skies* and *Crossed Genres*.

TEEN GRE

Grey, M.
The girl at midnight.

PRICE: $20.00 (3798/tfarp)